KU-541-285

If I Never See You Again

You Again

Niamh O'Connor

TRANSWORLD IRELAND

TRANSWORLD IRELAND
an imprint of The Random House Group Limited
20 Vauxhall Bridge Road, London SW1V 2SA
www.rbooks.co.uk

First published in 2010 by Transworld Ireland,
a division of Transworld Publishers

Copyright © Niamh O'Connor 2010

Niamh O'Connor has asserted her right under the Copyright, Designs
and Patents Act 1988 to be identified as the author of this work.

This book is a work of fiction and, except in the case of historical fact, any
resemblance to actual persons, living or dead, is purely coincidental.

A CIP catalogue record for this book
is available from the British Library.

ISBN 9781848270916

This book is sold subject to the condition that it shall not,
by way of trade or otherwise, be lent, resold, hired out,
or otherwise circulated without the publisher's prior
consent in any form of binding or cover other than that
in which it is published and without a similar condition,
including this condition, being imposed on the
subsequent purchaser.

Addresses for Random House Group Ltd companies outside the UK
can be found at: www.randomhouse.co.uk
The Random House Group Ltd Reg. No. 954009

The Random House Group Limited supports the Forest Stewardship Council (FSC),
the leading international forest-certification organization. All our titles that are
printed on Greenpeace-approved FSC-certified paper carry the FSC logo.
Our paper procurement policy can be found at
www.rbooks.co.uk/environment

Typeset in 11.5/15pt Sabon by Falcon Oast Graphic Art Ltd.
Printed and bound in Great Britain by
Clays Ltd, Bungay, Suffolk

2 4 6 8 10 9 7 5 3 1

Mixed Sources
Product group from well-managed
forests and other controlled sources
www.fsc.org Cert no. TT-COC-2139
© 1996 Forest Stewardship Council
FSC

Prologue

Even locked in the boot of a speeding car, all Stuart Ball could think about was how he was going to score his next fix. He was sick, that was why. Sick when he had drugs and sick when he hadn't. He was so used to being sick that even being folded in half in the boot of a cold and speeding car wasn't his priority. The gear was the only thing on his mind. The first turn-on of the day was always the best.

He tried to move his arm a bit to get at his back jeans pocket where he kept his morphine tablets. He needed his napps to stop getting sick. But his arm was jammed between his legs and a sharp, metal car jack. The car was jolting him about too much. He couldn't budge.

Stuart started panicking that he'd dislocated his shoulder. It was mad. He was fretting about the problems he'd have trying to score with a gammy arm instead of whatever the people who'd bundled him into the boot of a car were planning to do with him next. But what if his lighter didn't work? It had been acting up, kept blowing out.

He was sweating now. He liked everything right was why. His works – a spoon and lighter – were hidden in the sole of his trainer. His emergency gear was tucked in a condom up his jacksie. Lemon juice he could manage without and his belt would do as a tourniquet. But what if they didn't stop near a Spar, where he could buy a new lighter? He wouldn't be able to walk far with a bust shoulder.

It must be ex-Provos driving the car, he thought. Since the ceasefire, former members of the Provisional IRA had been muscling in on everyone's territory. Nobody else would have had the balls to burst into his ma's flat and abduct him. He was a Skid. They ran this town. When his mates found out it would mean carnage. The Shinners thought their war was over; it had only just started, man.

If it was them . . . he hadn't seen who whacked the back of his head. When he first came to he couldn't believe what was happening. He actually thought the sickness might be playing tricks on him. Then again, maybe it was the visitor who'd called to him earlier that morning asking one too many questions.

The only thing he knew for definite was there was going to be big trouble. Their biggest mistake was taking him from his ma's. She was from the country. She worked as a cleaner in Clerys and had never missed a day's work in her life. She didn't understand drugs. How did you explain horse to someone who got off on the smell of a chicken roasting on a Sunday? How did you tell your ma hurting people was easy when you needed a score? There were no words to describe a good goof. It was just a feeling. Like watching the best film you ever saw and being in it at the same time, without even having the telly on.

Suddenly his eyes were stinging like fuck as the boot of the car opened and the light flooded in. He hadn't even noticed the car stopping. He tried to cover them with his hands but the ex-Provos, or whoever the fuck they were, reefed him out. He was in agony. His shoulder was definitely dislocated now, if it hadn't been earlier.

'What the fuck is going on, man?' he roared, trying to get his hand to his shoulder to push it back where it should be. When he saw the shotgun he shouted, 'Not me bleedin' knees, no way, man.' But when he saw the vice the words just choked in the bottom of his neck somewhere. For the first time he wasn't worrying about smack. He was too busy thinking about dying.

MONDAY

1

Dublin Docklands. Late June. Mid-morning. Drizzle blew in from the slate-grey River Liffey across North Wall Quay and down Castleforbes Road. It smirred the hoists and jibs of a rusting old harbour gantry and coated the glass of the tilting barrel Convention Centre. Grit rising from a construction site squared off by lengths of blue-ply hoarding turned to grime. The building behind the barrier was an unfinished apartment block – abandoned, like a lot of other sites around the city, when the recession hit. Steel cables still protruded from the concrete. Clear blue plastic tape fluttered where it had come away from the seals of PVC windows and doors.

On the eighth floor of an east-facing balcony, Detective Inspector Jo Birmingham silently cursed whatever excuse of a foreman had downed tools before erecting any protective railing around the ledges. She reckoned within a matter of seconds the surfaces would become slippery. Running her fingers through her highlighted hair, cropped at the back, Jo took another small step forward. Directly in front of her, a little girl with eyes screwed shut was perched on the ledge, holding hands with a man in a pair of dirty trainers whose laces were undone. His knuckles had gone white.

'I want to go home,' the child said.

Leabharlanna
Fhine Gall

'We are going home, Amy,' the man answered.

'Sir . . .' Jo called. She moved stiffly towards him, one hand stretched out. 'Amy needs to come to me, so you and I can talk . . .'

He gave a quick glance over his shoulder.

Tight, confused sobs erupted and convulsed Amy's tiny frame. 'I want Mum,' she said.

'That bitch doesn't want us, don't you understand?' he answered.

Amy lost her footing and, with a sudden spray of gravel, was swinging from his hand. Her legs curled against the drop.

The man's back arched, he hauled her back quickly, shooting Jo a look that said it was her fault.

'Get the fuck away!' he warned.

'Back up, Inspector, he's losing it,' Detective Sergeant John Foxe directed through Jo's earpiece.

Jo saw red. She had two sons of her own plus a broken marriage under her belt. The thought that her ex-husband could resort to something like that so as to have the last, self-pitying word in the name of love . . . Bile rose in her throat. Pulling herself together, she made some quick mental notes.

She could see Amy was the man's princess. She was dressed all in pink; butterfly clips held her hair off her face; she wore pretty lace-trimmed socks under sparkling Lelli Kelly sandals that cost €50 even as 'authentic' fakes from the street traders. *Maybe too well dressed, like this is a special day.*

Advancing another hair's breadth, she said: 'My name is Jo Birmingham, what's yours?' Less than five feet separating them now. Close enough to see the way the man's limbs jittered. *Don't let him be on crack*. It was already over if he was on crack.

'Dad's name is Billy,' Amy answered.

Jo gave her a reassuring nod. 'Billy, I know you love Amy. She's beautiful. You must be very proud.'

'We're going to be together, just like old times,' he said, almost to himself.

Amy began to squirm. 'Daddy, stop it,' she said.

A megaphone boomed from the street below. 'Please stay still. You are at risk of falling.'

Jo drew a breath. Recovering quickly, she inched forwards again. Four-foot gap now. Amy was pulling back from her father, now gripping her upper arm.

'You've always protected Amy, always done your best for her.' Jo's voice was harder. 'You'd never do anything to hurt her. That's not what you want.'

'I can't leave her on her own.' Billy was panting with exertion. 'She needs me to keep her safe. She wouldn't be able to cope if something happened to me.'

Jo's stomach lurched. 'Ever hear a heart break, Billy?' she asked.

No answer.

'It starts off so low in the gut, it's hard to tell if it's human or animal. When it rises, the word "no" is in there somewhere . . .'

'Too much, Inspector,' the earpiece warned.

But Jo wasn't finished. 'You want to take your own life, Billy? Fine by me. But Amy wants to live, to have children of her own. Do you really think you'll be up there playing happy families, watching over her, if you take all that from her? Why don't you ask her? Ask Amy what she wants?'

'Step back, Birmingham,' Foxy remonstrated.

'You coppers, you're all the fucking same,' Billy hissed.

Jo could hear Foxy breathing. 'How's that?' she asked, sliding her weight on to the other foot.

'Persecute someone like me, someone who's worked his whole life even when I'd have been better off on benefit. Take my missus's word over mine soon as I put one foot wrong, and try and take everything from me. Put a barring order on me so I can't go near the house that I paid for, and force me into supervised visits with my own kid.'

Amy yelped.

'You're hurting her,' Jo said.

Billy didn't seem to have heard. 'And why? Because I'm an easy target, right? Your lot have got jobs for life, so what do you care about catching real criminals? You take the easy option. Threaten to lock up someone like me for not paying a television licence. Well, if you think I'm going to pay for a telly being watched in the house I'm not allowed to set foot in so my ex and her latest fancy man can cuddle up in front of *Corrie*, you got another think coming!'

'Plasma screen, right?' Jo asked. 'A thirty-two-inch, is it?'

Billy frowned.

'New man in your wife's life flash, is he?' Jo asked. 'Bet it's one of those state-of-the-art home-entertainment systems, right?'

'Birmingham!' Foxy growled.

'You ever think about the future, Billy?' Jo went on quickly. 'About what you'd really like to do with your life, I mean?'

No answer.

'Everybody has options. Sometimes people forget that. Me, I'd pack this gig in,' Jo said. 'If I had the choice, you know what I'd do? I'd become a stay-at-home mum. I'd give my right arm for it, do you know that? I'd do it properly, 'course. Make my own bread, pasta, jam. Go to seed? Yes please. Anything beats waking my little one at half six in the morning and handing him a slice of toast to eat in the car on the way to the crèche for breakfast. Might even get time to clean my car out, so it wouldn't have to carry a public health warning. My idea of heaven is to get a wash of clothes dry before I have to wash them again. I don't get time to pull them out and stick them in the dryer half the time.'

'Stand down, Inspector,' Foxy said.

Jo pulled the plug out of her ear. 'I'm sorry, here I am talking about me, when this is all supposed to be about you, isn't it, Billy? I haven't even told you yet that, until relatively recently, suicide was still considered a crime. I believe the correct legal term is *felonia de se*. Latin. Translated, it means if you do decide to jump, make sure you finish yourself off, because if you survive, I promise you that TV licence will be the least of your worries.'

Billy threw Jo a look as if she'd lost it. In that instant, Jo lunged and grabbed Amy, dragging her to safety. Jo looked over her at Billy. He was squatting like a skier at the top of a slope. She gulped in horror. And then he sprang – back arched, fists curled into balls at the end of up-stretched arms.

'Daddy!'

But Billy was gone.

2

Billy popped his head back over the ledge. 'No hard feelings, Sarge,' he said, pulling himself up and disconnecting the harness.

Jo took her trainee headset off. 'I'm a detective inspector.' Ideally, she'd have been able to add 'fuck you!', but Amy was still within earshot, so instead she added, 'I was promoted, remember?'

''Course you were,' Billy said with a wink.

Jo placed her hands on her hips and looked away. It was all she could do not to wipe the smug look off his face by telling him exactly how it felt to have colleagues with lower conviction rates promoted above her head just because they'd joined the right golf club. She bet he'd never given a victim his home number, or stayed up all night to hold their hand and listen, or even dreamt of offering them a bed. Mostly she'd have liked to test his knowledge of the names of the civil servants in the Justice Department, the people whose day she prided herself on making infinitely more difficult with a phone call sounding off about yet another failing of the justice system. But Jo knew she'd have been wasting her breath. She'd only be the butt end of a joke later. And 'fuck you' would have felt so much better.

She turned to face the half-dozen other gardaí on the

hostage-negotiation training course, some twenty feet away, grouped behind a monitor like on a movie set, and shouted over: 'Wrong bloody call, Foxy! And don't get me started on the mouthpiece on the megaphone . . .'

'Can I go now?' Amy asked, tugging her arm.

Jo knelt down on her hunkers and smiled, then waved Amy's Garda Reserve mum over, before unhooking the little girl's safety equipment. ''Course you can, sweetheart, and by the way you were absolutely brilliant.'

As soon as the two were reunited, Jo headed across the balcony to Foxy, dipping sideways briefly to cup her high heels back on – unsuitable, she knew, but her one-woman stand against institutional misogyny. Her rank entitled her to be in plain clothes so she also wore skirts as a rule, though they restrained her thighs a bit when she had to run.

Straightening up, she scanned the skyline. The city sprawled out from under the world's tallest sculpture – the needle-shaped Spire – like it had been pinned down. During the boom, the march of theme pubs and Michelin star restaurants with original art on the walls had driven the line between the city and the suburbs further out. In her experience, the cut-off point was not a street name; it was the choice between heroin or cocaine. Charlie was as social as a handshake among the Prada-clad professionals when there was money swilling around. But now that the bubble had burst, smack was claiming whole new territories in the suburbs.

The other members of the force dispersed rapidly as she continued on over, leaving only the slight, silver-haired John Foxe in her line of vision. 'I had him,' she said. 'He'd engaged.'

Foxy looked unconvinced. Jo sighed. She respected Foxy

– he'd taken her under his wing when she was a new recruit. He was old school – grouchy, but highly principled. As the station's 'Bookman', he was responsible for setting up all the major incident rooms, but his doggedness in applying the theory could be infuriating when on a job. Jo thought of herself as being the complete opposite. It was how she compensated for the gap between justice and the law. It hadn't done her career any favours, but nothing riled her like a system that didn't let the people most affected by the crime talk. The barristers could talk, the judge could talk, the accused could talk if they liked. But the family of a murder victim was expected to sit in court and listen while the person they'd loved and lost was assassinated all over again by the defence. If it was a headline-grabbing case, they were lucky to get a seat at all and had to stand through graphic and harrowing evidence . . .

Foxy gave a tired nod towards an area further down the balcony where they could get some privacy. Jo popped a plug of Nicorette she'd just about managed to rummage from the junk at the bottom of her handbag into her mouth. She chewed at a speed that let him know she was humouring him.

'If it was up to me, you'd have had him, okay?' Foxy said. 'But it wasn't up to me. We had a visitor. He left early.'

'Who?' Jo prickled.

Foxy gave her a knowing look.

'Come on, tell me. This is serious. If I fail this course, I've no chance of getting my transfer approved.'

Foxy held Jo's stare. Most people couldn't – the pupils of her glassy eyes had been permanently dilated since a childhood car crash.

'Who do you think?' Foxy said. 'The chief super, 'course.'

Jo groaned. Her work relationship with her ex-husband, Dan Mason, was becoming as difficult as their break-up had been. Since they'd split eighteen months ago, Dan had virtually grounded her, with jobs that carried no hope of upping her conviction rate, and now it appeared that he was sabotaging her contingency plan. She'd been signing up for every course going to keep as far away from him as possible. She'd hoped that by acquiring a new set of skills she could fast-track her transfer to some independent republic away from Dan and his cronies' sphere of influence – somewhere like the Garda National Drugs Unit (GNDU), or the Criminal Assets Bureau (CAB). But now it seemed that Dan was determined to interfere even with that. 'That's bloody well it, I'm going to kill him!' she said.

Foxy spread his hands to indicate that it was nothing to do with him. He was built like a jockey – wiry, with a head that looked too big for his body. He opened his mouth to say something – but Jo's eyes had moved to the apartment door to his right. She took a couple of steps past him, and ran her hand down its length.

'Looks like we've got a breaking and entering on our hands,' she said, pointing to the forced handle and scuff marks at the base of the door.

'This building is uninhabited,' Foxy answered, eyes worried. 'It's the only way the insurance would cover today's training.'

Jo pulled her hand inside her sleeve then pressed the handle down. She took a deep breath when the door gave way.

'Don't go anywhere. I'll get assistance,' Foxy said, glancing across the empty balcony and heading for the stairwell.

But Jo was already inside and patting the wall for a light

switch. 'Anyone home?' she called. She gasped and tugged her multicoloured Dr Who scarf over her nose, wincing at the bad smell. It was musty and invasive, like burning Bakelite. The heating was overpowering, and something else about the place she couldn't put her finger on was making goose bumps break out on her skin . . .

She jumped as Foxy, who'd doubled back rather than leave her alone, stifled a cough behind her. He had buried his face into the crook of his arm. 'Jesus, what's that stink?' he asked. 'Christ, it's rotten. You don't think somebody's popped their clogs in here, do you?'

Jo was on the move, surveying the small sitting room-cum-kitchenette. There were two doors to her right, one on the left, behind the kitchen area. No pictures hung on the walls; there were no personal effects, just a few bits of sparse, mismatched furniture on the laminate floor in need of a mop. She made her way over to a smudged, glass-topped coffee table, licked her little finger and dipped it into a line of untouched Charlie, then tasted.

Foxy whispered, 'Hey, have you forgotten everything I taught you? That stuff could contain anything – strychnine, for starters.'

Jo mouthed a silent whistle. She didn't have to worry about rat poison. The cocaine was uncut. This place was higher up the food chain than first impressions had suggested.

She registered the background sound that had been putting her on edge. Bluebottles had only ever meant one thing in her experience. *We're too late*, she thought.

She turned right and took the first door. It opened into the bathroom and it was empty. There were towels on the floor. She reached down. Bone dry.

She tried the second door: a single room with different outfits laid out on the unmade bed. A nurse's outfit; a leather jumpsuit and whip; a school uniform. It looks like a prostitution racket being operated from a vacated flat, she thought. All tastes catered for . . .

Backing out, she crossed the main living space to the third and last door, on the opposite wall, stalling briefly before flinging it open. The new and strongest smell hit her like she'd just walked into a butcher's shop.

'Foxy, in here, now,' she commanded. Shaking her head, she rooted around her bag for her small black hard-bound notebook. There was so much crap in the way – lip gloss, tampons, loose change, bloody nappy-rash cream. Her hand was shaking when she finally plucked the pad free and snapped the elastic off. She bent her left arm and held it up to eye level, read the time then noted it in the book. *The date is the thirtieth, right? What's today's date? Come on, keep it together, Jo.* She'd checked the date on the milk this morning against the calendar to see if it'd stretch to a cup of tea. *What was it?* The thirtieth. She wrote it down.

'Oh, Jesus!' Foxy said, appearing behind her then bending to throw up.

The body lay naked just inside the door, splayed on her back like she had been dropped from a height. The victim was in her early forties, maybe younger, junkie-thin with a mass of straggly long hair, dark at the roots, peroxide-blonde brittle everywhere else. Her legs were covered with infections around needle sores. Her arms were propped up over her head: the right wrist ended in a grisly stump where the hand should have been. Puce lipstick had seeped into the creases around her lips like scarlet stitches. Strands of hair had escaped and become matted with congealed blood across her face, blurring with streaks of smudged blue mascara. Blood had spattered and skimmed every surface, as far as Jo could make out.

'Jesus, Jesus, Jesus,' Foxy murmured.

'Minimum movement,' Jo warned, eyes darting around the room as she scrawled the physical details of what she was witnessing.

Foxy choked again behind her.

'Go back to the front door and secure the scene,' she instructed. 'Nobody comes through the cordon without my say-so. I mean, *nobody*. Contact base. Tell them we need the Tech Bureau asap and a doctor to declare death, and put a request in for the pathologist. Got that?'

Foxy nodded. She watched him go, over her shoulder, a maternal expression crossing her face. *There's a reason he's the bookman*, she thought.

Breathing evenly through her nose, she slowly and gently pressed her fingertips against the victim's midriff.

'Body cold to the touch despite stifling room temperature,' she wrote.

Kneeling, she tucked her pen behind her ear and gripped her notepad between her teeth, freeing up her hands to try and locate the sachet of sterile latex baby-blue gloves from her bag and put them on. They were greasy inside and the smell of plastic made the bridge of her nose sting.

Lifting the victim's arm up, she peered underneath, placing it back as delicately as if she were handling antique china. *Was she alive when you chopped her hand off, you evil bastard?*

'Pooling clearly evident on back of victim's right arm,' she wrote, adding, 'Rigor mortis has set in.'

She made a note of the ten-to-ten position of the arms and

the body's state of undress then placed the pen and pad back in her bag and leaned forwards to pick up a purse discarded on top of some clothes – a fake-leather mini skirt, a lime-green boob tube and a pair of knee-length red leather boots – a few feet away. She flicked open the clasp. Two €50 notes were rolled together tightly inside with a bus ticket dispensed in the city centre dated the twenty-ninth, a letter from the Social Welfare asking what job applications she'd made in the last month, and a plastic photo ID that turned out to be a medical card. She glanced from the picture to the bloody face on the floor and sighed. The victim's name was Rita Nulty, and she'd an address in Ballymun. She looked at her again, differently. Based on the income Rita was clearly not making, she appeared to have been a low-class hooker.

Jo turned around, focusing on a shape in a far corner, talking aloud to herself as she tried to process the image. 'Flesh in the corner . . . is . . . a hand . . . it's . . . Rita's hand.'

She swallowed and wrote it down, making a note of the bloodstain locations, their size and condition, and recording other details – how the lights had been off, the door forced before she'd entered.

She turned back to Rita and her mutilated arm. Her fingers hovered over Rita's candyfloss hair, and hesitated. She pulled a glove off, then touched Rita's face lightly. 'You poor love,' she whispered. 'What did you do to deserve this?'

She pulled the glove back on, slid the medical card back in the purse and placed it back where she'd found it. The two €50s she tucked in her coat pocket.

From the doorway behind her, Foxy said flatly: 'The lads are on their way.'

3

It was early evening by the time Jo pulled into the driveway of her home, a granite cottage with a For Sale sign outside it in Barnacullia, on the Three Rock mountain, six miles south of the city centre. Clutching her sleeping one-year-old, Harry, with one arm, Jo used the other, in sync with her elbow and foot, to battle the boot of her twenty-year-old Ford Escort open and take the M&S bag containing the groceries out.

The sloped lawn was only the size of a postage stamp, but it had looked permanently shabby since Dan had left. Much as she enjoyed gardening, Jo liked the idea of keeping potential buyers at bay for as long as possible even more. Even in a recession, she could never have afforded this place now that Dundrum town centre and the city's ring road had sprung up so close. But back when they were buying, this place had been considered the sticks, and the house in need of complete refurbishment. Times had changed, Jo thought as she struggled with the shopping. At weekends, a fleet of hip young professionals wearing shades on their heads and driving convertibles converged on the picnic benches outside Lamb Doyles or the Blue Light pub to drink cider and take in the view from the smog-line perch over the city. Jo had become adept at dodging the estate agent's calls.

She had a splitting headache and was having no luck

trying to shake the bag free of the stroller in the boot so as not to disrupt Harry, her mobile phone gripped between her teeth. There was a sixteen-year age gap between her boys and, on days like this, the having-it-all dream seemed more like a downright lie than a myth. Eventually, the bag containing the dinner crashed out on the tarmac, bringing with it the stroller and a stack of fluttering paperwork, and Jo snagged her finger in snapping metal in the process. She sucked and shook her hand miserably, stamping on the documents before bending sideways to scoop everything back up and in.

Once the balancing act had negotiated its way through the front door, Jo dropped her bags where she stood and carried Harry, who was still – miraculously – sleeping, to his cot beside the bed in her room. After tucking him in snugly, she flicked the baby monitor on.

Heading back down the hall, she swung into the sitting room and leaned over the back of the couch. She plucked a beer bottle and remote control from the armrest.

'Hey,' Rory protested, scrambling to his feet and turning around.

Her eldest son scrunched his eyes shut as Jo flicked the light on.

'Next time, I tell your father,' she warned, hitting the mute button. Incoherent gangsta rap came to an abrupt halt.

'Yeah, cos, like, he'll take the call,' Rory jeered.

She froze with her back to him and began the silent count to ten. 'Would you like your dinner now? Will Becky have some? And does her mum know she's here?' she said, walking into the kitchen, where yesterday evening's dirty dishes confronted her.

'Yes, please, and yes, Mrs Mason,' the body that had been

squirming under Rory on the couch called back. The pretty blonde teenager sat up and buttoned up her blouse quickly, smoothing her long hair back into place.

Jo glanced at the yellow Post-it stuck to the broken dishwasher door that was supposed to have been a foolproof reminder to Phone a plumber!!! for the last two days. She sighed, pulled up a sleeve and rooted under the bottom of the stack of dishes in the sink for the plug.

'We're starving,' Rory announced, arriving and asking behind her, 'Okay if Becky stays the night?'

'Spag Bol in approximately forty-five . . .' Jo said. 'And yes, if Becky puts her mum on the phone to clear it.'

Rory grunted.

Jo turned and eyed the handsome teenager towering over her. He looked so like his father suddenly that she caught a breath. Rory's shoulder-length hair needed a cut, his grungy clothes needed a wash and the swollen new piercing in his right eyebrow needed a doctor. His rebellious phase had kicked in the minute she'd brought Harry home and had culminated with him deciding to move in with Dan. It didn't feel like home without him.

'Don't you bloody well dare light that in here,' she warned, seeing the roll-up he was licking.

'I wasn't planning to, Mother,' he said.

Jo turned her back to him as she pulled open the medicine press and pushed horse-dosage pink and yellow tablets out of the blister pack and into her mouth, crooking her neck to gulp them back. She was so used to eating and drinking on the run, a glass of water didn't occur to her. The box also stipulated that you only took the yellow tab if the pink didn't work. *Who had time to wait?* Headaches were something she lived with on a daily basis.

'How was school today?' Jo asked, glancing over her shoulder to find Rory had gone again. She went into over-drive, squirting washing-up liquid in the sink and turning both taps on, wringing a J-cloth and wiping down the sur-faces, slapping a pan on the cooker. After losing count of the number of spoons of formula she'd spooned into Harry's bottle, she washed it out and started again, this time count-ing aloud and shaking it vigorously before placing it in the bottle-warmer. She'd just begun chopping an onion at arm's length, straining her head as far as it would turn away, when the sound of the doorbell made her frown. She wasn't expecting anyone.

'Rory, can you get that?' she called, wiping her streaming eyes on the back of her sleeve. 'Blast!' she complained when it chimed again. She cocked an ear to see if it had woken Harry, glanced from the pan sizzling on a hotplate to the door, then hurried down the hall, throwing her eyes up to heaven as she passed the sitting room and spotted Rory making out on the couch again.

Peering through the spyhole, she stepped back suddenly, muttering, 'Shit,' under her breath. It was Dan, with the baby's overnight bag slung over his shoulder. She'd forgotten it was his night for Harry. She tilted her head against the front door briefly, then pulled it open and stood aside.

Her ex-husband was tall and broad, with a boxer's nose and hands and Rory's blue-black hair, which he wore just shy of a crew cut to minimize his lightly receding hairline. His shirt collar was still buttoned closed, meaning he'd come straight from the station. She was still furious with him for showing up at the training session earlier when he must have had a million jobs that took priority, but, realizing that tension was practically steaming off him as he entered, she held her tongue.

Living with him before a suspect was nominated used to be a nightmare. It was like waiting for a pressure cooker to blow. Jo had left the murder scene as soon as the forensic team had arrived but she knew from the fidgety way Dan was behaving that he had been there too. Jo couldn't contain her feelings when she was working on a case, but Dan would bottle it all up. He'd nearly lost it after a child's body was found in the Phoenix Park a few years back. He had kept it together during the inquiry, and then when the case was finally solved he'd erupted over something incidental – she'd forgotten to set the video to record some match he'd wanted to watch after work. He'd reacted like it was the end of the world. He'd walked out on her and stayed away from home for two nights, refusing to answer any of her calls to his mobile. Afterwards, he claimed he'd stayed in a hotel to get his head straight, but refused to tell her which one.

They differed in other ways too. Dan got stressed by any deviation from routine; Jo liked change (as long as it didn't involve gadgets). Maybe they'd never have married if she hadn't got pregnant with Rory when they were both still students in Templemore Training College. But definitely they'd still be together if she hadn't got pregnant with Harry. Dan hadn't wanted another baby, not with jobs as demanding as theirs, he'd said, though Jo knew he now loved Harry every bit as much as she did. If he hadn't had a fling after they separated, while she was heavily pregnant, Jo would probably have taken him back the second she watched him take Harry in his arms for the first time. But then she'd found out the other woman was his secretary, Jeanie. And that she couldn't forgive. Too many lines had been crossed. Jeanie had been

Dan's secretary for ten years. Had those years been one long flirtation, and was there more to it, as Jo had regularly suspected? Why wouldn't he just tell her the name of the hotel?

'I'm just making dinner,' she told him, holding her hair off her face with her arm.

'Sorry, you go ahead, I'll wait in the car,' he'd said uncertainly. He'd been brought up in Manchester and his accent still had the twang.

Jo gave the door a flick behind him. 'Why don't you join us? You eaten?'

Dan managed a clenched smile. 'You're cooking?'

Jo pulled the dishcloth off her shoulder and whipped it off his leg. 'Very funny,' she said.

'What did you make of her?' he asked, following Jo down the hall.

'Rita?' Jo replied. 'The killer went to a lot of trouble.'

'That's what I was afraid you were going to say,' Dan said, glancing through the sitting-room door and calling, 'Oi, haven't you any homework to be getting on with?'

Jo began attempting to peel a clove of garlic at the butcher's block but was all fingers and thumbs.

Dan had spotted the Post-it and pulled the dishwasher door open. 'What's the trouble?' he asked.

'Won't work,' Jo said, studying the back of a tube of tomato purée.

He walked the machine out from under the bench as if it were as light as a feather and lifted the trays out on the floor, kneeling to inspect inside. Jo used to marvel at the span of his shoulders. She forced herself to look away.

'She was on the game,' he said, reaching behind the machine and jolting something.

'I gathered,' Jo answered.

He turned around to face her. 'You shouldn't have gone in there on your own. What if he'd still been in there? What if something had happened to you?'

'I wasn't on my own. Foxy was with me,' Jo said, abandoning the tube and scraping the onion into the pan. The hissing drowned out the sound of Dan snorting.

'The forensic team is not happy,' he continued, reaching across her to turn the heat down then pulling a screwdriver from a junk drawer.

'Yeah, well, levitation isn't something I've mastered yet,' Jo replied, trying to squirt the purée on to the spoon then aiming it directly into the pan.

Dan shook his head, straightened up and took it off her. 'We got an anonymous tip-off that a body was there – a unit of crime-scene examiners had been dispatched,' he said, going back down on one knee. 'That's how they were on the scene so quickly after you.' He closed the dishwasher door up, pressed the on/off button and nodded to himself at the sound of water flooding in, then turned it off.

Jo threw an arm over his shoulder as he stood up. 'Thank you.'

He gave her a sidelong glance that lasted too long and she moved away awkwardly.

Dan stepped behind her, placed his hands on her shoulders and turned her away from the frying pan and towards the table, pushing her back into a chair. He tucked the dishcloth into the sides of his belt like an apron and started tossing the pan around the heat. Jo wasn't about to argue. He was a great cook, while she had difficulty boiling an egg. 'What shall I do?' she asked.

Dan stretched across her to the cupboard over her head and pulled down two wine glasses. She suspected he knew the effect he was having on her because of the way he looked at her when he said, 'Make mine a small one, I'm supposed to be driving after.'

But when he tucked a strand of hair behind her ear, Jo pulled her head away. She hated that he could still make her feel like this after everything that had happened. 'I want you to put me in charge of the investigation,' she said tetchily. 'I've lost count of the number of murder cases I've been on, but I'm the only inspector in the division who hasn't headed one up yet.'

Dan returned to the cooker. 'It's tricky,' he said, handing a corkscrew to Jo. 'You know that.'

Jo had lots of appropriate expletives, but there was no point using them when she knew he was right. Her promotion had finally come only on the back of her threat to take the force to the High Court after she was repeatedly passed over on the promotion list despite a record conviction rate in Store Street station, the divisional drugs HQ for the Dublin Metropolitan Area (DMA). She believed she was being held back because she was too gobby with the staff of the Justice Department. But she couldn't help it – the system of social apartheid that operated in the courts drove her crazy. She couldn't bear the way the legal eagles looked down their noses at people, the convoluted language they used, the wigs and gowns they wore. Even the sign on the restaurant door when the criminal courts sat in the Four Courts stipulated 'Barristers only', informing them they were 'Entitled to free iced tea'. It all served to segregate people who were already intimidated enough by the whole process, people the justice system was supposed to serve. But she really wanted this case. If she solved it, she'd some hope of getting a transfer . . .

'I needed that hostage course under my belt, Dan,' Jo said, straining on her tiptoes to push the arms of the corkscrew down.

He placed his hands on her waist and slowly moved her sideways.

'I worked hard for it,' she continued, swallowing. 'I did it by the book. I was in command. I could have done a deal.'

Dan scoffed, popped the cork and poured, clinking her glass. 'You broke the cardinal rule,' he said. 'You started talking about angels, for Christ's sake! You left Billy between a rock and a hard place. His only way to save face was by going through with it. And don't even get me started on the shite you came out with about plasma screens!'

'You're wrong, Dan. I'd got his first name. I'd got him talking. I'd saved the kid. He wouldn't have left her, not on her own.'

She took a sip and felt herself instantly start to mellow. 'You sure you're not just trying to keep me around?'

'All right dad,' Rory said, sticking his head around the door.

Jo moved further away from Dan.

'Dishes,' Dan instructed, tossing the dishcloth at him.

Rory headed slowly towards the sink, removing and inspecting the contents of the half-open grocery bag on the island on the way.

'Do you have any idea how bad monosodium glutamate is for you, Mother?' he asked, studying the back of a soup packet, then lifting and dropping a block of Parmesan with disdain. 'Also, the smell of vomit is not conducive to appetite,' he said.

'Hey, a little more respect for your mother,' Dan

instructed, catching Jo's eye behind his back and straining to keep a straight face.

Jo heard a whimper upstairs and went to get Harry.

Dan and Rory were arguing when she got back, but they stopped talking as soon as they saw her.

'What's going on?' Jo asked, moving quickly to the cooker to turn the heat down. Gloopy water was overflowing from the pot of spaghetti.

'Go on, tell her,' Rory said, eyeballing his father.

Dan looked at Jo sheepishly and muttered something about Rory's school reports which Jo couldn't make out.

'Tell me what?' Jo asked, placing Harry in the high chair and handing him a rusk.

Dan opened his mouth to say something, but Rory spoke over him angrily. 'Okay, so my grades are down. Big deal. When your parents split, that's what happens. I'm a text-book broken-home kid. Shoot me.'

'Do not speak to me like that,' Dan said.

'Why not?' Rory asked. 'Because tonight we're playing grown-ups who get along? You want to get everything out in the open so much, Dad, why don't you tell Mum about the new place you're planning on moving into with your girlfriend?'

Jo looked at Dan. When he didn't say anything, she handed Harry his milk. As soon as he started guzzling, she left the room.

'I was going to tell you,' Dan said, following her to the front room.

Jo was sitting on the couch studying her hands, which lay on her knees.

Dan knelt down in front of her. 'Don't do this,' he said, clasping his hands over hers.

Jo stood up quickly, walked across to the door and lowered her voice as she closed it. 'How worried should I be about Rory's grades?'

'He's a bright kid, he'll be fine,' Dan said coldly. 'The move with Jeanie . . . it's not the way it sounds . . . It's temporary, until I find somewhere of my own. Her place is too small. She was moving anyway!'

Jo wanted to change the subject. 'We need to talk about my transfer,' she said.

'Not now,' he answered, sounding frustrated.

'When?' she asked, keeping her voice down. 'Your secretary keeps refusing to give me an appointment.'

Dan plunged his hands in his trouser pockets. 'Take it that Jeanie will book you in tomorrow morning.' He hunched his shoulders. 'All you have to do is say the word, Jo. You know how I feel about you.'

'And where does Jeanie fit in?' Jo asked calmly. 'You're just stringing her along in case things don't work out between us, is that it? And what if we did get back together . . . Would she stay on as your secretary, just like the old days?'

Dan's voice hardened. 'How many times do I have to tell you there was nothing between us before you kicked me out? And what's happened since isn't serious.'

He brushed past her lightly as he headed back into the kitchen.

When he called out, 'Grub up,' minutes later, she walked stiffly back to the kitchen and sat down alongside Becky, opposite Dan and Rory. She ate forced mouthfuls in between making light conversation. There was one humorous moment when Dan made Rory laugh by telling him about Jo's rooftop claim that she didn't want to be a cop, or to work. Jo tried telling them that she'd pack it all in at the drop of a hat if she won the Lotto, but they all just laughed harder at her, even Becky.

After Harry was winded and the strings of spaghetti removed from his hair, Jo pulled his hat on and kissed his rosy little cheeks before handing him slowly over to Dan, with a tube of Bonjela.

'I thought you were staying,' Jo said, as Rory began to follow his father.

Rory mumbled something before disappearing out the hall door. Becky tottered out behind him, telling Jo as she trooped out behind him, 'No offence. It's just that if my mum found out I was going to stay here, she'd, like, have a meltdown.'

Jo started to massage her neck. If Dan was letting Becky stay over with Rory in his place, they'd have to have the birth-control conversation. Something else to look forward to. She listened to Dan's car drone down the road and around the corner then went out into the garden, jostled the For Sale sign to the ground and dragged it around to the side of the house, where no one could see it. If Dan thought she was going to let him sell her family home just so he could use the proceeds of his half to buy one with Jeanie he had another think coming.

4

Unable to stay home alone, Jo spent the next half-hour perched behind the steering wheel in gridlocked Pearse Street trying to turn right on to Tara Street at the fire station but going nowhere. It was almost eight, but the only rush-hour rule that applied on one of the main feeder routes across the Liffey was bottleneck traffic. Her right hand was holding the choke at the only spot guaranteed not to flood the engine and her left foot was monitoring the clutch.

She was headed for the station, technically five minutes away. *Technically.* Her wipers slashed at the rain sheeting down, in high summer. The repetitive thump alternated with the throb in her head, which the pills had moved from the front to the back of her skull. When the lights changed but not a single car moved and her petrol warning light flashed up, Jo slid her right arm under her shirt collar to peel the nicotine patch off the top of her arm and relocate it on her left breast, directly over her heart, hoping for a maximum infusion. Seconds later, she leaned over to the dash where she stashed her emergency box of Silk Cut Lights and lit up. The car bunny-hopped until she grabbed the choke again.

After eventually managing to ditch it on a double yellow, she crossed the Luas tram tracks and hurried past the Victorian Coroner's Court, the last port of call for murder victims' families denied justice by the courts. Each morning, a new set of shattered faces could be seen heading into the building beside the station, arms linked, hands clutching photographs of the deceased, and clinging to the last hope – of restoring some dignity to the dead with a verdict of unlawful killing . . .

Entering the red-bricked, refurbished barracks, she swiped her ID card past the ice-block walls and solid beech doors and headed for the windowless incident room on the first floor. More desks than the room could accommodate were crammed in haphazard rows. A detailed map of Dublin city centre hung on the back wall, with little coloured pins highlighting the primary crime flashpoints. Immigrants were breathing new life into many of the no-go areas where marked cars would have been rammed or stoned in previous years, but the transition was creating a whole new set of tensions, especially now jobs were so thin on the ground.

Shiny white boards took up most of the end wall. A posthumous close-up of Rita Nulty's bloodied face had already been taped up, beside details relating to a previous case which somebody had made a half-hearted attempt to rub out.

Two men were working inside. She knew them both – liked one, couldn't stand the other.

Jo made a beeline through the fug of body odour and stale coffee towards Detective Inspector Gavin Sexton, who was studying some paperwork at the top of the room. He was sitting at the desk with the only computer. The other guy – the one with acne on his neck and an All Blacks fleece over his uniform – looked up when she entered. He was known as Mac. She hadn't a clue what his first name was or how his surname ended. Staff were split into four units to provide cover for twenty-four hours. You could go your whole career never having met someone working in the same station, but Mac she knew by form. He'd been the focus of an inquiry some years back after a mouthy juvenile died in a cell on his watch, but the DPP couldn't make any charges stick. Every cop on duty that night had suffered a collective lapse in memory. It made her sick to the teeth the way ranks closed whenever trouble loomed.

'Sexton,' she saluted, scooping up copies of *Evening News* splashed with the banner headline 'Murdered Hooker'. That was quick, she thought, dropping it on to the floor with a loud bang, managing to locate the keyboard that had been buried underneath in the process. Taking her arms out of the sleeves of her leather biker jacket, she slung it over the back of the chair.

Sexton looked up and grinned. He was short by police standards, and handsome, with Mediterranean good looks. It was only a few months since Jo had last seen him, but he'd aged so much she had to look twice. Grey slashes had appeared in his dark hair at the sides, and there were puffy bags under his eyes. He looked a lot older than his thirty-two years, Jo thought.

'Haven't seen you in a while, Sarge,' he said.

'That's Inspector to you . . . I got promoted, remember?' She plonked herself in the chair, wheeling it sideways with little steps, telling him to 'push over' with her elbows so she could work on the computer.

'How could I forget?' he replied.

The running joke that she'd cheated her way up the ranks was wearing very thin, but Sexton she let get away with it. He was three years younger than she was but the most instinctive cop she'd ever worked with, and rumoured to be on course for promotion when the next list came out. She knew first-hand how good he was and so she didn't begrudge him, especially when he'd also had to overcome huge personal tragedy – his late wife, Maura, had taken her own life, must be a year and a half ago now. Jo remembered it as happening at much the same time she and Dan broke up. Sexton hadn't taken a day's leave since, as far as she could tell, but he point-blank refused to discuss it whenever she tried to bring it up. She still hadn't been able to talk to him properly. She'd also heard on the grapevine that he'd only found out from Maura's autopsy report that she'd been expecting their first child.

'You need a shave,' she told him.

He rubbed his jaw. 'Did I ever tell you, you're the image of that actress . . . what's her name?' he asked.

Jo jabbed the keyboard, tabbing through the PULSE crime programme as she answered, 'Orla Brady – I wish, and yeah, you tell me all the time.' She didn't entertain it for a second. Sexton could charm the birds out of the trees.

'Wasn't she in *Mistresses*?' Mac asked with a snigger.

Jo shot him a look of contempt, but Sexton distracted her with another question.

'What are you doing?' he asked, linking his hands behind his head.

'I want to do a bit of research on the murder victim today,' Jo answered, still eyeballing Mac. 'You know, Rita Nulty – I found her.'

'I heard. Lucky for us. What were the chances of you being *in situ* at that location today, eh?' He stretched over to grab a novelty mug from her desk. 'So what have you been working on lately?' he asked.

'Don't ask. Deskbound, mostly.'

'What a waste,' he said.

'Pays the same.' Her eyes moved across the screen. The computer system was an exercise in frustration. The software had cost €50 million and was incapable of basic tasks. Unlike the HOLMES system in the UK, it didn't cross reference relevant information and, as the plan for a national DNA bank was in its infancy, it couldn't throw up the hits needed to solve crime. Plus there was the fact that, if the civil liberties crowd ever found out that the details of people who'd reported a crime were permanently stored with those of suspects who'd been long since cleared, there'd be hell to pay.

'Shit boring though, right?' Sexton guessed.

Jo shrugged.

'Milk, two sugars?' He held a mug up.

Jo pressed two pleading hands in his direction like she was praying. He nodded 'no problem'. She watched him as he walked towards the coffee machine on a bench on the opposite wall and thought how tired he looked.

When he realized the dregs in the coffee pot were burnt into a sticky glue at the bottom of the pot, Sexton clicked his tongue and headed outside to the toilets to clean it. As he did so, the phone on his desk rang.

'Sexton around?' a gravelly voice quizzed.

'Who wants to know?'

'Ryan Freeman.'

Jo looked at the newspapers on the floor and focused on the by-line on the murder story. She weighed this information up against the ten-odd seconds it would take to get Sexton back to the phone to take the call from the country's highest-profile crime reporter. 'He's not available,' she lied, ignoring Mac's open mouth and hanging up.

She returned to the computer search. 'Did you find out

who owned that apartment?' she asked when Sexton returned, adding, 'Cheers,' as he handed over a polystyrene cup from the machine outside. He held the coffee pot up to show her how the ring of glass in the bottom had come away when he'd tried to clean it.

'Yeah,' he said, sitting on the desk. 'Foxy actioned the job, but the key-holder was kosher. He'd bought it from the plans, never set foot in the place.'

'Had the victim any previous?'

'Lots – soliciting and shoplifting.'

'Drugs?'

He shook his head.

Jo wasn't surprised. The scale of the resources to tackle the drug problem was a joke, and with all the cuts to public-service pay, morale was at an all-time low. Nobody took chances with their personal health and safety when it came to drug arrests any more. 'How long had she been there?'

'Pathologist reckoned under twenty-four hours.'

'Could have told you that myself from one look at her bus ticket.' She blew on and then sipped the scalding coffee. 'Heard who's in the running for heading up the investigation yet?'

'Chief super's due to announce it in the morning. But between you, me and the wall, he's already given me the nod that it's mine. He wants this one solved quickly. Did you hear he's up for promotion? Assistant commissioner!'

It shouldn't have come as a surprise. Dan was one of only six chief superintendents in the city, which meant that he'd be a contender for the top job of commissioner in a few years' time. 'They'd have to move him out of here then, wouldn't they? It won't happen. I'd never be that lucky.'

Sexton laughed.

'Listen, just to give you the heads-up, I've asked Dan to

give me the Rita Nulty inquiry,' Jo said. 'Nothing personal, but I'm going to fight for it. You don't mind, do you?'

He nodded several times too often. 'If that's how things pan out, so be it. I've no problem taking orders from a woman, though a lot of men in here would. As the fella says, "May the best man win."'

Jo was typing with her two index fingers when PULSE miraculously threw back the information she was looking for. Sexton leaned over her shoulder to read from the monitor.

'What's your take on what happened today then?' he asked, leaning in close. He smelled of one of those trendy, androgynous aftershaves she didn't know the name of but liked. Too 'new man' for Dan. He'd even treated his wedding ring like jewellery and left it on the shelf beside his shaving mirror every morning.

Jo stretched across the desk for a pen. 'I get the feeling the killer hasn't finished yet. And I doubt today's victim was his first. I'm trying to dig out any old trophy-killer files.'

'Not just a punter coked out of his brain, taking things a bit far?'

She shook her head. 'The killer went to too much trouble.' She tapped the screen with her pen. 'See what's turned up. You were involved in this one, weren't you? It was put down to a gangland hit.'

'Stuart Ball?' Sexton asked, reading the screen over her shoulder. 'Yeah, I know him. His nickname was Git. He was a lowlife, a druggie. Used to be high up in the Skids until he started sampling the merchandise. What about him?'

'The thing is, he was found on New Wapping Street,' Jo said. 'That's just around the corner from where we found Rita today.'

Sexton nodded ambiguously and moved in closer to the screen. Jo knew he'd take an interest once she mentioned the underworld. The Skids were the biggest drugs gang in the country, so named because most had cut their teeth on the juvenile joyriding circuit.

'Here's the thing,' she continued. 'Git's eye was gouged out and left at the scene. Given what's happened to the victim we found today, I think it could be the same killer.'

Sexton straightened up. 'Interesting . . . You fancy a drink?'

Mac reacted instantly. He was on his feet, zipping up his jacket.

Jo checked her watch. 'Thought drinking on duty was your pet hate?'

'We're celebrating. Guess who's just been knocked off? Anto Crawley! Only happened a couple of hours ago – his body's still warm. Happy days, eh?'

'Really?' she said, understanding his euphoria. Anto Crawley was the country's top drug lord and the Skids' lynchpin. If he'd been taken out, it would be a major blow to the gangland.

'Yeah,' Sexton said. 'Someone just did us a big favour. Really had it in for him, whoever it was, and they smashed his teeth in before they killed him.'

Jo winced as she made a note of the numbers of the files she wanted to retrieve from the monitor.

Sexton put one hand on the back of her chair. 'You're taking this hooker's case a bit personally, aren't you? You got no home to go to? Where are your kids?'

Jo bristled. 'With Dan. You two go. I'm staying here.'

A couple of hours later, Jo had read and flattened all the dog-eared reports and newspaper cuttings arced around her on the desk. She leaned her forehead on her hands as she studied the victims' photographs closely. Stuart Ball had that hard look that came from seeing too much of what human beings are capable of doing to each other. At the same time, he had the unearthly expression people always seemed to assume when they meet a tragic end. That look was probably the only thing he shared with the dead prostitute, Jo surmised. Rita was at the opposite end of the criminal spectrum: she sold herself to survive. Stuart sold her the drugs that forced her on her back. For this reason, Jo kept all the information on their cases in two separate piles.

Next, she placed a sheet of A4 paper landscape on the desk and wrote both the victims' names on the left-hand side, drawing a line separating them from the space spanning the rest of the page. Alongside each name, in the larger right-hand column, she charted the element of spectacle in each death, listing the body part 'hand' beside Rita, 'eye' after Stuart.

A knot formed in her stomach as she realized that both had also been found in a state of undress.

She pushed the piece of paper aside and reached for the keyboard, running a broad internet search under the words 'murdered' and 'stripped'. The search engine threw back multiple hits. She qualified her trawl with the word 'symbolism' then clicked on a leaked CIA document entitled 'The Human Resource Exploitation Training Manual 1983', and read how some killers had been observed to take a sadistic glee in tampering with something as sacred as death by stripping or mutilating the corpse to instil fear in an enemy. This behaviour had become a recognized psychological technique of warfare. Deliberately humiliating the dead was a way of terrorizing the living.

Jo looked away from the screen. *Is this what you're up to? Are you forcing your enemy to submit?* she thought. She started rolling out a crick in her neck and was giving serious consideration to joining Sexton for a jar – after all, she was off duty – when she had a sudden idea. Scribbling 'Anto Crawley?' shakily at the bottom of her first list, she wrote 'teeth' alongside the list of body parts. Then she logged on to the intelligence wire posting bulletins between all the country's stations and learned that Crawley had been found naked just like the other two, a stone's throw away from the other two crime scenes, in an apartment off Spencer Dock, and that his teeth were not smashed but removed intact and scattered at the scene.

Jo scraped her hair back off her face and stared at the page, then entered the list of body parts into the search engine. What it threw up made her sit back from the screen with a start. She was staring at a parable from the Book of Exodus. 'A life for a life, an eye for an eye, a tooth for a tooth, a hand for a hand, a foot for a foot, a burn for a burn, a wound for a wound, a stroke for a stroke.'

5

Death would have been kinder, the crime reporter Ryan Freeman thought as he watched his daughter Katie's vacant face again fail to respond to the psychiatrist's gentle coaxing. But mercy didn't feature so prominently on the Skids' list of entry requirements. It was just over a month since the gang had abducted his nine-year-old to warn him to stop writing about them, and she hadn't uttered a word since. He still didn't know exactly what they had done to her. It didn't bear thinking about – but it was all he could think about. If Katie wouldn't tell him what had happened, it was up to him to find out. The only thing he had to go on was the CCTV footage recorded from her school. On the day Katie went missing, the Skids' boss Anto Crawley had sneered straight into the camera lens. It was as good as a confession. Ryan had gone from ridiculing Crawley in the paper and belittling him with the nickname Skidmark to trying desperately to contact him to beg him to release his daughter when, out of the blue, Katie had suddenly turned up, unharmed physically but utterly disorientated, on a street near their home.

'Can you draw a magic carpet for me, so we can fly up off the ground and away from things?' Dr Forte asked her.

Ryan glanced around the sterile office – filing cabinets and ornately framed qualifications were hardly likely to stimulate a child whose imagination had been delivered a fatal blow.

Katie looked at the crayons and paper on the table in front of her then back again at the light playing between the wooden slats of a blind opposite. She started to flick her fingers in front of her eyes, studying them intently.

Ryan sighed heavily and jumped to his feet, heading for the water canister to pour himself a drink. He couldn't stand this inactivity. He had to do something . . .

'Ryan,' his wife, Angie, chided.

He gulped the contents back, squeezed the plastic till it cracked and tossed it into the waste-paper basket before returning to his seat, shifting around uncomfortably. He felt every bit as powerless here in the shrink's office as he had been the day that Katie vanished.

Dr Forte took Katie's hand and pulled a puppet over it, inviting her to let it speak on her behalf. But her hand might as well not have been connected to her body, because she stopped moving it and began to rock gently instead. There was no room for flying carpets or puppets wherever she was. Ryan tapped his foot steadily against the leg of the desk.

'Ryan,' Angie said again.

Ryan placed his hand on his leg to remind himself to keep it still. Everything in his life had been spinning out of control from the second he'd switched from being the reporter to being the story itself. But only the people he'd have trusted with his life knew about the nightmare. He'd managed to keep Katie's attack out of the papers because, instead of reporting the crime, he'd called a personal friend in the gardaí when she went missing.

The head of the emergency services was also a long-time associate, and had reassured him that the ambulance crew who'd transported Katie to the Sex Assault Unit of Crumlin Children's Hospital for tests after she was found would keep the incident quiet.

The neighbours had been given a cock-and-bull story about the ambulance having been called because she'd suffered an asthma attack.

No one at the paper knew what had happened. They'd only have found some way of turning it into a story, their 'exclusive'. Ryan knew only too well how it would have read – 'Scum Target Ace Reporter's Kid'. The subheads would have referred to it as the worst attack on the freedom of the press since the murder of his colleague, Veronica Guerin. If he'd been the one reporting a story about someone else's child, he'd have made sure to get Katie's age up near the top to lure the voyeur on and in. It wasn't that he didn't care about the people in his stories, just that human misery was the currency of the newspaper business. If he'd got personally involved in every tragedy he'd covered, he'd have been unable to get out of bed in the morning.

He tipped the swinging-metal-ball gadget perched on the doctor's desk and watched the chain reaction it set into play. Angie shot him an angry look. Nothing new there. Most of the looks he got from her were angry now.

Katie stood up and walked over to the door, ready to leave. She was so broken-spirited that she reminded Ryan of a kicked dog and made him want to punch the wall. Instead, he swallowed the bile rising in the back of his throat as Angie and the doctor tried to persuade Katie back to her seat. *What had been done to her? Why wouldn't she tell him so that they could help her get better?*

'I'd like to know how long Katie will be like this,' he said.

'For Christ's sake, not in front of her,' Angie said despairingly.

'There's no way of knowing,' Dr Forte said, taking the little girl's hand and opening the door into an adjoining playroom, in which Katie could be seen through a wide, one-way window.

When he returned, he continued where he'd left off as they watched her through the glass. 'As I've already explained, we don't know what we're dealing with here. It may well be that Katie suffered a trauma that would have fractured the strongest of adult minds. You have to be patient and prepare yourselves for the fact that she may never recover enough to speak.'

Angie groaned. Ryan put his head in his hands.

'She's not responding to the treatment yet because she's blanked out what happened,' Dr Forte went on. 'It's a classic coping mechanism, where the survivor finds it easier to deny that anything has happened than process the reality. Unfortunately, by disabling the cognitive part of the brain, her ability to communicate has also been paralysed.'

Dr Forte paused and knit his fingers across his chest. 'To put it another way, if Katie's case ever results in a conviction and I am invited by the court to give a Victim Impact statement, I intend to give the view that Katie's mental condition is by far the most devastating I have ever experienced in the twenty-three years that I have been providing therapy to juvenile victims of serious crime.'

Ryan winced. Forte had counselled kids who'd survived rape, attempted murder, seen their parents murdered. What the hell had happened to Katie? He looked at her in the playroom, rocking again, and then tuned out of the rest of Forte's summation, fidgeting with the handle of his chair, picking at a hole in his jeans, scratching at the back of his neck till it stung. When Angie ferociously locked her eyes on his, he focused again.

Katie would almost certainly experience flashbacks, the doctor was saying, and that was why, despite her youth, he was treating her with high doses of medication. She was on child's anti-depressants, and paediatric sleeping tablets to get her through the nights.

'But it's vital that the two of you stay calm and close in front of her,' Dr Forte concluded. 'Katie needs to feel secure if she's ever to relax enough to speak again.'

Angie looked at Ryan expectantly, and he nodded his acceptance of the terms. Dr Forte took it as his cue to bring Katie back into the room. Ryan sat silently through the rest of the session, thinking back to the day it happened, remembering where he'd been when he'd first received the news of Katie's disappearance. He'd been standing at her empty bed when the implication had hit home like a concrete block. *It was all his fault.* The dolls, the diaries with heart-shaped padlocks, the angel figurines Katie collected – all had swirled into props from a horror movie. He really believed, sitting in her bedroom that terrible night she vanished, that she would never come home.

Ryan looked to Katie. She had begun to spin on the spot, faster and faster, head bowed, hands stretched behind her back like little wings.

'Stop, stop, stop,' Angie pleaded, her voice becoming gradually more panic-stricken as she looked from Ryan to her daughter, before running across the room and holding her.

Ryan was thinking about that look he kept seeing in his garda friend's eyes when he'd first called to take down the details of the abduction. He knew the cop was thinking Katie might be better off dead than being kept hostage and suffering, but Ryan was convinced that, no matter what had happened, if he could just get her home, he could fix anything.

For the first time, as he looked at his wife and Katie, the elation he'd experienced when his daughter had returned was replaced by the suspicion that his friend may have been right. What if Katie really was gone for ever anyway?

6

It was dark as Jo steered towards the address she'd found in Rita Nulty's purse. 'Who are you?' she asked aloud, flicking the radio off as if it would help the killer hear. 'And who are you avenging?'

She tried winding the window up, but the handle came off in her hand. She tossed it on to the passenger seat, hitching her collar up against the night air. 'Bloody marvellous,' she groaned. The car was like a fridge as it was because the heater didn't work. A cassette in the deck caught her eye, and she pulled it out, squinting to work out what it was from the handwritten scrawl on the side. It turned out to be one of Dan's compilation albums, which had gone wonky from being played to death. She chucked it on to the seat too, and tried to concentrate on the case.

A couple of minutes later, Jo rubbed her forehead miserably. It was no use, and she knew exactly why. Dan had given her that tape as a present one Christmas years back when they hadn't had a penny. It had meant the world to her. Every song had been picked for a reason, and he'd bitten her ear as he whispered the reminders – the one playing in the pub on their first date, another that they'd been dancing to when he proposed. She had lain curled up in his arms in bed feeling like the luckiest woman on earth. Next morning he'd led her into the driveway, holding his hands over her eyes, until they reached the rest of her present – this bloody car. Jo felt her heart sink. It was hard to believe they could have grown so far apart since then . . .

She pulled up outside a block of flats. A billion euro had been pumped into the rejuvenation of Ballymun, a black spot on the north side, but she was still parked beside a lorry container doubling as a grocery shop. Its corrugated, windowless steel was fireproof and, as it weighed several tonnes, it couldn't be stroked either. The worst part was that the original tenants allocated a place here by the corporation thought they'd landed on their feet. It was a black joke, like the name of the local pub – The Penthouse. The only thing more depressing than the view was the soundtrack, as Ballymun was situated under one of the city's main airport flight paths.

Jo climbed out, discovering that she couldn't even lock the door from outside any more, as the window pane had wedged itself against the lock. *You'd be doing me a favour*, she thought about any would-be joyriders.

She watched two kids ride by on a horse, as if on cue. They were riding bareback, holding on to its mane and causing havoc with the traffic. A double-decker bus was trying to pass, but the driver kept losing his nerve and swerving back. It was only a matter of time before someone and, most likely, the horse, got killed. 'Urban cowboys' they called kids around here. The thought of bringing her kids up somewhere like this made Jo shudder.

She walked over to the tower block and ducked into the stairwell; the lifts were permanently out of order. The smell of urine hit her taste buds at the same time as it did her nostrils. Jo almost jumped out of her skin when a group of youths in hoodies taking the stairs three at a time almost knocked her over. She called, 'Oi!' after them, ignoring their hand gestures and taunts. Fortunately, Rita's flat was on the second floor. Jo blew into the space between her hands, and rubbed as she continued on up. Even in summer, her feet felt cold with all the concrete. If you grew up in this part of town, life presented you with only two choices to escape it, she thought: sell drugs or take them. Like Rita.

Finding the door, she rapped a gleaming brass lion's head and stepped back, checking her shoes and brushing specks of fluff off her jacket. Catching sight of her reflection in the knocker, she realized that old habits die hard. She used to go through the same grooming routine before every death knock. She'd done more than most, as women were considered better purveyors of bad news. Some were; some weren't. She remembered one who always got a fit of giggles on the doorstep. Formal training for family liaison officers tasked with comforting a family, usually in cases of murder, had only been introduced after a male FLO working with the family of Raonaid Murray – a schoolgirl killed yards from her home – allegedly urinated in the spot where she had been knifed to death.

If Jo'd been the one dispatched here earlier today to break the news of the death, she'd have been practising what to say at this point – not that the words mattered. Most people guessed the second they opened the door.

'Mrs Nulty?' she asked the chink of white-haired, spindly pensioner peering behind a safety chain, after she heard the sound of a bolt-action lock.

'Who wants to know?' the old woman answered.

'I'm Detective Inspector Jo Birmingham,' Jo said, reaching into her bag for her ID then changing her mind, depressed by another reminder of the amount of crap she carried everywhere. 'I'm so sorry for your loss . . . I need to ask you some questions about your daughter, if you feel up to it.'

'Come back tomorrow,' the old woman whispered. 'It's late.'

Jo held up Rita's two €50 notes. 'She'd have wanted you to have these.'

The door closed momentarily, then swung open. Jo stepped inside and carried on past the woman, down the hall a few steps, left into the front room. Foxy's first rule of thumb when it came to interviewing hostile witnesses was, the further inside you got, the more time you had to bring them around to your way of thinking. Procedure required a visit just like this to find out about the victim's habits, associates, vehicles and movements prior to death, and to obtain particulars of his/her clothing, jewellery, personal effects, recent whereabouts and time of last meal. Ideally, you examined the victim's bedroom and took possession of photographs, documents, diaries, etc., for potential use in the investigation too.

But Jo wasn't attached to the investigation, at least not yet anyway.

Inside, the room was small and cheaply furnished but spotless. The air had the dry feel of gas heating, making the sickly-sweet smell of air freshener overpowering. Life-sized porcelain King Charles spaniels sat on either side of a tiled fireplace. Plastic flowers were on display in the window – hydrangeas.

Mrs Nulty was wearing a shiny, navy button-up pinafore over her clothes, and a pair of trendy Uggs that all the teenage girls were wearing. They didn't lift off the ground when she moved.

'You'll have to keep it brief,' she said.

Jo scanned her face, thinking that her kind of chippy, know-my-rights attitude only came with experience, especially after the news she'd got today. The woman's eyes were not red-rimmed or puffy, she observed, and Mrs Nulty's hands and voice were steady. *Because her murder came as no surprise to you*, Jo concluded. *You lost her years ago.*

Jo sat down on a floral-patterned couch and unbuttoned her coat. Foxy also believed in making yourself at home. It helped people to open up. 'How are you?' she asked.

'Like I said, it's late.'

Jo's gaze travelled to the Belleek china models of dancing milkmaids on the TV and a brass carriage clock over the fireplace positioned on a crocheted doily. If Rita had lived here, she'd have hocked them long ago to pay for her habit.

'Please, sit down, Mrs Nulty. This won't take long.'

'You asked me if I was up to it. Well, I'm not. Come back tomorrow.'

But tomorrow an investigation team would have been assigned to Rita's case and, if Jo wasn't on it, she'd have no business being here. As it was, she could be disciplined for making an unauthorized call-out. She cut to the chase. 'I need to know if your daughter had recently found God.'

Mrs Nulty shook her head.

'Maybe she started going to church out of the blue or took up Bible classes?' Jo persisted.

Still nothing.

'Mrs Nulty, I'm sorry to press you, but I believe whoever killed Rita may have been some sort of religious fanatic, and it's really important you think hard about what I'm saying.

Do you remember Rita describing any of her clients as a "holy Joe", or maybe a "religious freak"?'

Mrs Nulty grappled for the armchair like she was about to break a fall.

Jo took a breath. She couldn't believe she'd come out with something so insensitive. It looked like Mrs Nulty hadn't known her daughter's occupation. Jo had seen other officers harden to the job over the years, and it always shocked her. She was determined not to go that way herself – the justice system was clinical enough. She had lost count of the number of times she'd seen some member of a victim's family shout out in distress in a courtroom, get held in contempt and be transported to a cell and held there until they purged their contempt by apologizing to the court. Mostly how they felt came pouring out on the steps of the court, to a waiting scrum of journalists, after the trial ended. Usually, all they'd wanted to say in the first place was who they'd lost, and how different the victim was to the person described in court, information treated by the judges and barristers as if it would cause the pillars of the temple to fall. Jo had a big problem with the idea that it was necessary to trash the victim's character to prove the defence of provocation. The criminal system was going to have to take a leaf out of the civil code and follow the principle 'You wronged me and I seek rectitude' if it was ever going to give bereaved families a sense of justice.

'Tell me about Rita . . .' Jo said, deliberately softening her voice.

Mrs Nulty stared at her blankly.

'The kind of person she was, I mean,' Jo continued. 'What made her laugh? What made her cry? Who was she?'

Mrs Nulty pulled a length of stringy tissue from her sleeve

and ran it over her eyes and nose. 'She was a good daughter
. . . Until drugs got her. You know, she got leukaemia when
she was seven and survived it. And for what?'

Jo shook her head. 'I'm so sorry.'

'Started on aerosol cans when she was ten. Had her first
hit of heroin at thirteen years old. She told me once she had
to get wasted so she could forget.'

'Forget what?' Jo asked.

Mrs Nulty shrugged. 'What does it matter now? My husband's dead. Rita's dead. It was between the two of them.'

Jo leaned forward and took her hand, placing the money
in her palm. 'Look, maybe you could have a think and ring
the station if anything occurs to you? I'm sure Rita would
have wanted you to have this.'

A set of fingers bent at a right angle from swollen knuckles closed around the money. 'It's probably nothing, but
there was something a couple of days back,' Mrs Nulty suddenly said. 'Not a priest exactly. But he said that I could
trust him because his twin brother was one . . . a priest, I
mean. He called looking for Rita.'

Jo frowned. 'Did he give a name?'

Mrs Nulty shook her head.

'What did he say, exactly?' Jo asked.

'That's just it, he didn't say anything. He just asked if Rita
was here, and when I said she was out he asked if I knew
where she'd gone. He joked that I could trust him, and then
he said it . . . that his twin brother was a priest. I didn't
know where she was. That's what I told him.'

'What age was he?' Jo asked.

'Late thirties . . . I don't know, I'm no good at ages, but I
never forget a face.'

A defence barrister would have a field day, Jo thought.

He'd ask all about your cataracts, glaucoma, not what you saw. But still, it was a start. 'Can you give me a description?'

'Dark, not bad-looking, if you like that sort.'

'What sort?'

'Like those gypsies living on the roundabout.'

So most likely to be Eastern European, Jo realized. 'What about a mobile number?' she asked. 'Did Rita have one?'

Mrs Nulty shook her head again.

Jo was losing patience. 'I need to know where she really lived,' she persisted.

Mrs Nulty looked surprised. 'Rita lived here, she just wasn't in is all. That's what I told him.'

Why don't you want to tell me? Jo wondered. Are you scared of losing face with friends and family? Or is it because you don't want to tell them you turfed Rita out on to the streets? Maybe because of some dodgy social-welfare claim that had her here as a dependent.

'Mrs Nulty, we can't catch whoever killed her if you're holding back on us. She was your daughter, for heaven's sake!'

'You must be mistaken,' Mrs Nulty replied sullenly. 'This was Rita's home.'

7

The fourth victim lay naked on the flat of his back, arms and legs stretched and tethered to the corners of the bed, mouth stuffed with a dirty rag. He could squirm and moan, but barely. Beads of sweat flickered to life across his wrinkled forehead and rolled down the sides of his face.

'If I tell you one of the things he told me, you will pick up stones and throw them at me; a fire will come out of the stones and burn you up,' the killer said as he leaned over to inspect the binds, his face hidden by the flaps of a pointed hood attached to his cloak. Satisfied, he sat his bag on the bed, opened the clasp and pulled out a hypodermic needle.

The victim's head bolted sideways, frantic eyes following his captor's every move. The killer reached into his waistcoat pocket, removed a vial of liquid, turned it upside down and flicked it with his index finger to tap an air bubble towards the top. The needle pierced the foil lid and sucked the contents up slowly.

The victim's head bobbed as the killer eyed then pinched the pulsing vein running down his neck.

With a prick the needle penetrated the artery.

The victim exhaled deeply through his nostrils as the last twitching muscles in his neck grew still.

The killer stopped breathing himself, waiting for the

moment he knew was coming, savouring the anticipation. It hit like a tidal wave, endorphins surging through his veins and giving him an overwhelming feeling of omnipotence, the whole point of the exercise. When the ecstasy subsided, he got back to work, removing a knife, chisel, pliers and screwdriver from his case to set about the ritualistic aspect of the proceedings.

Tuesday

8

Next morning, after only managing a couple of hours sleep, Jo drove to upmarket Merrion Square. After checking the car seats for valuables, she got out of the car, slotted an exorbitant amount of loose change into the meter and criss-crossed her handbag over her shoulder. The Georgian terraces with their wrought-iron balconies and fanlights over brightly coloured doors looked magnificent, but by night the area turned into a notorious red-light district. If she'd had a penny for every time she'd had to argue against men – especially ones she worked with – that women didn't sell sex to fund their college education or even because they were turned on by danger, the cost of the parking wouldn't have been an issue. There was one overwhelming reason she knew of why women went on the game, and whether it suited men's fantasies or not, it was to pay for drugs.

Crossing the street to the National Gallery, she glanced right, where a street away a cricket match would be getting a gentle clap from the crowd on the lawn in Trinity College, and left towards St Stephen's Green, where parents brought their toddlers to feed the ducks. The last squalid moments of the murdered prostitute, junkie and drug lord seemed to belong to a different city. If Jo'd had her way, every white-collar worker who believed they'd *earned* the right to party with the so-called recreational drug of their choice at the weekend would have been forced to attend the latest gangland autopsy and made to understand that the trail of responsibility led directly back to the market principle of demand and so straight to them.

Having scrolled through the contacts in her mobile phone as she walked, with one hand she dialled Gerry in Justice and with the other rummaged out a Nicorette tab, which she almost couldn't bring herself to put in her mouth.

'You don't bring me flowers . . .' she announced, chewing hard as the call connected to the minister's spin doctor.

'What happened . . . You run out of flies to pick the wings off?' he answered.

'That's funny, Gerry, but don't quit the day job . . . The Separate Legal Representation report . . . where are we on that?'

Jo could hear Gerry drumming his pen on his desk.

'Lawyers for rape victims in court,' she continued. 'We've got to rebalance the scales of justice to stop victims feeling like they're the ones being put on trial. I sent the minister a briefing document. I don't touch-type, Gerry. That means it was a lot of work for me. It's been on his desk the last six months . . . All fifty-five pages of it, which works out at less than ten pages a month to read. Maybe our boss should consider one of those adult-education programmes . . . When's he . . .'

'Birmingham, he's been a little busy. Thought you'd have noticed. Murder rate goes up, so does the number of times his name appears in a column inch. Speaking of which, they're all in your district. Where are we on that?'

'You had your bagel this morning, Gerry?'

'I'm salivating as we speak, just waiting for you to hang up.'

'Cream cheese?' Jo guessed.

'Bacon and guacamole.'

'Guacamole repeats a lot – maybe try a croissant tomorrow.'

Jo removed the phone from her ear and glanced at it, then pressed it back to be sure. 'Nice talking to you too,' she said, shoving it into her pocket and entering the main entrance of the National Gallery.

Inside, she pushed her shades up into her hair and walked with a spring in her step. She knew that no sex customer who'd been about to pay Rita Nulty for oral, anal, a hand job, titty-wank, or whatever it was he was prepared to pay her to perform, would have called to the prostitute's mother's home. That meant the man who told Mrs Nulty he was a 'priest's twin' had not been seeking Rita out for sex, which also meant he could have been the killer. If he was someone legit, why the mystery? Why not just tell the pensioner his name? The timing fit too . . . right before the slaying.

It also meant the killer had made his first slip, because now she could possibly have him ID'd by Mrs Nulty in a line-up – once she found him. But first she'd have to work out how he was choosing his victims, because there was no doubt in her mind he would strike again. He was only halfway though the list of body parts . . .

Jo's heels clicked along the gleaming parquet floor of the gallery. She knew the layout like the back of her hand. Four wings, two levels, the prized Picasso on the mezzanine, and the symmetry of the six archways in the central Milltown wing tricking the eye like a mirror. She'd come to study the religious themes which dominated the Italian collection. This was where she'd come to terms with the car crash that had killed her father. She had been fifteen years old. In the two decades that had passed since, she'd learned to live with the grief, but nothing could change the simple fact that it had all been her fault.

That night, she'd gotten drunk for the first time. First disco. First fag. First snog – some guy in blue suede crepes into The Cure who asked her to dance to Bros then put his arms around her waist for the slow set. She'd written her number on his arm in black eyeliner after standing still for the national anthem at the party's end.

She was supposed to have used her last fiver to travel home with her sister Sue, just as she'd promised their dad before heading out. But she was having too good a time. Instead of filling her empty bottle with tap water in the ladies to make it look like she still had something to sip, she'd used her taxi money to buy two more bottles of Budweiser.

She'd had to ring home to ask her father to come and collect her, from a phone box outside. She'd lost her sight temporarily after the crash – maybe that was why the memory of the sounds of what happened were so amplified in her memory: the phone box where she'd rung home being shelled by rain; a moth thrashing off a light bulb over her head, the static twitching after each bash; her change clinking into the slot; the pips ticking like a heartbeat; the round dial whirring back after each number; her father's sleepy voice agreeing to come and collect her from the disco . . .

He'd found her sitting on the kerb, head hunched between her legs – the whole street swimming. She'd never got the chance to panic about what he thought of finding her in that state. That little rite of passage was supposed to come the next morning, along with the hangover from hell, Sudocrem on her beard rash and obsessing with her friends about whether

Curehead would ring. Instead, she was lying in a hospital bed praying to God that at any minute she would wake up and her father would not be lying in the morgue downstairs.

Later, she couldn't bring herself to tell her mum or sister what had happened. The truth was, she'd pulled the handle of the passenger door open while her father was driving so she could lean out of it on the carriageway to vomit . . . His pyjama-sleeved arm had lunged across her to close the door, and the car swerved straight into an oncoming lorry.

Jo never told a soul. Not even Dan. What would she have said? That the reason she was so good at getting into a killer's head was because she was one?

After she'd recovered, she used to come to the gallery because it was the only place it was socially acceptable to stand absolutely still without looking like a weirdo. All around her, life went on regardless as the sounds of that night kept playing over and over, like one of those tunes you can't get out of your head: a single heel clicking with every second step as she walked to her dad's car – she'd lost a shoe; the lorry's horn blowing that deafening foghorn noise; tyres screeching; metal ripping and glass shattering; a hollow brushing sound as her dad was sucked through the windscreen; and the sound of someone crying, almost drowned out by the car alarm – herself.

Who was she before the night her dad died? Jo asked herself. Someone she'd never got the chance to know.

Who was she after? Someone completely different, who'd have traded blindness in a heartbeat – she'd needed cornea transplants – if it had meant freeing herself of survivor guilt.

Her mum and Sue had moved to Australia a few years later, when she was eighteen, to try and 'put the past behind them'. They'd begged Jo to come, but she couldn't leave her father on his own, not in a grave, not when she'd been the one who'd put him there. And she could never shake the feeling that they'd have a better chance of starting over without her.

The smell from the exact same ratio of dust to polish hadn't changed in twenty years, Jo thought as she stepped out of the lift on to the second floor. As she crossed the Beit Wing, she realized that everything in her adult life could probably be traced back to the accident. The birth of her son, Rory, and marriage to Dan when she was still in her teens: a quick-fix solution to replace the family she'd lost. The connection she felt to victims of crime, because she knew first hand what the agony of grief felt like, and even joining the force, so she could start fending for herself.

Out of the side of her eye, the painting hanging on the furthest wall through the last of the six open arches caught her attention, and she turned to face the Caravaggio, the gallery's major new addition. She hadn't come across many works by Caravaggio before, but this one she knew all about because it had been presumed a fake and had been hanging in a Jesuit dining room in Leeson Street since the 1930s, until its recent rediscovery created a furore in the art world.

Jo approached until she was close enough to reach out and touch the paint. Not so much as a brass-slung rope separated her from the moonlight bouncing off the faces of seven life-sized figures, all in profile except for the downcast head of Christ, second from the left, straining away from Judas's kiss as three soldiers on the right moved in to take him. On the far left, a figure was fleeing, his arms outstretched, his fingers splayed, his open mouth conveying the horror of what was unfolding. On the far right, a man – Caravaggio himself – was straining a lantern over the soldiers' heads towards Christ, blocked by a human wall of gleaming, buckled armour.

But it was Christ's posture that intrigued Jo. In all the panic, he was the only one perfectly still, his hands joined limply in prayer. Only his creased forehead betrayed any torment. Gaunt shadows danced across his face, making flickering hollows of his eyes and cheekbones.

She knew the painting was telling her something about the case but, stealing a worried glance at her watch, Jo realized that if she didn't leave for the office right now, whatever it was would be irrelevant, because she might not even make the investigation team.

9

By mid-morning, Jo was standing outside Dan's office trying to muster the courage to enter. It was originally an L-shape, but the leg had been annexed off to accommodate Jeanie's work space. This was the reason Jo was hesitating outside the door. She hated the way Jeanie would try to make her wait in that claustrophobic little space until she'd cleared her entry with Dan first. Jo got the same treatment when she dialled Dan's direct number: Jeanie always picked up first and asked who was speaking.

Swallowing her resentment, Jo rapped twice and entered. Breezing past Jeanie with a captain's salute, she ignored the loud protests and continued on through the adjoining door into Dan's inner quarters, pressing the connecting door closed with her back.

Dan looked up over his computer monitor and motioned to the chair in front of his desk. Jo's gaze shifted from the lemon geranium that had appeared on the window sill behind him to his suit jacket draped on a coat hanger on a hook on the coat-stand, and settled on the back of an ornate photo frame propped on the corner of his desk.

'You wanted to see me,' he said, taking some papers from the In/Out tray and banging them together before putting them back in exactly the same position.

Folding her arms across her chest, Jo wondered who had selected his chunky pink tie, the type preferred by the younger, sharper solicitors in the courts, the ones who specialized in personal-injury claims, the kind of people she thought he regarded as sharks.

Pushing her shoulders back a fraction, she said, 'I'd like to formally enquire if my transfer's been processed.' No reply. No eye contact. Dan reached for the mouse and began clicking files shut on his monitor. 'It's been six months now since my latest submission and I still haven't . . .'

Dan's presidential black leather chair creaked loudly as he shifted position. 'I'm afraid I find myself unable to recommend it at the moment,' he said.

'Why? This is insane. Your life has moved on, Dan. Why can't you give me the chance to do the same with mine?'

Rows of tired crinkles appeared at the sides of his eyes. 'I need you to head up the Rita Nulty investigation,' he said. 'Solve it, and you get to go whenever you like.'

'What?' Jo sat down in the uncomfortable cup chair Dan kept for visitors.

He reached for a sheet of paper from the top tray and slid it across the desk. 'These are the officers I can spare.'

A murder brief. Jo felt a jolt of excitement. 'Thank you, Dan. You won't regret this, I promise.' She knew he'd take flak for this – be accused of giving her special treatment – but she also knew that she could solve the case.

Reaching over to take the list from him, she overturned the picture on his desk with her elbow. It fell, face up, revealing the snap behind the framed glass. Dan was standing behind Jeanie with his hands on her shoulders. Jeanie was nuzzling Harry on her lap. Rory stood to one side, looking a hair's breadth off the centre of the lens, making him seem removed. Dan had a high, forced smile on his face and a round-necked jumper on – the kind men only wore at Christmas, the kind he didn't wear, the kind that left her in no doubt that this was not a case of waving at a passer-by and asking them to take their picture. This was a posed shot, and she could tell from the background it had been taken at a photographer's studio.

Dan stared at the picture as if he were seeing it for the first time too, then caught Jo's eye guiltily. In that split second she saw the old Dan, the one who would say or do anything rather than hurt her. He reached over quickly and slid the photo towards a desk drawer. 'I didn't put that there . . .' he began awkwardly.

'You told me last night it wasn't serious,' Jo said, her breathing short.

He glanced to the door behind her then lowered his voice. 'You still haven't said you want me back, Jo. I can't wait for ever.'

Jo focused on his hands gripping the desk and pictured them on Jeanie. 'I've taken the house off the market,' she said. 'The boys have had enough upheaval. I'm sorry.'

Dan leaned his chair back as far as it would go then stood up and walked over to the window and stared out. Jo wanted to go to him, press her face against his back and wrap her arms around his waist, beg him to come home and tell him that everything would be all right.

'Don't you mean you have had enough upheaval?' he answered.

Jo blinked rapidly, but held her tongue. She made a big effort to concentrate on the names on the page. As she did so, she realized her big break came with a big catch. Dan was assigning Mac and another of the station's nonentities,

Merrigan, to the case. If Rita had come from some nice leafy estate on the south side with an SUV parked outside and had not had a shitty life nobody cared about, he'd never have pulled a stunt like this. Mac was a liability and would need babysitting so as not to get into any more trouble, and Merrigan was about as politically correct as Bernard Manning. Sending either of them to interview the girls working on the street would be a disaster. 'No,' she said. 'I can't work with these guys.'

Dan turned around.

'I need Foxy,' Jo said. 'I know he hasn't been on a live case in years but he's such a stickler for detail, I could do with a mind like his. And I want Sexton, because of his contacts on the street. As many mules as I need to cover the door-to-doors and checkpoint questionnaires, obviously, and every detective that can be spared.'

Dan loosened his tie and unbuttoned the top button of his shirt, revealing a neatly trimmed arc of chest hair. 'Foxy, fine. Sexton, for now. But Mac needs the experience and Merrigan is doing nothing else.'

'I don't like Mac's history, and Merrigan is bloody useless,' she said.

'Fine, forget Merrigan, but Mac stays,' he said, adding, 'Final answer.'

She opened her mouth to protest, but he wasn't having any of it. 'Get me something to go on and I might even let you keep Sexton for the duration.'

Jeanie burst into the office to ask if he intended to keep his lunch appointment, making Jo wonder if she'd had her ear pressed to a glass on the door outside. She noticed how perfect her hair and make-up looked. The wraparound dress she was wearing emphasized her fantastic figure. If Dan hadn't been her ex, she'd have taken Jeanie aside and told her not to try so hard, because the odds were stacked against the relationship working. Jeanie was a civilian, and that meant she was going to take every anniversary dinner he missed because of work and every romantic weekend he cancelled at the last minute personally.

Jo stood to leave. 'Can you contact these members?' she asked Jeanie, holding Dan's list out. 'Tell them I intend holding the first case conference on the Rita Nulty case in the incident room straight after lunch, and I expect everyone there. No excuses.'

Jeanie turned away, so Jo pressed the list down on Dan's desk, saying 'asap,' in a tone that said she was the one who called the shots on this case now and that she intended to find out who had murdered Rita Nulty in record time. That meant that, from this point on, Jeanie was the least of her problems.

10

Ryan Freeman lay spreadeagled on his couch, studying the TV screen. The new addition to the family – Cassie, a border collie bought for Katie in the hope that she would help reawaken her social skills – was lying on the rug watching him, her head tilting occasionally as if she had tuned into his pain.

Ryan was watching the CCTV footage taken outside Katie's school on the day she'd disappeared, as he had a million times before, convinced he had to be missing something. He believed that, once he found it, he'd have the link he needed to begin unravelling Katie's problems.

The sepia images moving across the screen were so grainy they had a phantom feel. The now dead drug lord Crawley was wearing a trucker cap pulled low over his eyes, the peak barely visible under his hoodie. He wore this under a black leather jacket, elasticated at the waist, with a pair of blue jeans and white trainers.

Ryan pointed the remote at the TV angrily, fast-forwarding to the point when Crawley moved robotically, owing to the slow snapshot speed, towards a mystery car which had pulled up outside the gates. Only a corner of the vehicle could be seen; the rest was just outside the frame. It was impossible to work out the make of the vehicle, though the right tail-light and last number of the plate were just about visible in the upper left-hand corner.

Four swift frames later: Crawley bending over and into the driver's window . . . gesturing like a madman by jabbing his index finger in at the driver, his elbow in and out of shot . . . recoiling from an invisible shove from the driver, his cap spinning off his head behind him. Ryan watched Crawley try to reef open the driver's door then have a change of heart and grab a clump of his hair through the window instead. Long, fair hair came momentarily into view.

A vicious row, but with whom, Ryan wondered, as he had constantly, since first seeing it. What did the woman driving the car know about Crawley's presence? What were they fighting over? Had she provided him with information about Katie's movements or helped Crawley identify Katie just before the abduction? And most importantly, if he found her, would she help Ryan unlock Katie from her world of silence in return for immunity from prosecution?

He paused the screen, searching for any new clue as to who the woman was, anything that he might previously have missed. He had already drawn up a shortlist of all the mothers who had collected their daughters that day and had run background checks, but none had anything shady in their past that could be linked to the gangster.

He hit play and felt his stomach constrict like it was about to take a punch. On the screen, Crawley was turning back towards the school and walking, in that cocky, swaggering way he used to have, directly up to the camera fixed to the wall above the main entrance. Once he was as close to it as he could get, he looked up and gave a sneering salute to the person he knew would end up watching this film – Ryan.

Ryan froze the image. Crawley was situated no more than three feet below the lens, the skin taut on his face, his expression one of defiant hatred, his message unmistakable – 'You get to me, I get to your daughter.'

'R.I.P.,' Ryan said.

Katie entered the room, and he hit the stop button quickly and sat straight up. Cassie stood, wagged her tail and went over to her to nuzzle her hand.

'Okay, sweetheart?' he asked.

She moved, oblivious to him, cornflower-blue eyes trance-like, as if she had earphones in and was listening to some secret soundtrack. She knelt beside Cassie and wrapped her arms around the dog's neck, lying her head on her neck. Cassie wriggled free to lick her face.

Katie began methodically to brush the dog's coat.

Ryan was smiling, but his eyes were brimming.

'Daddy?' she asked, suddenly sitting back on her hunkers.

'Yes, my darling?' he answered automatically.

'Do dogs cry?'

Ryan stared. Had she actually spoken? He wanted to leap up and whirl her round. He looked from her to the dog.

'Do they dream like we do?'

'Yes,' he said, gently, kneeling down beside her. 'In their own way.' His chest started to heave.

'What kind of things make them cry?'

He reached for her hand. 'Being lost, my darling. And scared. And hurt. The same as for us.'

Katie hugged Cassie tightly again. He saw the glaze spreading across her eyes and began kissing the top of her head to try and keep her with him. But she had begun to shake in his arms, slowly at first then more violently.

Angie appeared in the doorway and lunged, trying to pull

him away. 'Let her go. Ryan! What are you doing . . . Stop! We need to lie her down flat.'

He stood up, trying to explain. 'No, you don't understand. She spoke . . . She said . . .'

But Katie's eyes were rolling in her head.

'Call an ambulance,' Angie ordered. 'She's convulsing. Ryan, for Christ's sake, call one now!'

11

After speaking to the officer keeping the cordon on the balcony and waiting for him to log her time of entry, Jo ducked under the 'Garda No Entry Crime Scene' navy and white tape and entered the apartment where she'd found Rita, closing the door behind her. The body was gone, the forensic work finished. Jo was back because she believed that, if the killer had made any mistakes, her best hope of finding evidence of them would be here. If it was him who'd called on Rita's mother, he was overly cocky and, hopefully, by the time he'd got Rita here, he would have grown careless.

Jo's fists clenched as she braced herself for what was coming next. She wanted to see the world through his eyes, to feel what he had. She dreaded putting herself through the emotional wringer, but she was going to do whatever was necessary to find him. For the last eighteen months, her professional life had languished because her personal life was falling apart. This was the first chance she'd had to get her teeth stuck into a case, and her adrenaline levels had risen. Dan had been right to laugh at her the previous day – work was a huge part of who she was.

Yesterday, when she stood on this spot, Jo had reached for the light switch. Today, she kept her eyes screwed shut as she thought about what she knew about Rita. She pictured the kind of looks Rita must have got when she boarded her last bus, dressed in the kind of clothes that would have revealed her occupation as well as any sign around her neck. If the bus had been crowded and Rita sat down beside someone on a double seat, Jo presumed they'd have stood and walked away rather than be associated with her. She wondered how young Rita was when her father first hurt her so badly. Jo was ready . . .

She opened her eyes and held her hand against the apartment door. 'You're already angry with her by the time you get to this point, aren't you?' she asked out loud. 'That's why you forced entry. You both know what she is. Rita Nulty has no right to say no. So why does she? It's because she already knows you, doesn't she? She knows what you're capable of. You're someone she's frightened of. Otherwise, why would you have to break in?'

Jo lifted her head. She reached into her leather jacket for her notepad and pen, and scribbled: 'Ask street workers about recent violent attacks?'

Her eyes roamed to the coffee table where she'd seen the cocaine, now covered with metallic-grey fingerprint dust. 'Do you keep whatever you used to break in with in your hand or put it down?' she muttered. 'Yes, you put it down, for now. You need her calm. The art of ceremony requires preparation, so you've brought a peace offering. But you can't risk her actually taking the coke, can you? Might fire her up for a fight. You've too much work to do. That's why we found it untouched.'

She headed across to the bedroom and flung open the door. She swallowed: the bloodstains were still there, more disconcerting without the body.

Jo held her own hand up at arm's length, spreading the fingers out, turning it from back to front. 'Do you take what she owes you while she's living or dead?' Jo knew the forensic analysis of the blood spatter would yield the answer. In her experience, only a pumping heart would blood-spray every surface – even the ceiling. She looked up and saw the telltale signs. 'You need her alive, of course, because justice requires punishment. What did you use? An axe? A cleaver? You'd have needed to hide it, though, wouldn't you, along with the crowbar you used for breaking down the door.' She turned to a new page of her notebook. 'Long coat? Bag?' she wrote.

Jo hurried over to the bathroom on the right where the towels had lain before they'd been bagged and taken to the lab. 'Who washed?' she asked. 'You or her? The clock is ticking. Any stray or pre-booked punter could come by at any point . . . her pimp, for example. Why was washing so important? It could have risked the kill . . .'

She reached to the tap in the bath to turn the shower on, but the lever was damaged and the water kept flicking out the bath spout.

She looked around the bath but could see no stray peroxide strands. 'It's you who's in the bath, isn't it?' Jo asked the killer. 'Not all of you, there isn't time, just your feet . . . like in the Bible? Did you want Rita to dry them with her hair, like Mary Magdalene?'

Jo wrote in her notebook: 'Have samples of Rita's hair from PM sent to forensics for contact analysis.'

'If she's the whore,' she asked aloud, 'who is it that you think you are?'

A knock on the door made her start. The garda who'd been on duty outside stuck his head around the door. 'You asked me to remind you about your conference, in case you lost track of time,' he said.

12

Sexton hadn't been notified that he'd lost the investigation to Jo Birmingham because he was in the interview room with a skinny scrote who had just confessed to murdering the Skids' drug lord, Anto Crawley. Sexton didn't believe for a second that 'Skinny', as he was known, had executed Crawley. He hadn't asked Sexton for a brief yet. Guilty parties always wanted their brief. Sexton suspected that, with the Skids' succession battle heating up, Skinny here was making a bid for the leadership. Crawley had been tortured, an old underworld way of sending out a message: there were worse things than death – there was a hard death. If Skinny presumed Crawley had been caught touting to gardaí, maybe he figured that he could gain a lot of ground in the Skids' pecking order by owning up to a crime he didn't commit.

Sexton leaned across the desk. 'Tell me what happened,' he said again.

Skinny wasn't hunched in the plastic chair because of an attitude problem. He just didn't have any shoulders. The sum of his parts, as far as Sexton could see, was an Adam's apple and a bum-fluff excuse of a moustache. There was a jerkiness to him that Sexton associated less with drugs and more with the kind of man who liked to hit women; he had something to hide, and it was making him jumpy, but he was certain it was not Anto Crawley's murder.

'I heard Anto Crawley was in the area so I –' Skinny said.

'Hold it,' Sexton cut in, straightening up and pressing his hands into the small of his back. 'Where are we talking about?'

Skinny rolled his eyes and sighed. 'I already told ya, Spencer Dock.' He turned to the overweight detective on his left, who was sitting on a chair beside the door. 'Can I have another cup of tea? One with sugar in it this time?'

The detective stared straight ahead. His only purpose there was to offset any allegations of garda brutality, which had become par for the course in the days before everything was recorded on camera and audio tape.

Skinny cleared his throat, looked around for somewhere to hawk, caught the glint in Sexton's eye and swallowed.

'Address?'

'Can't remember, mate.'

'Time?'

'I'm no good with times.'

'Then what?' Sexton pressed.

'Then I got a knife and I –'

'Wait . . .' Sexton cut in, lighting up a cigarette. 'Where did you get the knife?' The smoking ban wasn't enforced when it came to the country's prisons, which meant a blind eye was turned to scenarios such as this – encouraging prisoners to talk.

He turned his back on Skinny and studied the view from the window. The city's bus terminus was directly opposite, the Customs House sat further back, there was a diamond-shaped sculpture of mirrored glass on the forecourt outside, and a couple of nice restaurants had sprung up recently too.

Not that Sexton ate out since Maura had died. It just reminded him of who wasn't there with him. They'd married in a church just around the corner from here, held her funeral mass there too. 'By her own hand,' the bastard of a priest kept saying. Like Sexton needed reminding . . .

'I got the blade off a fella and I –'

'What's the "fella's" name?' Sexton interrupted.

'I'm not grassing me mates up, no way, man.'

'So you took the knife,' Sexton said, 'which your anonymous friend gave you, and you . . .'

'Anonawha'?'

'Then what?'

'Then, when I saw Crawley coming, I went in after him. Crawley was a prick. He was a snout. He had it coming to him, and I made sure he got it. That's why I smashed up his teeth.'

'You can't remember where this was?' Sexton enquired.

'It was one of those old warehouses.'

'What's it used for?'

'Nothing, it's a crack den.' Skinny puffed out his chest and went on. 'That slapper who was murdered the other day used to squat there. Even the homeless fellas won't stay there. It's a kip.'

Sexton turned around slowly. Had this nonentity just linked two murder victims to the same location? 'Oh yeah?' He looked over to the detective. 'You can get him that tea now.'

'Great,' Skinny called after the detective leaving the room. 'Got any biscuits? HobNobs over Jersey Creams if there's any going. You coppers only ever have Jersey Creams.'

Sexton grabbed the plastic seat opposite and pulled it around to the side of the table. *Less confrontational*, he thought. He leaned back, stretched his legs out and took a few drags on his fag, then stood it on its butt so the ash started piling up on itself. Old trick, never spilt a flake, unless someone knocked it. *Keep it nice and casual*, he thought. *Soon as he knows he's got me, he'll start playing games.*

'You heard of Stuart Ball, or Git, as I think he was known?'

Skinny nodded. 'Him and that slag used to go out when she worked as a lap dancer, before she got real bad on drugs. Heard the pair of them kidnapped a kid for a day and kept her in the warehouse where I knifed Crawley. All the junkies were talking about it. Sick, so it was. I wouldn't be surprised if that's why Git and his old mot were killed.'

'When was this exactly, can you remember?'

Skinny opened his mouth to say something then ran his thumb off the pads of his first two fingers instead. 'It'll cost ya.'

Sexton reached into an inside jacket pocket for his wallet but slipped an empty hand out quickly when the detective laboured back in and placed a plastic cup in front of Skinny with a paper plate of miniature Jaffa Cakes.

'Can't eat them Lidl ones, they make me teeth hop, man.'

The detective threw his head at the door. Sexton hesitated, then followed as Skinny blew a mouthful of tea in a wide spray. 'Fucking hell, you can't make tea in a microwave, it's bleeding wrong, man,' Skinny roared.

'What is it?' Sexton asked the detective impatiently in the corridor.

'You're not going to believe who you're going to have to answer to on this one,' the detective told him.

Sexton frowned.

'The chief's just given Jo Birmingham the Rita Nulty murder investigation,' the detective said.

Sexton gave a half-smile. 'Did he now?' As the detective tried to continue on into the room, Sexton took a step sideways to block his path. 'Don't bother, I'm about to send him home.'

His hand on his wallet, Sexton went back in to speak to Skinny alone. It was nothing personal, he thought. He liked Jo Birmingham, she was one of the most instinctive cops he'd ever worked with. But Ryan Freeman was a close friend, and Sexton had been helping him try and find out what happened to his daughter. And if that meant bribing one of the scrotes who knew the people who had hurt her, then so be it.

13

Jo sat on the edge of the top table in the incident room, legs crossed at the ankles, arms folded, fingers drumming the sleeves of her plain white shirt. A dull throb had struck up in the back of her head the second she'd stepped into the killer's skin, but this wasn't the cause of her darkening mood. Having prepped the room for the briefing, arranged the desks into a semblance of order, cleared the wipe board and organized posthumous pictures of the two other victims of recent murders to stick up alongside Rita, there was still no sign of her crack team of detectives, although the room was packed with a dozen-odd officers who were now at her beck and call.

Twenty minutes after they were due, Mac sauntered in without so much as an apology, shrugged off his fleece and threw it across a desk. He couldn't but have noticed Jo's presence, but the way he didn't bother to salute her – just swivelled a plastic chair back to front before straddling it, and then peeled an egg mayonnaise sandwich out of its plastic container before getting stuck into it – told her he considered it deserved more respect than she did.

Jo dialled Jeanie's extension to see if she'd passed on the message. Jeanie said that she had, adding that Foxy had gone home sick.

'Good of you to tell me,' Jo said, slamming the receiver down.

Sexton arrived seconds later, not bothering to remove his trench coat, and took the seat beside Mac. Folding his arms, Sexton rested his chin on his chest and settled in like he was about to grab a snooze. After eyeing the three photos on display, he nudged Mac's shoulder with his own curiously.

Jo headed for the door to close it as Mac muttered to Sexton, 'You were after this case, weren't you? You'd be a damn sight better than that! A murder brief for riding the boss, that's a good one.'

Jo slammed the door. 'Phones on silent,' she ordered, before returning to the wipe board.

Mac made great play of rooting out his mobile and doing what she'd asked – squinting and angling the phone into the strobe light overhead, sticking the top of his tongue out as if he were concentrating on a task that required dexterity.

Sexton shoved his phone into his coat pocket.

'Right, you're probably asking yourselves what a dead prostitute, a junkie and a drug baron have in common?' Jo said, pointing at the pictures.

Mac took it as a cue to discuss possible answers with Sexton and didn't stop when she banged her fist on the table. 'Oi! You got any ideas about how this lot are linked?'

She may as well not have been there. Mac carried on regardless, as Sexton sighed heavily and studied his shoes.

Jo walked over to Mac's table and leaned across it, stopping short inches from his face. 'Very funny. I'm glad you can still find the time to have a laugh considering I'm looking for the first opportunity to turf you off the case. You don't have what it takes to be here. So by all means, keep it up . . .'

She headed back to the wipe board. 'Meet our victims.' She turned around and held up her index finger. 'All linked by one killer.'

'Sorry?' Mac asked through a mouthful of sandwich.

Jo pointed at Stuart Ball's picture. 'The Skid, murdered a couple of weeks back.' She swiped a couple of photocopies from her desk and handed them out. 'Name was Stuart Ball and, Sexton, you already know his incidentals.' She watched the heads lower to the paper. 'You can read up later. Only thing I want you to note at this point is that Stuart's eye was removed at the scene.'

Mac winked dramatically at Sexton, who was clearly growing tired of him.

One step sideways took her to Rita's bloodied face. 'As you know, we found Rita yesterday.' Two-beat pause. 'Minus her hand. And last, but by no means least, Anto Crawley,' Jo continued.

'There's a million people wanted Crawley dead, and with good reason,' Mac protested. 'His killer did the rest of us a favour, if you ask me.'

'I didn't,' Jo answered. 'Now, in Crawley's case, the teeth were extracted.' She looked directly at Sexton. 'And not smashed in his mouth as first thought and reported in the press.' Pulling the cap off a fat red marker with her teeth, she wrote her Book of Exodus quote up on the board. The pen squeaked as she worked.

'Meet our killer,' she said. 'Looks like we've got our very own Bible John.'

Sexton got up slowly, walked over to her desk and pulled a chair up in front of it. 'Okay, Inspector,' he said, 'where do we start?'

Jo gave him a grateful smile. 'We need to go through the

paperwork the team of uniforms on the house-to-house enquiries have brought in, and also trawl through the information gleaned from the checkpoints in the vicinity. I've done up the questionnaires . . . the usual: Did they see any working girls that night? Anyone matching Rita's description? Was she alone? Priority is to get Rita's mobile number sharpish – we might strike lucky on data analysis. Then there's the collection of any CCTV in the extended area. The location has been bugging me most. I mean, you said it yourself – what were the chances of our training exercise taking place in the same location that the killer decided to kill Rita? We know our man puts a lot of thought into symbolism. I think he chose the place deliberately.'

'Someone who knew we'd be there and wanted to leave us with egg on our faces?' Sexton asked.

Jo nodded. 'Looks like it. The building was, technically, unoccupied . . . So our priority is to find out where Rita was actually living before she died.'

Sexton studied a ballpoint pen he was walking through his fingers.

'Also, it has to be more than coincidence that all three were involved in criminality. Two were Skids, so it's fair to presume Crawley and Ball knew each other. We need to find out if Rita was also mixing in their circles.'

'Oi,' Mac said. 'Anyone remember the name of that victim knocked off a couple of months back out near the airport?'

Jo and Sexton looked at him blankly.

'White . . . That was it,' he went on. Heading over to the back wall of filing cabinets, he pulled open a screeching metal drawer. 'Don't you remember? That bloke found – there was a page ripped out of the Bible at the scene. Here it is.'

'I never read anything about a page from the Bible in the notes on any of the recent cases,' Jo said, shocked.

'Kept quiet for operational reasons,' Mac replied. 'You'd have found it on PULSE.'

Jo gave him a 'pull the other one' face. 'Was there mutilation at the scene?' she asked. 'And where exactly was the body found?'

Mac licked a thumb and riffled through the pages. 'Some disused shed near the airport,' he said.

'Not our district,' was Jo's reaction.

Sexton put his hand on her shoulder. 'Why don't I leave you two to argue the toss while I try and find out if any of our victims knew each other?'

Jo nodded. 'We'll meet tomorrow in the morgue for Rita's autopsy. I want everyone to start feeling some empathy for her instead of just seeing her as a tart. Oh, and Sexton, she was a working girl, so she must have had a number for clients. We get it, we can GPS her last movements.'

Sexton hurried out.

'My victim was *burned* to death,' Mac said, pointing to what Jo had written on the white board.

'I dunno,' she said. Why hadn't the case come up during her searches yesterday? she wondered. She glanced at the door, which had swung shut behind Sexton. Dan was peering in through the small, rectangular, wired-glass panel, rapping it lightly. She waved him in to join them, but he stayed put.

'Dan, I'm in the middle of conference,' she complained, joining him in the corridor outside.

'My office, now,' he answered.

'I'll be along as soon as we're finished,' Jo replied, still holding the door open.

'That's the least of your worries,' he said. 'You're off the case.'

Jo let go of the door. 'You winding me up?' She looked at her watch. 'I've only had ten minutes on it. On what grounds?'

'We've got a witness who says you thieved from Rita Nulty.'

Jo crinkled her nose in bewilderment.

'The dead hooker, Jo!'

'I know who Rita Nulty is,' Jo said through gritted teeth.

'Good, because you're accused of robbing her last few quid,' Dan said, looking past her. 'I'm sorry, but there's nothing I can do to bail you out of this one. This is way too serious.'

14

Rory's principal phoned on Jo's mobile just as she was pulling up outside Foxy's allotment in Tymon Park in Tallaght, shortly after 3 p.m. After yanking the handbrake, she hit call connect and reached for the takeaway coffee she'd bought after finally stopping off for petrol on the way. The car had been running on bloody air since yesterday, but having reminded Dan before leaving the station that there were protocols in place for serious allegations and having just about managed to swing another twenty-four hours to clear her name, every second now counted. On the other end of the phone, Mr Montague told her to hold.

Jo exhaled impatiently through her nostrils and took an extra-careful sip as she ran through the scenarios of why the school would be calling, while watching Foxy down on his hands and knees, working. He was turning the earth around some lettuce, fenced in by barbed wire high enough to fend off either teenage vandals or rabbits on stilts, with a trowel.

Foxy spotted Jo as he headed for the pavement to retrieve some tools which he had left beside a neatly trimmed border.

'Heard you're feeling a bit peaky,' Jo said, leaning across the passenger seat and swinging the passenger door of the car open to block his path.

'Excuse me?' Mr Montague asked her suddenly on the phone.

'No, not you . . . Is everything all right?' Jo said, sitting back up.

Mr Montague explained that there was no need to be alarmed, but he wanted to arrange an appointment to talk about Rory's problems. Right now, he'd only got five minutes.

'What problems?' Jo asked warily.

Foxy looked back at his allotment then leaned inside the car, scooped up the window handle, cassette tape and several chocolate wrappers and deposited them in the back seat. Climbing in, he swung the door shut and stared straight ahead.

'Obviously, I'd prefer to do this face to face,' Mr Montague was saying.

'Sorry – do you mind?' Jo asked Foxy, nodding at the door and raising her eyebrows.

'Yes I bloody well do mind,' Foxy barked. 'You wanted me to get in, now I'm in. We get this over with here and now, or I'm off to see to my tomatoes.'

'Jesus wept!' Jo pulled her own door open so she could step outside for some privacy.

'What?' Mr Montague asked.

'No, no, no not you!' she answered, slapping the roof of the car in frustration.

'Look, it really is better if we do this in person,' Mr Montague said.

Jo sighed heavily. 'Mr Montague, I work full time. After work, I battle through traffic to get to the childminder's to collect my baby. By the time I get home, generally an hour and a half after leaving work, and ten since seeing my infant, he needs feeding. Getting it ready takes at least half an hour. Sometimes he's too tired to eat and has nodded off by the time I dish it up in front of him. So any chance you could cut me a bit of slack here and, whatever it is you have to say to me, tell me now?' She paused for breath.

'That's five minutes up,' Montague said, not unhappily. 'Ring my secretary if you feel Rory's truancy is worth fitting into your schedule.'

Jo kept the phone pressed to her ear for a few seconds after the call disconnected. *Truancy!*

Foxy had also got out of the car and was gathering up his tools.

'I want to talk to you,' she said.

'I'm feeling ill again,' he replied, gathering his tools into a wheelbarrow and marching off.

'Hi ya, Sal,' Jo called, spotting Foxy's daughter sitting in the open door of the shed. Sal had Down's. Her mother had left not long after she was born, and it was just the two of them. Foxy could have afforded a house with its own garden, but he lived frugally so as to put as much aside as he could spare for a fund for Sal when he was gone.

'Hi Jo,' Sal answered. 'Want a cup of tea?' She shook a teapot good-humouredly.

'No thanks, sweetheart, I've got to rush today. You see *X Factor* at the weekend?' Jo asked.

'Yes,' Sal said. 'I have it on video if you missed it. The fella I like looks like Rory. He's gorgeous.'

Jo laughed. 'We can watch it together when I've got a bit of free time, if you like.'

'Great,' Sal said.

Foxy handed over the tools to Sal, who began to put them away. Every inch of space in the shed had some labelled recycled container with different-sized nails and reusable wire. Foxy was the kind of man who could make appliances last a lifetime and was more at home in the shed than his house. It was covered in graffiti, and scorched from a couple of attempts to burn it down, but somehow it had survived.

'Why did you tell Dan that I'd taken money from Rita?' Jo whispered to him.

'I told you from day one that there are bad apples in every walk of life and there's only one way to deal with them. Did you honestly think I'd do nothing?'

'If you'd bothered to ask me, you would have learned there was a perfectly reasonable explanation. You know exactly what happens to cash that's found at a crime scene,' Jo said, her voice still low.

'Nothing you can tell me can justify what I saw with my own two eyes,' Foxy said. 'The sad thing is, if anyone else had reported you, I'd have said they were barking, gone out of my way to help you defend your good name. But I was there. I witnessed it for myself. And what's even worse is, I think I would probably even have forgiven you if it had been just a case of sticky fingers . . . But you saw the lines of cocaine. That money was rolled up like a vacuum hose, and you took it anyway. What if the killer used them to snort some of it before paying Rita? A single sweat cell is all they need to get DNA nowadays.'

'The coke hadn't been touched and, anyway, no court of law would have allowed that money as evidence! Not at the rate currency changes hands.'

'So that's your justification, is it?' he replied. 'What if it had given us a new lead? Thrown up someone's name we could have gone after?'

Sal emerged to ask what was wrong.

'Nothing, lovely,' Foxy answered. 'What time you doing my fish fingers?'

'Can start them after mass if you like,' Sal said, checking her watch. 'Better hurry up, Dad, or we're going to be late. Do you want to come with us, Jo?'

'Next time,' Jo promised, pulling her notebook out and scribbling an address on a piece of paper. 'I've got to get to Rory's school before it closes.'

She turned to Foxy. 'When you're feeling better – after your dinner of course – I want you to head to this address. It's Rita Nulty's mother's. Tell her you need to take a statement concerning my visit there yesterday. Key question is if I handed her any money. When she tells you the amount, I want you to write it down in that notebook of yours.' She held the page out to him.

'You're saying you gave it back?' he asked. 'You bloody fool, Jo. You've left yourself wide open . . .'

'Don't you get it?' Jo asked, leaning in close. 'Rita Nulty died because she was prepared to do anything to make that €100. The way I see it, that means the pocket it ended up in mattered, and in my book that means her mother's. I'm sorry it's not up to your high standards, but would I do it again? Damn right I would. If you want to discuss this any further, ring me later, and not the chief.'

Jo headed over to the shed and gave Sal a hug. 'Bye, sweetie. Why are you going to mass on a Tuesday anyway?'

'I have a special intention,' Sal replied. 'I need to find Dad a girlfriend. You sure you don't want to come? Jesus forgives all sinners.'

Jo couldn't resist returning Foxy's grin. But as she climbed back into the car, that niggling feeling she'd had since seeing the Caravaggio in the gallery hit her like a tonne of bricks.

'That's it, isn't it?' she said to herself. 'The killer doesn't worship Jesus Christ, he blames him . . . Before he came along, justice meant "an eye for an eye" but, after him, it was a case of turn the other cheek. Jesus forgave the whore, the downtrodden, the criminals. But our killer is turning back the clock.'

15

It was gone 4 p.m. when Jo arrived at Rory's school. As she entered the main corridor, she stepped up to the framed photos on the wall showing the different classes dressed in the same rugby strip, all the pupils with the same open-legged, arms-folded-high pose, the same hail and hearty grin on all their faces.

She scanned the lads' faces for any sign of Rory and recognized some of his mates among the sixth-formers. *Where the bloody hell was he?* she wondered. *Was he on the bloody mitch that day too?*

Continuing on down the hall to the staircase, she felt her hackles bristle at the sight of the sports trophies on display. Jo liked sports – it was just the type of sports this school preferred made her feel like a hypocrite: tennis, horse riding, bloody polo! Rich kids' games designed to set the students a class apart and, in their own minds, above the rest. Jo had believed in a free and equal education system for all, until the time had come to enrol Rory somewhere. Then her ideals went out the window. Dan hadn't been happy. It wasn't the money, though it took a sizeable chunk out of their income. He believed a free education was as good as any, but Jo hadn't been quite so sure. She hated that money could buy the best teachers, a network of friends on course for the best jobs and a social life that attracted the kind of girls who spoke with the right accent and were on the pill from sixteen because they had ambitions of their own. But she'd wanted to give her son the same chance in life as the ministers' and judges' sons.

When Rory first started here, she'd spent a lot of time in his ear reminding him to be his own man and to never condescend because somebody had less than they did – they hardly had much themselves. But she'd backed off when he'd reminded her that the rate she paid a Polish woman to come into the house once a week to clean was, strictly speaking, extortion. An Irish woman wouldn't have done it for three times as much.

'It's easier to be a hypocrite in a clean house, isn't it, Mum?' Rory had ribbed, before turning the telly back on.

In any event, the days of hiring help went by the wayside after the Budget, and the split from Dan.

Jo walked straight into Mr Montague's office and watched him struggle to come up with any one of a hundred reasons why he couldn't see her unannounced. But the confrontation with first Dan and then Foxy had left her in no mood for the runaround, and Mr Montague appeared to pick up on as much. As she took a seat in front of his desk, she reckoned she could have done a pretty accurate BP readout if she'd counted the twitches per minute in a vein in his temple as he straightened his tie then smoothed his thinning hair with the heel of one hand.

'Right . . . Rory Mason, here we are,' he said, pulling a manilla file free of the cabinet to the left of his desk. 'Anaemia last September; Granny died in October; November, chest infection; December, ah yes, this one I thought particularly creative, "twisted gut"; Granny did a

Lazarus act in January but unfortunately didn't make it, and it took Rory two weeks to get over the trauma.'

'No,' Jo corrected. 'Dan's mother did pass away.' She held back the fact that Dan's mother had died the previous August, was in her nineties and in the advanced stages of Alzheimer's and that her own mother was still very much alive and kicking. 'And he was very close to his grand-mother,' she added. Rory was a good kid, with a kind heart, and when it came to it, this was all that mattered, she told herself. He may not have been the world's most academic kid, but he'd held Dan's mother's hand every time he'd vis-ited. Jo'd take kindness as a quality for her son over his bloody attendance rate any day.

She looked at the letters Rory had forged, and sighed. He hadn't even tried to copy her signature.

'Oh, my condolences,' Montague went on, not sounding remotely sorry. 'Still, I'm presuming these are fake.'

'Far from it,' she lied.

'My apologies again,' Montague lied back.

'I really do feel you should have alerted us to your con-cerns about Rory's truancy a lot sooner.'

'I've spoken to your husband several times. He sat in that very seat you're sitting in now,' Montague retali-ated, little filaments of spit pooling in the corners of his mouth.

Jo began to fidget with her hands. Constant rows were building up the distance between her and Dan. It was differ-ent when you lived together, when you couldn't leave something unresolved or it would eat into the following day and sour the atmosphere for the kids. When you were together, you put things behind you, accepted when you were wrong or tried not to parade the fact that you were right. But right now, whatever they'd had was so lost that he believed her capable of robbing a murder victim.

'What's the bottom line here?' she asked, reaching into her pocket for her mobile, which had been vibrating persistently since she'd come in. A quick glance, and she registered Sexton's name flashing. She'd have to take the call.

'Bottom line? Rory is below the quota of days necessary at school to sit his exams.'

'But it's his Leaving Cert next year! You can't hold him back . . .'

Mr Montague raised his voice over hers. 'If he makes a concerted effort to attend school for the short time left between now and the exams, I won't flag a problem with the Department of Education. But if he misses another day, and I really do mean a single day, I'm afraid drastic measures will be taken.'

'I understand,' Jo said, glad she had the phone as an excuse to get away from him.

'You'd better come quickly, Birmingham,' Sexton said as the call connected. 'We've got ourselves another body. This one's still alive, but he's hanging on by a thread. And we'll have a hard job linking him to the Skids. The victim's a priest.'

16

Sexton's tie was hanging loose when Jo approached him at the outpatients entrance of St Vincent's Hospital, where a group of poorly patients in pyjamas and dressing gowns who should have known better were gathered under the bicycle shelter smoking. Jo would have happily joined them, if there'd been time. She walked briskly with him down the hospital corridors, past the medics still robed in theatre gowns and the luridly painted concrete statues of various saints.

'The matron's refusing point-blank to let us in,' Sexton explained, blowing his nose. 'ICU's a closed ward. It's relatives only, and only then on the matron's say-so.'

'We'll see about that,' Jo said. She stopped in her tracks, causing him to pause too. 'You looking after yourself?' she asked him intently as he turned in surprise.

'It's nothing, just my rhinitis,' Sexton answered.

Jo looked unconvinced.

'The victim's name is Father Reginald Walsh,' Sexton said quickly. 'His foot was sliced clean off, within a half-mile radius of the other slayings.'

Jo was on the move again. 'I want you to contact hospital management,' she told him. 'Tell them this city's got a serial killer on the rampage and they've got his latest victim on their premises. Tell them that, if they don't co-operate, we're leaking the details to the press, who'll be all over the place like a rash. It's not beyond the tabloid journalists to arrive donned in white coats to get what they want. No way will management risk that kind of a security breach. Tell them I only need five minutes.'

Sexton nodded and pointed out the door to ICU up ahead before parting from Jo.

She headed for the door to the unit, which was covered with warning signs about using mobile phones. A couple of fraught relatives clutched each other's hands, and there were more distraught people crammed in a tiny waiting room opposite. Shelves of blankets and pillows indicated that the couches doubled up as beds at night. The health system in this country made Jo see red – the sick and elderly were left to sleep on trolleys in A&E while wards with beds never slept in had never been opened because all the bureaucrats in middle management were too desperate making sure the cuts never put them on the dole queues.

Within less than ten minutes of Sexton's departure, a squat matron emerged from intensive care. She seemed to have no problem identifying Jo as the one she wanted. 'The minute I say leave, you leave.'

Jo entered a poky wash room and followed the instructions pinned to the wall, squirting pink Hibiscrub on to her hands and rubbing her hands with a white, alcohol-based gel that smelled like white spirit and dried instantly – super-bug repellent. Unfurling a white plastic apron, she hooked it over her head and knotted it behind her back, pulling a mask over her mouth before finally entering the ward.

It was loud and fluorescently lit. Four glass cubicles provided screens for three beds, affording a modicum of privacy to the relatives of those patients closest to the end. The fourth cubicle was being used as a nurses' station. A television elevated on a wall bracket was tuned to a soap and being watched keenly by some nurses on a break, even though the sound had been muted.

The matron was writing information on a large chart balanced at eye level on a wheeled frame that overlooked the bedside of the priest. He was running to fat and the colour of candle wax. He was rigged up to a mesh of wires and tubes which were attached to flashing monitors that beeped intermittently. Rosary beads dangled from one. His mutilated right leg was held inches above the bed by a sling attached to a pulley in the ceiling.

'How is he?' Jo asked.

'He's been anointed.' The matron knelt down at the side of the bedframe to unhook a clear catheter bag and, after measuring the fluid ounces, she made a note on her chart.

Jo scanned the priest's face.

'No questions,' the matron warned, reading her mind.

But the priest was as remote as an embalmed body. His jaw was trussed back horribly off centre with a length of white cotton string double-looped around his chin and tied roughly in a knot at the back of his neck. It held open the throat passage for a clear ventilator pipe that plunged down his windpipe. A nasal gastric-tube-feed travelled through the back of his nostrils and into his stomach to deliver basic nutrients. A dialysis machine beside the bed groaned like a machine being tortured. Cogs spooled rhythmically, cranking pumps as they churned the priest's blood in and out. An artery in his neck delivered a central line into his heart. It vied for space with a cluster of drips that bunched like stalks out of the tiny space. A plugged cannula inserted into the back of his hand was at the ready if any of the other lines kinked or were rejected by the body.

Jo noted the high bluish colour on his cheeks, bleeding into the circles under his eyes. 'What's causing this?' she asked.

'It's usually a sign that the temperature is spiking and the body overproducing white blood cells to fight an infection. You can give him this if you like.' She thrust a sponge stick that looked like a lollipop into Jo's hand in a way that said this was a place for families. 'The mouth gets very dry when it's open like that all the time.'

Jo knew she was making a point. She dipped the pink sponge in a plastic cup of water, pressed it against his parched lips and watched how they instinctively twitched. She scanned the equipment that was pulsing average statistics of his heart rate, blood pressure, breathing rate, temperature and the cardio-vascular pressure on the intravenous line. Then, aware it was only a matter of time before she started thinking about her own personal tragedy, and her father's death, she said goodbye to the matron and left.

A few minutes later, she was outside with Sexton in the car park. 'Can you take over until tomorrow?' she asked him. 'Something's come up I need to deal with.'

Sexton nodded. ''Course. What do you want me to do?'

'Find out if Father Reg has a brother,' she said, remembering what old Mrs Nulty had told her about the man who'd called looking for Rita describing himself as the brother of a priest. 'We also need to talk to the girls on the street, see if any of them knew anything about Rita and her last client.'

'Leave it to me,' he said, offering her a cigarette.

She took it, and leaned into the lighter in his cupped hand. 'Call me tonight if Father Reg starts to speak. I don't care what hour of the night it is.'

17

Jo chainsmoked through Rory's explanation of *Grand Test Auto: San Andreas* from the far side of the fully opened front-room window. She stood in the front garden, turning away for every guilty drag as she listened to him. He was sitting in front of the telly, consol in hand.

She had found him by phoning Becky, who'd suggested she start looking in Dundrum town centre. Sure enough, Rory had been leaning on a railing staring at the water fountains, looking like an ASBO waiting to happen, his trainers open and the waist of his trousers showing half a foot of boxer shorts. He hadn't even bothered to change out of his school uniform. Jo had coaxed him home with a bribe – €20. She'd put Harry down for a nap, and was trying to humour Rory so that she could build up slowly to the serious conversation she needed to have with him. When he'd finished giving her the lowdown, she stubbed the fag out with her foot, headed into the kitchen, pulled a tub of Häagen-Dazs from the freezer and scooped a few dessert-spoonfuls into her mouth before heading back in and plonking down beside him on the couch.

The virtual screen featured a bouncing car.

'So the gangster's in there having sex with a prostitute?' Jo asked.

'Yep.' Rory was twiddling the controls furiously.

'And to win, you have to rob people, cars and banks to make yourself rich, killing anyone who gets in the way?'

'Yep. See those numbers in the top right-hand corner?' Rory pointed, as the car stopped bouncing and a hulking Hell's Angel with a bandana on his head and tattoos all over his neck climbed out.

'Yeah?'

'They're keeping track of my health and my wealth. Now, as you can see, the bad news is my money has just taken a nosedive but, on the plus side, my health's gone shooting up.'

'She robbed you?' Jo asked.

'Technically, I paid her for services rendered, but it doesn't matter, because I'm about to rob her back,' Rory said.

'Jesus,' Jo muttered, looking away from the screen. 'And the cops – they're fair game too?'

'Five stars if you kill one,' Rory answered.

Jo took a few deep breaths. 'Doesn't it feel . . . creepy?'

Rory hit pause and turned to face her. 'No, Mother, it doesn't make me want to go out and shoot people, if that's what you're asking. Drive faster, sure, but kill? No. It's just a laugh. Anyway, there's a new one out ages ago now. This one's ancient already.'

'Okay,' Jo said slowly.

'And as you haven't yet figured out how to set the video to pre-record, you are in no position to judge the noughties generation's toys,' Rory said, reading her mind. 'Or Bebo.'

'They can prosecute parents for a child's truancy, did you know that?' Jo said casually, after another long pause.

Rory stayed focused on the screen.

'I get a criminal conviction, that's the end of my job.'

Still no answer.

111

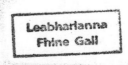
Leabharlanna
Fhine Gall

'You do still want to go to college?' she asked, frowning. This time he shrugged.

'I thought law was your first preference.' Jo could hear the panic in her own voice.

'What's the point?'

'I can show you if you want. I can bring you out in a squad car some night and show you why education is everything. I can bring you into one of the prisons and give you a breakdown of the corresponding literacy rates. I can . . .'

'I can read and write, Mother,' Rory said, his voice rising. 'I'm not going to end up a smackhead sleeping on the streets because I don't go to college. Loads of successful people didn't go to college . . .'

'You *don't* want to go to college? Since when?'

Rory sighed, turned the game off but kept staring at the blank screen. 'What's the big deal?'

Jo stood up and headed back out the front door. Out in the front garden, she lit up another fag and spoke to him more calmly through the open window. 'I just don't want to see you waste your potential.'

'If you cared so much, why did you walk out on us?'

He sounded so young and vulnerable suddenly, Jo felt a pang of guilt. 'Rory, I didn't walk out on you!'

'Yes you did.'

'Things weren't working out with Dad, that's all. I never wanted you to leave. I want you to live with me full time. You have no idea how much I miss you.'

'Did you really think I could leave Dad on his own? It was bad enough you walking out on him without me rubbing his nose in it. He can't even work the bloody iron.'

'So I should have stayed with him to do his ironing?'

'No, but . . .'

'Dad's life has moved on now, Rory. He has Jeanie.'

'Don't get me started on that cow.'

'Don't call her that!' Jo snapped. She leaned in through the window and caught Rory's eye. 'Why, what's she done?'

'She just makes me feel like . . . I'm in the way . . . all the time . . . in my own, or at least in their, house!'

'Cow,' Jo agreed.

Rory's face softened.

'Move back with me.'

'Dad says you'll just turn me into a glorified "manny".'

Jo pursed her lips. 'No manny of mine would kill cops for fun.'

Rory laughed. A short half-laugh, but a laugh.

He sat back in the sofa and flicked the game back on. 'Okay,' he said. 'For a bit, see how it goes, yeah?'

Jo headed back into the room and hugged him. 'Would you start turning up for school if I get you the latest version of this God-awful game?' she asked.

'Subtle, Mother. Why not offer me some shiny stars while you're at it?' He grinned. ''Course, if you were talking about a pair of tickets to Oxygen . . .'

'It's really important you knuckle down now with the exams coming.'

'On one condition . . .' Rory cut her off.

Jo sighed.

'You give up smoking.'

Jo reached for the box in her pocket, and crunched.

He was high-fiving her when the landline rang. Jo was still smiling as she headed into the hall to answer.

It was Dan, explaining that, on his solicitor's advice, the only way to maintain his stake in their house was to move back home.

18

Sexton sat at the back of Heaven, a lap-dancing club in a Leeson Street basement. His legs were planted wide apart, his expression completely blank, as a chunky, semi-naked dancer combed scarlet fingernails through his sweat-drenched hair and shimmied between his legs. Madonna's 'Like A Virgin' blared in the background, speaking volumes about the demographic profile of the clientele. In their teens twenty-five years ago, they were now trapped in dead-end nine-to-five jobs and not getting any at home.

The dancer loosened Sexton's skinny tie to mid-mast with a pair of streaky, false-tanned hands and jiggled her tasselled boobs inches from his face. Sexton surveyed the tacky room, wondering what Maura would say if she could see him stranded in the middle of this bunch of sad bastards. It would probably be something non-judgemental like, 'Live and let live.' She hadn't had a cynical bone in her body. The first time he'd laid eyes on her, she was busking with a guitar on Grafton Street, her hair in plaits, friendship bracelets and bangles stacked on both wrists. He'd only stopped to watch out of amusement, because she hadn't a note in her head. Then someone grabbed the cap at her feet, robbing the few miserable quid she'd managed to collect, and Sexton had set off after them. That's how it had started between them . . .

The dancer was determined to get Sexton's attention. She pawed his inside thigh then brushed against his cheek, leaving a graze of thick make-up on his shirt collar. He took another swig from his wine glass and grimaced. The plonk had cost almost €100 – he'd had to pay with his credit card – but it was so piss-poor it could have stripped paint. He wiped the corners of his lips self-consciously with his finger and thumb in case they'd turned blue.

The dancer coiled a cerise feather boa around his neck, and he grabbed her wrist. 'I want a word . . .' he growled, adding with emphasis, 'Frank.'

'I'm taking my break in fifteen,' a deep voice snapped, trying to jerk free.

Sexton spotted one of the bouncers heading over, shoulders braced for the 'hands off the skirt' routine. Smashing his glass off the floor, he jumped to his feet, bawling 'Gardaí' and demanding to see the proprietor and his licence. The 'raid' wouldn't have seen the light of day in a court of law; he was off duty and well over the limit, but try telling that to the punters emerging from the foam pool and scurrying for their trousers, socks and shoes, running for the exit.

The music came to an abrupt halt. Frankie gave Sexton a dagger look and minced into the dressing room. Sexton followed him.

Frankie's tacky dressing room was the size of a broom cupboard. A large theatrical mirror surrounded by light bulbs made the space even more depressing. Plucking a postcard from San Francisco off the mirror, Sexton read the back idly as Frankie covered up in an oriental, raw-silk dressing gown and whipped off his flowing mane. His short hair was scraped back off his face with a hair net, and flattened down by sweat. Plonking himself on to a stool, he pouted at his reflection and dotted blobs of gloopy cream on his face, then made a swipe for the postcard. But Sexton held his arm up and out of reach.

'Temper, temper,' he said.

'This is police harassment,' Frankie said, peeling off false eyelashes.

'That's exactly what it is,' Sexton agreed. 'We have an ombudsman now, you should file a complaint.'

'So your old boys' club can make my life a complete misery – give over. What do you want?'

'I want to know all about Rita Nulty.'

'Never heard of her.'

Sexton took hold of Frankie's chin and forced his neck around. 'Look me in the eye and say that again,' he said. 'Only she was all over the papers yesterday and today. Last time a hooker was murdered, your lot were up in arms, forming a union to protect yourselves, sending out press releases to the papers. So let's start again, shall we? Rita Nulty. I'd say this place was full of talk tonight about the murdered slag.'

'Lap-dancers are not prostitutes,' Frankie responded. 'Prostitutes work in parlours or on the streets. Lap-dancers are artistes.'

Sexton released him and bent over his shoulder to talk to Frankie through the mirror. 'Let me put it another way,' he said, pulling open the dirty dressing gown. 'I presume these are courtesy of the Social, yeah? Let me guess how you pulled that one off . . . Your shrink wrote and told them all about your suicidal feelings from the time you realized you were trapped in the wrong body at the age of five . . . You've got no income because you can't work because your self-identity is shattered, you're so desperate to be a real woman. Do you think they'll keep forking out for your hormones when the Revenue discovers you've got all this going on? How long does that treatment take anyway? Years, isn't it? You had downstairs done yet?'

Frankie covered his face with his hands and started to shake. 'You bastard.'

'Rita Nulty?'

'She was hooking for the Skids. Anal, dogging, group – anything went with her, long as she got her supply. She did anything they wanted, but she was way out of her depth. She owed them money, couldn't pay.'

Frankie looked up at Sexton, his mascara running down his face like black tears. 'You want to know who Rita Nulty was? A junkie. That's all. Now fuck off before you get me killed.'

Spotting the look on his own face in the mirror, Sexton took a step back, feeling a pang of shame. Maura wouldn't have recognized who he'd turned into.

He pulled open the dressing-table drawers and rifled through them quickly, stopping when he found a little black contacts book. By now Frankie had covered his face in his hands again and was wailing. Flicking through the pages, Sexton stopped to study a page then tucked it into his inside pocket.

'Nice boobs, by the way. Very natural,' he said before he left.

19

Jo was standing at one end of the hall with one ear cocked, making sure her boys were finally asleep. It was near midnight, but she'd been up and down all evening with Harry, who was unsettled with his teeth, the poor love. And Rory had only conceded defeat of their doubles match on the Xbox after Jo's victory jig had made him cover his eyes and beg her to stop. The way he'd cringed had made her laugh aloud. It felt really good to have them both with her under the same roof again, where they belonged. She would make up for the hours she'd missed off the job tomorrow. Her boys always came first.

Satisfied all was quiet, she moved down the hall to the kitchen, rotating her aching shoulders and stretching her arms up over her head. What she needed now was one of Dan's shoulder rubs, she thought. That said, if he'd laid a finger on her after the things he'd come out with today, she'd probably have swung for him.

She pulled open one of the Mexican pine presses, noticed the hinge was slipping and realized it was at least ten years since Dan had fitted the units. *Where had those years gone?* She pulled out a bottle of Powers and a whiskey glass and poured herself a stiff drink. It had taken them the guts of two years to scrimp and save for the traditional, country-style units, she remembered, taking a sip of the whiskey and admiring the room reluctantly. Meals out, holidays, even the odd bloody blow-dry had gone by the wayside during that time, as they'd penny-pinched enough to get a loan from the credit union. They'd never have afforded it at all if they'd had to pay the same again for a carpenter, but Dan was brilliant at DIY. He'd put in the floor as well – though he'd had his doubts about Jo's choice of tiles: dark-red and bottle-green check, which in the end had worked a treat. And if anyone had seen the way they'd celebrated when they'd salvaged an original Victorian Sally rack from a car-boot sale they'd have presumed them barking. For years afterwards while she was still married, Jo had felt a little surge of pride every time she walked into the room and glimpsed the home they'd made for Rory.

She studied the drink she was swirling around in the bottom of her glass. Back then, she'd presumed this kitchen would be the heart of a home that would fill with more children over the years. What had happened? she wondered. Why had there never been a right time for Dan? The old excuse, that he wasn't getting any younger – he was ten years older than her – hadn't been a factor when he was still in his thirties. Then it was always the pressure of the latest case. During one of their last heated rows before they split, he'd finally admitted that he resented the prospect of rearing another child when they were just starting to get their lives back. The way Jo saw it, without kids, you had no life. Family meant everything to her. *So how did I manage to lose mine then?* a voice inside her head asked.

She knocked back the last of her drink, organized a pen and notebook from a drawer and pulled a high stool up to the breakfast bar. She needed to get working on her defence for having taken that money from Rita Nulty. After staring at the blank sheet of paper for a few seconds, she sighed and twisted the cap off the whiskey bottle again, helping herself to another glass.

The liquid warmed her insides, and her thoughts moved to the sense of joy she'd felt at the sight of the little blue cross appearing on the pee stick, telling her she was pregnant again, with Harry. A flush spread across her cheeks as she remembered the shock and hurt – and yes, bloody humiliation – of realizing Dan's reaction was the precise opposite. He'd actually asked her to have a termination! Right there, at the kitchen table. He'd knitted his fingers in hers, looked her in the eye and come straight out with it. He'd said, 'You don't have to go through with it. We've got a good life. Why ruin it?'

Jo put the back of her cold hands on her cheeks to stop the heat from the anger spreading, even now, almost two years later. She'd told him it wasn't going to happen, tried to explain how much she'd longed for the baby, thinking he'd see it her way. But instead he'd dug his heels in, refusing to talk about it, until the long silences between them just wore her down. Eventually, it got so bad she'd asked Dan to leave. She wanted to enjoy what she knew would be her last pregnancy. She'd never meant the separation to be a permanent arrangement; she couldn't look further than one day to the next without him, that was just how things had turned out.

For a very brief time – twenty-four hours, to be precise – she actually thought they would sort everything out and get back together. The day Harry was born, Dan had taken him in his arms and asked her to forgive him and to allow him home. Jo agreed, only to have Jeanie pay an unexpected visit to the hospital. After she'd gone, Jo remembered looking at the card on the bouquet of flowers she had brought, wondering why Jeanie had signed them from Dan too. As she waited for Dan's visit that night, Jo had written her sense of panic off as postnatal paranoia: her hormones were all over the place, after all, and there were plenty of men called Dan. Then Dan had come in, a big blue teddy under his arm, and Jo had made a joke of the card. The moment she'd glimpsed his reaction, she realized Jeanie had not called to see her out of the goodness of her heart at all. That was how she'd found out her husband was seeing someone else – from a congratulations card on a bunch of bloody carnations signed off by his girlfriend with a string of kisses.

And now, just as things seemed set in stone, life was taking another twist and he was coming home after all, she this time having managed to foist her pride out of the equation, and giving her back everything she wanted – her family. So why couldn't she shake the hole in the bottom of her stomach, stop feeling that it was all too late?

She reached up and adjusted the pots and pans hanging from the Sally rack they'd bought together in that car-boot sale so he wouldn't start bashing his head into them, like the old days.

Pressing the nib of the pen against the top left-hand corner of the page, she tried to focus on her case. Nothing could happen between her and Dan until she'd sorted the business of what she'd done with Rita Nulty's money. She would have to tell the truth, no matter how unpalatable. But what did any of it matter when three victims were dead and a fourth battling for his life? Dan's adherence to procedure was keeping her from doing the only thing that mattered – finding who was responsible.

Harry let out another cry, and Jo pushed the pen and paper aside. She turned out the lights as she made her way down the hall. The inquiry was a complete bloody waste of energy. She wasn't wasting another second on it.

Wednesday

20

Next morning, the only one running late for Rita Nulty's post mortem was Jo herself. Jeanie had rung while she was banging on Rory's bedroom door to get him up and into the shower. As Jo listened to the message she'd left, saying that Dan intended to hear her appeal before lunch, she chose her best lace bra and matching French knickers. She lost a good quarter of an hour ironing her best suit, a tailored navy pinstripe, and fitted white blouse, and another twenty dropping Rory directly outside the school gates. And so as to catch up on the murder inquiry before the hearing, she'd detoured to Swords garda station, losing the guts of another hour. She'd called to see the officer who'd headed up the investigation into the death of the victim Mac had mentioned, the case where the page of the Bible was found at the scene. As it turned out, the dead man had a history of psychiatric illness, had made several previous attempts to set himself alight and was a fanatical born-again Christian. After rooting the original file out of her briefcase to establish how she'd missed this information first time round, she'd discovered from the numbering that there were pages missing. *I'm going to bloody well kill Mac*, Jo thought, as she sped back down the Malahide Road towards the morgue in Marino.

Backed up in the traffic at the Griffith Avenue crossroads,

she rang Gerry in Justice but got straight through to his answering machine. She left a message reminding him of a case in which an accused man had got a suspended sentence from the courts after being found guilty of perpetrating an aggravated rape on a twelve-year-old schoolgirl. 'The judge accepted the defence's case – that the child's school uniform constituted an act of provocation,' Jo said, signing off. 'Separate Legal Representation, Gerry. Call me.'

Jo steered to the back of the fire-brigade training grounds, past shells of buildings called 'toy shop' and 'fireworks factory' that were burned out regularly for the exercises, and pulled up beside three Portakabins ring-fenced at the back of the grounds, which looked more like a used-car sales lot than the city's morgue. Two of the prefabs were used by the state pathologist for admin purposes; the third was where autopsies were carried out. Jo sighed as she parked the car. The use of the premises had been 'temporary' for the best part of a decade, but if the families of the victims whose lives had been cut short by violence could see just where they'd ended up, there'd be uproar. In Jo's eyes, it was typical of the Justice department's 'out of sight, out of mind' attitude to victims.

The team was waiting for Jo in a squad car outside. Mac and Sexton were tucking into full Irish breakfast rolls, but Foxy had declined all food offers, even a cup of tea. The morgue's 'canteen', as it was jokingly referred to by staff, consisted of a toaster and a kettle on top of a photocopier in the crammed admin cabin. 'On The Run' logos on the wrappers on the food told Jo they'd picked up breakfast in a garage up the road.

'How'd you get on? Was it our man?' Mac asked, as she climbed into the passenger seat.

126

Sexton, behind the wheel, turned sideways, waiting for Jo to answer.

Jo was not amused. 'A bloody wild-goose chase, as you already bloody well know, Mac,' she said, twisting back to face him 'And you can wipe that smile off your face while you're at it. You're off the case.'

Mac looked around for some support, realized none was coming, opened the door and banged it shut after him. He stormed off, firing his breakfast roll at some wheelie bins as he left.

Jo pulled the door shut. Foxy unplugged a coffee from the carton tray balancing between the front seats and leaned forwards to hand it over to her. 'I need to talk to you about what happened when I called to Rita Nulty's mother yesterday,' he said.

'Why? What happened?' Jo asked intently.

Sexton pointed through the windscreen to a young man with a neat trimmed beard in a white coat who was waving them into the post-mortem Portakabin.

'You can fill me in later,' Jo said, taking the coffee from Foxy and holding it clear of her best clothes as she climbed out.

After gowning up in white Tyvek jump suits and skimming the area under their nostrils with scented Vaseline, they filed into the neutral grey cabin. The space measured thirty feet by forty-five, and contained five fridges, each of which could hold three bodies. A shore in the ground drained the sluices slicking in through a grid. Three stainless-steel slabs on wheels gave the business of death a conveyor-belt feel, though, in actuality, only one post mortem was carried out at a time.

Standing over Rita Nulty's remains was Professor Michael

Hawthorne, the white-haired state pathologist who'd been the country's foremost expert on murder and suspicious death for the last twenty years.

Jo had already briefed him on the circumstances of death over the phone. It was Hawthorne's job to tell her the probable time that Rita died, the age of the injuries, whether they were inflicted ante or post mortem, and how she died. Jo was also hoping for a description of the weapon used, the interval between wounds received and death, and drug or alcohol content in the blood. She had lost count of the number of PMs she'd attended. They were never easy – the smell was the worst part – but skipping them was a cop-out. Questions always came up when you were there witnessing it for yourself that would never have sprung to mind otherwise.

After the PM, Rita's face would be 'naturalized' to ease her family's distress and in order to be able to obtain a more 'lifelike' photograph for the records. Her hair would be cleaned and combed, her face washed, the lips coloured with carmine in alcohol and a little rouge applied. The lividity stains would be powdered over with talc. Eyes were only fixed open when a body hadn't been ID'd, so that posthumous photographs could be released to the public.

But, right now, Rita appeared to be the last thing on Professor Hawthorne's mind. He was scrolling agitatedly on a mobile phone which, based on his comments, had just alerted him to the details of a hit and run he was expected to attend at the first opportunity. 'Bloody waste of bloody time . . .' he grumbled. 'I mean, what do they think I'm going to do – rule out drowning, a knife in the back or bloody poison in a clear-cut road death? As if resources aren't stretched to the limit as it is! You know what my main function will be when I arrive there? To pat the hands of the gardaí and say, "There there, everything will be all right!" I've had the country's biggest drug lord in a fridge over there since Monday, and it'll be Thursday at the earliest before I can get to him.'

He flicked a switch on the wall and the *enfant terrible* of Irish radio, Gerry Ryan, started ranting in the background about how the only thing bullies understood was a smack of the fist.

'This one doesn't exactly require rocket science either,' Foxy said, leaning back as he pointed to the laceration just right of Rita's breastbone.

Jo nudged him in the ribs. Hawthorne was very easily wound up, and Foxy knew it.

'Actually, the X-rays showed us that the knife fell short of the heart,' Hawthorne replied, hooking his index finger into the wound and poking around, nodding to himself in satisfaction.

Jo raised an eyebrow. A similar wound had been referred to in Stuart Ball's autopsy report. She stared at Hawthorne's fingers as they probed.

'Cause of death: a sudden catastrophic drop in blood pressure caused by this' – he pointed to the stump of Rita's arm – 'not this, I'm afraid,' he finished, indicating a stab wound under Rita's right breast. 'The good news is, she would have passed out before death, and the level of adrenaline produced by the shock – probably from the point in time when she realized what was going to happen – would also have minimized the pain.'

'Sorry,' Foxy muttered, and ran for the door.

Jo sighed, still watching Hawthorne. He turned to a tray of implements and reached for the scalpel then sliced through Rita's chest like butter, making a wide V shape that tailed down her torso into the leg of a Y. He peeled and clamped back the layers, like meat. The sound of the ribs separating was like a creaking door. With a slippery scoop, Hawthorne manoeuvred out the glossy stomach, sliding it into a kidney-shaped dish and snipping it free then opening it with scissors, squeezing the contents out into the tray.

The stink hit all of them at the same time – sickly-sweet, like a bag of rubbish left in the sun combined with raw sewage. 'Looks like her last meal was sausages,' Hawthorne declared.

Sexton made his excuses and, looking grey and sick, also left.

'Any defensive wounds?' Jo asked, conscious that she was the only one asking questions now that it was just her left in the room with Hawthorne and his bearded assistant, who was working quietly in the background.

'Absolutely none,' Hawthorne said, re-examining the wrists. 'Not so much as a bruise.'

'How did the killer keep her still?' she asked.

'This is the interesting bit,' Hawthorne said. 'I managed to fast-track the blood tests because of your concerns over links to previous killings – of course, if we had our own toxicology unit, that wouldn't be an issue. Bloody disgrace that we have to send them to Beaumount for preliminary screening, then the lab in Celbridge. Bloody weeks it takes! Pointless . . .'

The assistant coughed, and handed Hawthorne a sheet of headed paper listing the blood-test results.

'Yes, I was just getting to that . . . the bloods showed up the presence of myrrh and gall.'

He stared at Jo's blank face. 'You Catholics should be

ashamed of yourselves. Like bloody sheep, practising blind faith, with no interest in the actual history.'

'Myrrh and gall,' Jo prompted. 'I don't quite see –'

Hawthorne paused, then sighed in irritation. 'A combination commonplace in the Roman empire, and specifically during crucifixions. Don't you remember John Wayne as the Roman centurion at the foot of the crucifix: "Truly this was the son of God"?'

Jo clenched her fists. She did remember, and she understood exactly why it was important.

'The sponge passed to your King of Kings,' Hawthorne continued, 'was believed to have been soaked in myrrh and gall, which was used as an early form of pain relief. That's what your killer was using on the victim. I expect he didn't want her to pass out on him. By deadening the pain, he made the whole experience last longer for her, I'm afraid.'

21

By mid-morning, Jo was back in the station, sitting straight-backed, knees and ankles pressed tightly together, hands clasping the note she'd managed to scribble in the car park outside five minutes earlier. She was a lot happier with her account of the reason why she had taken the money from Rita Nulty's body than she'd have been if she'd spent hours poring over it the night before, because it was truthful: 'So no one else would'. But one glance at the set-up was making her palms clammy. First, Dan had arranged to meet her in a non-entity of a room at the back of the barracks normally used as a dumping ground for old filing cabinets. *I didn't even merit the conference room*, she thought. Second, a sheet of A4 paper had been stuck to the door outside and read: 'Hearing in Progress'. *Handwritten as an afterthought, not worth typing*, she concluded. And last, but not least, he'd made sure his arse wasn't going to be left hanging out afterwards by bringing witnesses – the in-house expert in law, a cop with a night degree named Brown but known by the rest of them as 'Brown Tongue' because he was like Dan's shadow, and Jeanie, ostensibly to take minutes and studiously avoiding Jo's eye. Jo wondered how she felt about the new living arrangements; Dan was due to move back home at the weekend.

Leafing through her file, Jo tried not to check Dan out. He was dressed in full uniform and perched on the middle of a wide table, which he'd managed to have propped on some sort of temporary dais, giving him a height advantage – as if he needed it.

'We're here in a formal capacity . . .' he began, speaking exaggeratedly slowly, pausing until Jeanie's pen stopped darting '. . . to give Detective . . . Inspector . . . Jo Birmingham the opportunity to appeal my decision to replace her as head of the Rita Nulty murder.'

Jo felt her heart rate quicken. *He's laying on the formalities a bit thick*, she thought.

'Now, the original situation has changed somewhat in that we did have a witness . . . who was prepared to claim Detective Inspector Birmingham had removed a sum of money from the crime scene . . .' He poured himself a glass of water from a decanter, looked up to see if Jo wanted one and, when she gave a stiff nod, swiped Brown Tongue's empty glass, filled it for her and handed it over the table. 'Am I going too fast, Jeanie?'

Jeanie put her pen down and poured herself a glass of water.

'You can insert the date and location of the scene when you're typing this up. But the witness has now withdrawn his statement and suggests he must have made an error in judgement.'

Jo swallowed hard and put down her drink. *Foxy, you beauty*, she thought. Now at last she was in with a chance.

'Now, however, we have some concerns about Mrs Nulty's whereabouts,' Dan went on.

Jo sat forward.

'Although she's not formally a missing person, we have been unable to contact her today, and her neighbours say she did not return home last night, and it's highly unusual for her to go away without telling them first. Detective Sergeant John Foxe yesterday forced entry and established that nothing seemed out of order; however it seems unlikely that she'd leave of her own volition before her daughter's funeral, so that inquiry is also ongoing.'

Jo opened her mouth to speak, but Dan was still in full flow. 'However, until what happened to the missing cash . . . can be explained, the charges against Detective Inspector Birmingham remain in place. Until that time, I am going to recommend that Detective Inspector Gavin Sexton should take over the investigation into the recent murder cases. I understand he agrees with Detective Inspector Birmingham's assertion that the cases are linked.'

Jo stood up quickly. Foxy had just given her the perfect get-out clause, so why did Dan seem so dead set on persecuting her? So much for any prospect of reconciliation. 'Write this down, Jeanie,' she said. 'My reputation has been grievously impugned by the spurious allegations made against me in this sham of a hearing. As these allegations can no longer be substantiated, the suggestion that there should be any onus on me to prove what happened afterwards is untenable. Rita Nulty's mother's whereabouts are unknown. She's now the only one who can corroborate my version of events, which is, in any event, no longer necessary, as Detective Sergeant John Foxe has withdrawn his statement. If I am removed from heading up this inquiry as Chief Superintendent Mason suggests, every one of my colleagues out there is going to believe the accusations against me have been substantiated. That is not just tantamount to constructive dismissal, it's slander and, make no mistake, I will sue.' She paused. 'Have you got that?'

Dan looked at her, stony-faced, then tilted his head towards Brown Tongue, who nodded slowly.

She tucked her paperwork under her arm and walked towards the door.

'I heard you threw Mac off the team,' Dan called after her. 'I've told Merrigan he's the replacement.'

Jo kept going. She may have won herself the right to hold on to this case but, in her head, she was drawing yet another line under her marriage.

22

Jo was still talking herself down as she queued up for food in a greasy spoon in Smithfield, where she'd hastily arranged to meet the team for a working lunch. Only when she finally slid the tray loaded with plates of fried eggs and chips on to a pine table where Sexton, Foxy and Merrigan were sitting did she finally manage a smile, because the lads had struck up a little round of applause.

'Is that because I got the grub in, or because I'm still your boss?' Jo asked.

'What do you think?' Foxy asked, putting his arm across her shoulders to give her a reassuring squeeze as she sat down.

She smiled at him, then shrugged him off. She didn't want any schmaltz in front of this lot.

'The food of course,' Merrigan joked.

Jo glanced at Sexton. The shade of his skin suggested that he still hadn't recovered from watching the autopsy, and he seemed distracted, gazing out of the window at the wide, cobbled street. The area had had a multi-million-euro facelift in the days when there was money for such things, and now sported hotels with marble floors and Art Deco-style interiors. But the horse traders still considered it their first home and converged here with hundreds of horses every month, despite the protests of local businesses and the council.

'They'll have told you that old Mrs Nulty is gone AWOL,' Foxy said. 'That's what I was trying to tell you this morning before the PM.'

Jo bit the top off a chip and reached for the vinegar. 'It's irrelevant, anyway. I felt something was wrong the second I met her. My gut is now telling me she doesn't want to be found full-stop.'

Foxy wiped the corners of his mouth with a napkin. 'That's a big assumption to make, Jo.'

'You didn't see her. Hard as nails, she was, and dodging questions left, right and centre. Surely at a time like this, with your daughter murdered, you'd do anything you could to help catch her killer?'

'We don't exactly have a good record with solving working-girls' murders,' Foxy replied. 'The last three are still open.'

'What's your point?' Jo asked.

'I'm just saying that you'll have to forgive Mrs Nulty if she doesn't take us at our word,' Foxy said, dipping a chip in his yolk.

'Well, I'm in charge now, and Rita's death will be treated no differently than if she'd been the Irish Country Women's Association knitting champion, let me assure you,' Jo said. 'Sexton, can you concentrate on the interviews with the victims' families? We've linked the victims in death. I want to know how well they knew each other in life. We need to establish why our man's choosing these particular individuals to display his talents on, as against anyone else. Got that?'

Sexton, who looked unsure about the food in his mouth, gave her a thumbs-up.

'How'd you get on last night with the working girls?' she asked him.

'I got talking to one of them, and she said Rita was working for the Skids,' Sexton replied.

'Fantastic,' Jo said. 'Now we've got three of our four victims linked to the drugs gang. Well done, Sexton. I wonder if we can link Father Reg to them.' She clicked her fingers as she thought through the implications of what Sexton had told her. 'That also explains why the coke in the apartment where she was killed was uncut. They hadn't even mixed it with anything to maximize the profits yet. They trusted her.'

'Do you think Bible John is a Skid?' Foxy asked.

'Not necessarily,' she said, taking a mouthful of coffee and wincing. It was that instant muck and would leave a bitter aftertaste for the afternoon. 'Did you find out if Father Reg had any brothers?' she asked Sexton.

'No brothers, and no friends resembling a pikey . . .'

'I've been thinking about Father Reg,' Foxy said.

'Kinky!' Merrigan cut in, ripping some salt sachets open with his teeth and scattering salt liberally.

Jo sighed. 'Go on,' she said to Foxy.

'Maybe I'm off the wall, but it sort of struck me as a possibility from the word go. Father Reg ministered in Sheriff Street, right? Maybe Rita came and gave him a confession. Priests swear a vow of silence, don't they? What if the killer found out Father Reg knew something?'

Jo nodded. 'It's possible. The location's been bothering me from the start. By the way, I contacted the hospital on the way here, and Father Reg's condition is still touch and go, so I've organized protection out there, just in case. We need him to talk to us as soon as he regains consciousness.'

'Nice,' Merrigan said, watching a girl walking by in a tight dress.

'Merrigan,' Jo said, 'I want you on the door-to-doors on Sheriff Street with the uniforms. See if you can back up Foxy's theory and put Rita Nulty in the confessional. And don't start giving me excuses. Plus, you could do with the exercise.

'Sexton, I want you to interview Anto Crawley's wife and see what you can get out of her. Foxy, can you hit the library after this and find out everything you can about the killer's Bible fixation? This is a personal crusade. If we can find out who he thinks he is, it may help us work out who he thinks his enemies are.' She stood up. 'Let's aim to meet up in the station afterwards to compare notes. We've got Anto Crawley's post mortem first thing in the morning, so we need to be on top of things by then.'

'Here, what are you going to do?' Merrigan asked.

'I'm going to work out why the killer doesn't like the Skids,' Jo said, pulling the collar of her jacket up and stepping on to the street outside.

23

Sexton was waiting for Ryan Freeman to show. He was standing around the corner from the derelict harbour warehouse on Sheriff Street where Anto Crawley's body had been found. The street was a mismatch of squat harbour outhouses and brand-new high-rise office and apartment buildings. Developers had been snapping up derelict harbour outhouses just like the one where Crawley was killed, the kind of places you couldn't have given away ten years ago – until they couldn't give them away again. The whole area had an abandoned feel. 'Office To Let' signs draped down entire sides of brand-new buildings. When it came to projections about how long the economic recovery was going to take, Sexton reckoned that a head count of the dwindling number of cranes on the quay was proof enough that the politicians were lying.

He kept his head down. It would be just his luck to be spotted deviating from the job Jo had given to him by someone from the station.

He glanced at his watch anxiously. Ryan was late. Sexton rummaged in his pocket for his mobile. If Ryan didn't come soon, he would never be able to talk to Anto Crawley's wife and get back for the next briefing.

His friendship with Ryan went way back. They'd gone to

the same school and palled around together for a few years afterwards, but they'd lost touch until Maura's funeral, a year and a half ago, when Ryan came to pay his last respects.

Then, when Katie was abducted, Ryan had asked Sexton to investigate what had happened on the QT, so it wouldn't appear in the papers. Sexton knew Angie, but he'd never set eyes on the little girl. But as soon as he saw her, he knew he couldn't walk away, not since he knew Maura had been expecting a little girl. Ryan believed Crawley was responsible for Katie's kidnapping, and had asked Sexton to show him where he had died.

He clicked his tongue as he hit a wrong digit on the phone's keypad trying to ring Ryan. He was all fingers and thumbs today. He looked up and down the street again for any sign, gripping the phone tighter as he cleared the number to start again. The rattle of lorries hurtling by wasn't helping, and neither was the fact that his sinuses were giving him jip and he was in dire need of the hair of the dog. He'd overdone it on the vino again last night, and his stomach was in shit from a staple diet of TV dinners.

'You've got acid reflux,' a quack had told him on a recent visit, before launching into a lecture about how he needed a biopsy and to start looking after himself but, first and foremost, what he needed most urgently was grief counselling.

'Just give me the pills,' Sexton had answered. What he had really wanted to say to the quack was that remembering to eat five portions of veg didn't register when there was only room in his head for regret. Last night's flashback had been a particular doozy. It was the putdown he'd delivered to Maura in what would turn out to be their last Christmas together. He'd been moaning on for months about being the only breadwinner and how it was all very well her being a free spirit, but couldn't she do it after hours? Next thing, she appeared with freckles drawn on her rouged cheeks, wearing a silly costume, and announced she'd got the perfect job, as Santa's elf in the local shopping centre. He'd flipped, said something like 'grow up'. He'd gone to watch her at the shopping centre after, staying at a distance so she didn't know he was there, and had seen the way she'd brought a smile to people's faces. She'd always had a gift when it came to making people happy. So why was she so unhappy herself?

Sexton felt his windpipe start to burn and rubbed his chest painfully. Hunching his shoulders, he scanned up and down the street again – still no sign of Ryan. He crossed the street to the warehouse, winking at the uniform keeping the cordon as he approached. Together they worked the rusting bolt-lock sideways, clanking the rusting door along on its rollers.

Natural light flooded into the opening, making Sexton wince. Inside was a long, narrow hovel. The brick walls had turned a slimy black from rusty water dripping down the sides; the floor was covered in different-sized mattresses partly littered with broken slates, glass and empty cans. As he took a step inside, the stink hit the back of his throat. It was like a dog's coat drying.

He groaned, taking a step back.

'Wait till you see what's on the back wall,' the uniform said. 'I'm going to have to close this door, mate – regulation.'

'You got a torch?' Sexton asked.

'There's a light on down the back. Keep an eye out for the hypodermics – they're everywhere.' The uniform laughed. 'If the syringes don't get you, Weil's disease will.'

Sexton nodded, and tucked his trouser legs inside his socks as he began to pick his steps. The door cranked shut behind him, making the place look even more sinister. An exposed light was throwing out bald light, but patchily.

'Jesus!' Sexton stopped as he reached the darkest part of the warehouse. Four metal shackles were set in the wall, the word 'bitch' spray-painted in between them. Was this where they'd held Katie? His stomach lurched.

Sexton's eyes moved to a series of rusting implements. Hooks and serrated edges – shapes that were frightening just to look at – were set in holders along the wall. He walked over for a closer inspection. What had they been used for here? Something brushed his shoulder, and he turned and saw a hand.

He spun, swinging his arm back, fist back.

'Woah!' a woman's voice said.

Sexton's hand stopped mid-air. It was Jo Birmingham, who was looking as pale and drawn as he felt.

'You scared the life out of me,' he said, bending down and putting his hands on his knees.

'What's going on?' she asked him icily.

Sexton took a couple of deep breaths. He wasn't sure what had shocked him more: the state of the warehouse, or Jo being there. 'I just wanted to see for myself where Anto Crawley died.'

'I told you I wanted you to interview Anto Crawley's other half. You should have cleared it with me first.'

Sexton reached for his Benson and Hedges and offered her one, aware that his hands were still shaking.

Jo noticed too. Taking hold of his elbow, she guided him out of the warehouse and into the bright light outside.

24

Jo was fit to kill Sexton as she led him out on to Sheriff Street, but bar the fraction too long she spent jotting questions for the job book in her notebook, she didn't give it away. The light had been working inside. Jo wanted to know who'd bother paying the electricity bill in a derelict building being used by junkies as a shooting-up gallery. She made a note to have Foxy action it as a job. The location also had to be highly significant: the street where Crawley's body was found intersected both Castleforbes Road, where Rita was killed, and New Wapping Street, where Stuart Ball was murdered. She sketched a rough outline of streets, approximating the angles where they met, and placed an X at the points where she estimated the dump sites to be in relation to each other.

Jo looked around her, aware that, beside her, Sexton had sunk his hands into his trouser pockets and was shifting from one foot to the other. He looked wretched – his shirt was creased and there were broken veins under his eyes. But if he thought she was going to let him use that as an excuse . . .

'Well?' she said, when she was good and ready. 'Are you going to tell me what the bloody hell you were doing in there?'

Sexton opened his mouth to answer then turned his head. Jo followed his gaze and saw a man approaching. She knew the face, but it took her a couple of seconds to recognize Ryan Freeman out of context. He was wearing a donkey jacket and had a reporter's spiral notebook tucked under his arm. He looked a lot shorter in real life than on the telly spouting on about scumbags, and was carrying some weight in his jowls and belly, which hadn't spread to the rest of his frame, suggesting it was recent. Judging by the hollow look to his eyes, he hadn't slept properly in a while either.

'Detective Inspector Birmingham, isn't it?' he said, giving Sexton a quick nod. 'I'm Ryan Freeman, and I've learned from a source that you believe Anto Crawley was killed by the same person who murdered Rita Nulty and Stuart Ball.'

Sexton flicked the fag on to the road and stared after it.

Jo looked at Sexton, noting his blank expression, then turned back to Freeman. What possible advantage to the investigation had the motormouth who'd briefed him thought they'd achieve, apart from scaring the public witless and telling the killer it was time to change his modus operandi?

She offered Freeman a stick of gum, which he took.

'Sick son-of-a-bitch,' he remarked, staring at the ware-house, as he folded the gum into his mouth.

Jo didn't know if he was talking about the killer or the victim. 'You lose someone to crime?' she asked.

Freeman turned to Jo and shook his head. 'So, can you give me a comment on the Anto Crawley killing?' he asked.

Jo sighed. 'Here's what I don't understand. If you've got a story, why haven't you used it yet? What do you need me for?'

Freeman said nothing.

'Come on,' she cajoled. 'Your source is telling you a serial killer is on the rampage. It's a tabloid editor's wet dream, isn't it? You get to go on all the breakfast shows, pull that face you're so good at – you know, the one of measured fury – the news bulletins run your outraged soundbite, the analysis programmes flash your front page. In two months' time you've got a bestselling book, and a year down the line you've a movie contract in the pipeline. You're seriously expecting me to believe that you care if I confirm it or not?'

'I don't. I just thought you'd like the opportunity. And don't look at me like that. What you and I do is not so very different after all.'

'You know, my mum used to have this friend, and when she'd call around for a cuppa' – Jo made a talking mouth with her hand – 'it was "Such and such has cancer", "So and so is having their house repossessed". You know why? Because it made her feel like there were worse things than having four cats for company. Don't compare what we do. You sell misery to make your readers feel like they're having a good day.'

'Funny that,' Freeman snapped back. 'Only my auld one used to have a brother. It was back in the fifties, and my uncle, he got himself into trouble for robbing a loaf of bread because he was hungry. Seven years old he was. He got a warning, but he was still hungry and he kept robbing – never the luxury stuff like chocolate, just what he needed to stay upright. Got himself sent to an industrial school for his trouble in the end. He was sodomized by a priest on and off for five years. He developed a stammer and had a lot of problems with incontinence from the damage done to him. When he was got out, he was a headcase, but he went to the bishop and complained. Your lot arrived at his door and threw him in a cell for a night, where he hanged himself. The priest continued to fiddle with little boys until a newspaper ran his name, his photograph and his address to warn parents.'

Jo hunched her shoulders. He'd trumped her, and he knew it.

'How about I give you some new information?' she asked. 'With quotes.'

Freeman's eyes widened.

Jo waited till he'd his pen and paper ready then said: 'As head of this investigation, I want to tell the killer I know he thinks what he's doing is honourable.'

'What?' Freeman asked, looking up from his pad.

Sexton took a packet of Rennies from his pocket and put one under his tongue.

'We're dealing with a *muti* killer,' Jo answered.

'*Muti?*'

'You know,' Jo said, waving her hand, 'the African tribal ritual of harvesting body parts in order to assume the victim's powers . . . penis for sexual prowess, that kind of thing. The screams of the victim make the *muti* more powerful.' She checked to see he was buying it.

'Penis?' Freeman said, alarmed.

Sexton nudged the base of his breastbone forcefully.

'Not yet,' Jo answered. 'But it wouldn't surprise me.'

Freeman pulled out his notebook and wrote something down.

'You remember the case of Adam – when the torso of a boy was found on the Thames,' Jo went on, watching Sexton rubbing his chest. 'Cuts on the body, candles at the scene . . . exactly the same scenario as with our victims, did you know that?'

Freeman shook his head.

'Off the record,' she said out of the side of her mouth, 'we're examining asylum lists for immigrants from the specific regions of Africa where it's practiced. But that can be our follow-up.'

Freeman nodded, waved goodbye to her and Sexton then crossed the street and climbed back into his car.

'What did you tell him that bullshit for?' Sexton asked, as they walked away from the warehouse.

Jo took a couple of seconds to react. She was still staring at the spot on Sexton's chest that he'd been rubbing. It had just occurred to her – she knew exactly who the killer thought he was.

25

Having told Sexton to get on with the job he'd been given, which was to interview Anto Crawley's wife, Jo headed back to the station. Once inside the noisy incident room, she walked past Merrigan and the two rows of detectives collating the questionnaires and answering the phones, heading straight for Foxy, or at least the neat stack of books on the desk in front of him. She picked one up and began flicking through the pages.

'Oi,' Foxy protested. 'They're my Sal's books. She's been collecting anything to do with saints.'

But Jo had already found what she was looking for. Curling her finger, she indicated to him to follow her, throwing a look of intense irritation at Merrigan, who was on the phone telling his wife what he wanted for dinner.

Book under her arm, she led Foxy down the fire escape stairs, where she could be spared the sound of Jeanie on the Tannoy paging her to Dan's office. Satisfied the coast was clear after a quick recce up and down the corridor, she ducked into the cleaning lady's store room.

'That's him,' she told Foxy excitedly, holding the book open for him at eye level. The room was so small she couldn't fully extend her arms.

Foxy looked around awkwardly.

'That's our killer!' Pointing at something in the book, she handed it to Foxy. 'He only thinks he's bloody well Doubting Thomas!'

Foxy cleared some space between some toilet rolls and sat down on a shelf. Removing his reading glasses, he let them dangle from a string around his neck and adjusted the book to the spot in his vision where the painting became clear.

The image was of a robed Christ holding his tunic to the side of his chest to accommodate three bearded spectators straining to see his open wound. The nearest one was crouched up at eye level, prodding the flesh with his finger. He was the figure Jo had been pointing out.

'*The Incredulity of Saint Thomas*: aka Doubting Thomas . . .' She paused. 'A work by Caravaggio.'

Foxy put his glasses back on quickly. 'Jesus is telling him, "Reach hither thy hand and thrust it into my side: and be not faithless, but believing."' He peered at Jo over the tops of his specs.

'The wounds on all of our victims,' she explained.

Somebody rapped on the door outside, making them both jump. Sarah, a female officer with a round, rosy-cheeked face, stuck her head around the door. Jo knew her from indoor soccer, though she hadn't played with the team since Harry had been born. She didn't have the time any more.

''Allo, 'allo,' the officer said, giving Jo a wink. 'Thought I saw you two lovebirds coming in here. You know the chief's looking for you?'

Jo nodded. The messenger grinned and ducked back out.

'I need you to get me everything you can on Doubting Thomas,' Jo told Foxy. 'Who was he? What did he do? And what is his relevance to our killer? Got it?'

'Who was Doubting Thomas?' Foxy repeated. 'Sal did a project on the apostles some months back, so I can tell you that he didn't just doubt the Resurrection, he doubted Christ at the Last Supper. And, according to the Bible conspiracy theorists, he was a brother of Christ . . .'

Jo opened the door then stopped. 'So that's why the killer told Rita Nulty's mother he was a priest's twin!'

'But what about Caravaggio? Is the killer taking a lead from him?' Foxy asked.

'I don't think so,' Jo said. 'Caravaggio just helped me piece it together.' She looked at Foxy. 'What time you get to bed at last night?'

Foxy opened his mouth but Jo silenced him with a prod of her elbow because, after a quick rap, Merrigan had poked his head around the door.

'Ho, ho,' he said. 'So this is the bolthole you've locked yourselves up in.'

Jo could tell from the smug look on his face he was pleased about something.

'Just letting you know the boys from NBCI have just arrived and they headed straight for Dan's office.'

'Who's there?' Foxy asked, pulling the door open and pushing past him into the corridor.

'Frank Black's there, and he does not look happy,' Merrigan explained with relish.

'Well, he can bloody well wait,' Jo said crossly, running her fingers through her hair. The National Bureau of Criminal Investigation was the force's equivalent of the UK's Special Branch and had subsumed the old murder squad. She didn't need him or Merrigan to tell her that the NBCI's arrival meant that her days heading this investigation were very probably numbered.

But Merrigan had more news.

'Did I mention a tray of tea and sandwiches was delivered in to the chief? You know what it means if he's organized catering: he must have known they were coming.'

Jo stepped closer to him. 'Between you, me and the wall, I think the killer could be black.' She watched his eyes light up, ignored Foxy clicking his tongue behind her and went on. 'Can you start cold-calling some of the refugee centres, see if you can round me up any possible suspects?'

Merrigan nodded with an open mouth, then took off like a man possessed.

Foxy was shaking his head.

'Somebody's been feeding the press, and I just want to see whether it's Merrigan.' She filled him in on how she'd found Sexton in the warehouse where Anto Crawley had been killed, and how she'd fed Ryan Freeman the same line. If Freeman's source was Merrigan, he'd double-check it with him and get it corroborated, meaning that her red herring would appear in the paper.

'You're the only one bar me who knows who the killer thinks he is,' Jo concluded. 'And that's the way I want it kept for now. Right?'

'Without a team behind you, you're peeing in the wind,' Foxy replied. 'Two of us won't solve this.'

'We may have to,' Jo said. 'I've got a horrible feeling he's closer than we think.'

'What makes you say that?'

'Don't you think it's more than coincidence that all our victims have turned up in our district? Rita Nulty was right on site, waiting for us to find her. Stuart Ball, Anto Crawley and Father Reg . . . all in our jurisdiction. That's the only reason we've held on to the inquiry this long. We will need to brainstorm these locations as soon as possible.'

'Want me to set up a conference?' he asked.

She nodded and checked her watch. 'Once I've faced the music in Dan's office.'

Foxy put his hand on her arm. 'I've ordered the records from Customs showing any importations of myrrh. It's an aromatic gum which grows in Arabia, India or Abyssinia, did you know that?'

She looked at him appreciatively. 'You look exhausted. I'd be happier if you'd go home to Sal and get some kip. I don't want you running yourself into the ground because of me.'

'There isn't time,' Foxy said.

'That's an order,' Jo said. 'Merrigan could do with missing a dinner. I'll get him on the records. And I'll ask him to find out about who's paying the ESB in the warehouse where Crawley was found. I don't want you staying up all night any more. You won't do anyone any favours if you get sick, least of all me and Sal.'

Jo was walking towards Dan's office when her phone trilled to life with that ring-ding-a-ding Crazy Frog tone. 'I'll bloody well kill him,' Jo muttered. Rory must have been fiddling with it.

'Not quite sure how to put this,' Hawthorne said when the call connected.

'Not like you,' Jo said, giving a thumbs-up to a colleague asking had she heard Dan's page.

'Before I go on, I want it understood that what I'm about to tell you is completely for your background information,' the pathologist went on. 'If you try and call me to court to relay this conversation, not only will I completely deny this conversation ever happened, I'll –'

'Understood,' Jo interrupted.

'The thing is, I've got a PhD student from the university who's tech-ing here when we need a dig out,' Hawthorne said. 'You may have seen him when we were doing the Rita Nulty autopsy. Decent fellow. Obliging. You don't get that any more. They're all too busy socializing . . . It's just there'd be all kinds of ethical problems and permissions required if the student tried to do it by the book, you see . . .'

'To do what?' Jo asked.

Hawthorne coughed. 'The technician – his name is Walter, by the way – has been studying the effect death has . . . ahem . . . on semen.'

Jo took a quick breath in. 'You mean the killer didn't use a condom?'

Hawthorne gave a short hum.

'This changes everything.'

'The bill for the DNA database was only published in January,' Hawthorne reminded her. 'The odds of us having his profile on record are nil.'

'I'm talking about the way our man thinks. In the States they call it the CSI effect . . . You know, the way popular culture has schooled the ordinary criminal in the advances of forensic science. Burglars wear gloves; joyriders burn stolen cars; rapists wear condoms. Nobody leaves a DNA sample. Unless . . .'

'He wants to be caught?' Hawthorne asked.

'Not wants,' Jo said. 'He knows exactly how far behind we are. We're looking for someone who not only knows the law here, he's also confident we're not going to trace him.'

'There's something else . . .'

'Go on.'

'Walter's convinced that, in Rita Nulty's case, the degen-
eration which would have been caused to the semen upon
the release of certain chemicals had she been alive was not
present . . .' He paused and coughed self-consciously again.
'And that the said same semen, if you will, had aged less
than the time which had passed since death.'

There was a pause as Jo worked this out. 'You're not
saying our killer had sex with his victims after they died?'

'I don't know about the rest of them,' he replied. 'As you
know, we are PM-ing Anto Crawley in the morning, but
don't start thinking about an exhumation order for Stuart
Ball. It's something I could never corroborate, even with this
information in mind. It's true that bruises can only appear if
the blood is circulating. And certainly there was tearing in
Rita's perineal and genital area, but that in itself does not
mean sex has not been consensual, especially given the
victim's profession – well, I don't have to spell it out. It
would never stand up in court. However, I thought it was
something that might be of use to you.'

Jo was too shocked to say anything.

Hawthorne seemed to pick up on her reaction. 'It's a prac-
tice as old as civilization, by the way. It was widespread in
Latin America and Ancient Greece,' he said, trying to put
her at ease. 'Did you know that the Ancient Egyptians never
entrusted the dead to embalmers before decomposition had
set in? And in parts of India it was believed that a dead
virgin would never rest in peace, so the men folk obliged,
posthumously, of course. So you see, necrophilia is not *that*
extraordinary.'

'Yes, thank you, I appreciate it.' Still reeling from the
news, Jo made her way slowly towards Dan's office. She was

just about to knock on his door when Foxy called her on her mobile. He'd been flicking through another of Sal's books on his way to the car when he'd seen it. If she was right about who the killer thought he was, there was something she should know, he said. Tomorrow – July 3 – was Doubting Thomas's feast day.

26

A four-storey terraced house of fine-cut granite. Derelict –
the once-grand French windows blocked up; the Regency
door sealed over with sheets of chipboard.

Entry is through a rusting iron grate set in the flagstones
on the street. The location has been chosen because of what
lies underneath the car park it overlooks – an ancient grave-
yard.

Inside: dim, fragrant, bloody. A tabernacle in the centre of
a makeshift altar, the burst of glinting brass spikes shooting
from the point of intersection on the cross like an exploding
meteorite.

On the grimy wall behind, a life-sized crucifix, damaged
in the places where the mutilated carving of Christ was once
fixed but has since been chopped free. The carving now lies
face down on the ground in front of the altar, head closest,
feet furthest away, prostrate. Around it is an array of gleam-
ing implements – an axe, knives, crowbar, hammer and
chisel. Lined up on the altar, the wooden hand, claw-like,
the foot complete with nail, the eye.

A figure dressed in a hooded monk's robe glides across the
room. He chants as he prepares the noose, slung from an
exposed beam in the ceiling. The words are not discernible,
but the sound is hypnotic.

And now he drags the Christ figure up, a dead weight carved from sacred yew. The neck in position, the weight drops and the wooden figure swings like a pendulum because of its outstretched arms. The rope holds.

The killer pushes his hood from his face, raises a meat cleaver and delivers it to the chipping torso with a whocking noise. The fifth ceremony has begun.

27

It was only 5 p.m., but even so Sexton was dog-tired by the time he reached Anto Crawley's missus's doorstep. Shielding a fag under the flap of his jacket, he took a deep drag and lit up, then pressed his finger on the bell and jabbed impatiently. It was one thing trying to get through the day with the hangover from hell, but ever since Jo Birmingham had scared the living daylights out of him in the warehouse, his nerves were also shot.

He squinted through the smoke the wind was blowing back into his face, making his eyes water. Anto Crawley's former home was a corporation flat in Oliver Bond, near Christchurch cathedral in the Liberties. In the old days, Crawley would have had his bird shacked up in a sprawling mansion in salubrious Foxrock on the Southside, or Malahide on the Northside, the kind of place that boasted a rhododendron border and an Italian cyprus driveway. The barristers' and builders' wives would have invited her to their fondue parties out of curiosity then shot each other horrified looks behind her back at the sound of her accent or the sight of her table manners. But with the successes of the Criminal Assets Bureau, the gangsters were now flaunting their lack of ill-gotten gains, staying in corporation flats and concealing all property acquisitions under other people's names.

The irony for the locals was that, by having a scumbag like Crawley ensconced in the vicinity, the usual lawlessness and antisocial problems associated with the building complex stopped and the place ran like clockwork. The joyriders' ramps were removed, the boarded-up flats filled. The prospect of prison didn't deter scumbags, but having to answer to Anto Crawley – that made them think about the consequences.

Sexton leaned sideways and shouted through the letterbox to open up. A bunch of kids who'd spotted him the second he'd entered the complex came for a gawk, all kitted out in their back-of-a-lorry designer trainers and hoodies.

'Who are you?' an obese youngster asked him.

Sexton put him at ten and, with a lip on him like that, he could see his future like it was mapped in his palm, leading straight to the 'A' wing in Portlaoise – where they kept the likes of John Gilligan, suspected of ordering the murder of Veronica Guerin.

'You're a copper, aren't you?'

'Piss off,' Sexton told him.

'I could have you up for that,' the kid said.

Sexton looked at the boy's burger-fed face. He had so many freckles they were joining. Sexton held his hand up in an Ali G salute. 'Booyakasha,' he said.

The kid forked his fingers back, said 'Respek' with a grin and slouched off.

Glenda George pulled the door open, rubbing sleep from her eyes and flattening her bed head. In the front room, Sexton could hear the TV on. She'd got up for Oprah, Dr Phil, then Richard and Judy, he reckoned.

'Yeah?' she asked.

Sexton eyed her up and down. She was early thirties, with

long, thin, jet-black hair and a body to die for, including tits too gravity-defying to be real. Dressed in a pink-velvet track-suit top, denim mini and a pair of long black FMBs, she had enough make-up caked over her hard expression to convince him that he recognized her from a dodgy porno tape he and the lads had seized in some raid a couple of years back.

He put his foot on the step, inside the door.

Something caught Glenda's eye on an adjoining balcony, and she let out a roar over his shoulder. 'What the fuck are you gawking at?'

'He's a copper, Glenda,' a kid shouted up from the forecourt.

'Tell me something I don't know,' Glenda replied. 'Come in,' she said. 'Can't bear these nosey bastards knowing any of my business.'

She turned and led him down the marble-effect hallway, the word 'juicy' inscribed on the arse of her skirt rising and falling with each click of her heels.

They went into the front room, where a wall had been knocked through to give it an open-plan feel. It was untidy – clothes strewn about – but Sexton noticed the state-of-the-art fittings and fixtures: the Olsen and Bang & Olufsen stereo system; the gas fireplace set in the middle of the wall with its heap of pebbles; and the new windows. On paper, this place should have been worth a small fortune. In actuality, an address like this was worn like a badge of criminality.

Glenda lowered herself into a shiny red-leather armchair, zipped off her boots and transferred her perfectly French-manicured toes into a pair of fluffy pink open-toe sandals. 'You've got a fucking nerve,' she told him. 'How can I organize a wake with no body? Cheeky bitch in the morgue keeps hanging up on me. What are you holding on to Anto for?'

'Leave it with me, I'll sort it out,' he said, offering Glenda his card.

She kept up the indignation routine for a bit, but the bite was gone out of her bark. Sexton sighed and settled back in the chair. He kept picking up this sexy little siren vibe she was giving off through it. His tart radar could recognize one through frumpy clothes, a plummy accent and hobbies like flower-arranging and singing in the choir.

'Yeah, well, last night should have been his bloody send-off,' she said, stretching over to take the card, giving him a flash of her sizeable rack. 'Two hundred people I had calling, and no Anto. You pigs are all the same.'

By now Sexton had placed her accent in Dublin 1, where women were so at home that they shopped in their pyjamas and slippers and liked to remind people who worked how much free time they had.

'Late night?' he asked her, offering her a smoke.

She took it with a nod and another generous flash. This time it was not accidental, he knew.

He flicked his lighter and held it up for her to light up. She leaned in and took a succession of little puffs then a slow drag, playing with the zipper on her top, up an inch, down two, up again.

'Got any theories as to who's behind it?' he asked.

'Take your pick,' she said, combing the ends of her hair with her fingers.

'Heard he owed the Yardies money,' Sexton said. 'After a trip to Holyhead a few months back.'

She sniggered in an 'as if' way and announced, 'I'm no rat.'

Startled by a noise behind him, Sexton turned around

quickly. A kid aged between two and three years had appeared at the door in a pair of dirty pyjamas and bare feet. His nostrils were caked in snot. 'Mammy, I'm hungry,' he whined.

'Not now,' she answered. 'Now get back in there and close the door until I'm fucking ready.'

It took every cell in Sexton's body not to grab her by the hair and force her into the kitchen to give something to the kid. Instead he pulled out a photograph of a woman with long fair hair from his inside blazer pocket. It was a snatch photo he'd taken himself – the woman hadn't even been aware of the lens pointing at her as she climbed into her car. 'How well did Anto know her?' he asked.

Glenda barely glanced at it. 'Not his type,' she said.

Sexton moved closer to her and put the photo on her lap.

'Why don't you look again? Only I've just had a call from someone who's been busy unscrambling the make of this lady's car, which was caught on CCTV camera. In that particular film, Anto seems to know her very well.' Two-beat pause. 'Did I mention we've got someone who's confessed to killing him?'

Glenda looked at him in astonishment.

He tapped his nose, pointing to the pic.

'It was strictly business between them,' she said.

'Didn't look that way in the film,' Sexton said.

'You've got it wrong. Anto was making sure no harm came to her or her family, and in return she was making sure no harm came to his. Now who's confessed to killing Anto?'

Sexton stood up, and flicked his fag at her gas fireplace. 'Afraid I'm not at liberty to say.'

She swore and picked up the glass paperweight on a nearby coffee table.

'I'll let myself out, shall I?' he said, ducking just in time. It smashed on the wall inches above his head.

The kid came flying out into the hall to see what had happened. Sexton thought about slipping him some money, but knew his ma would have smelt it from the other room and it would only cause the kid problems. Feeling even sicker than when he'd arrived, he went back out to his car, inspecting it for damage before getting in.

As he gunned the engine, Sexton knew he couldn't keep protecting Ryan Freeman. He was in enough trouble with Jo Birmingham already. If she found out what he'd been keeping from her, it wouldn't just be the investigation he'd lose out on: his job could be on the line. And that was all he had left since Maura had died. But having seen for himself the warehouse where Katie had been held, he was going to talk to one last person first. The woman in the picture.

28

Dan took Jo by the elbow, turned her around and walked her straight back out of his office. In the corridor outside, he planted himself straight in front of her. 'Where the hell have you been? Have you any idea how long I've been calling?'

'Why didn't you tell me Rory's been mitching?' Jo snapped.

Dan looked like he'd misheard. He'd nicked himself shaving, Jo noticed, but forgotten to remove the paper blotting the blood. She put her hands behind her back and held them there.

'We don't have time for this now. Don't you realize . . .'

'I'm his bloody mother!'

He raised his arms and headed inside, glancing behind her after a couple of seconds to make sure she didn't disappear again.

On the other side of the door, Jeanie was touching up her make-up with a compact.

'You missed a bit,' Jo told her, following Dan inside.

None of the backs of the three heads facing Dan's desk turned as Jo came into the office. There was no greeting, and none of the officers from the National Bureau of Criminal Investigation outranked her either, but the way they had joined their chairs in flank told her they all thought they did. A fourth, free chair sat at the end of their row, but Jo walked to the far side of Dan's desk so that she was facing them, and remained standing.

The way they were continuing to make small talk amongst themselves was more than just condescending: it showed a level of contempt. Jo knew that the same superior attitude could be found in every specialist group in every police force in every part of the world – from the Feds in the States to MI5 in the UK. There was out-and-out hostility between customs officers and the gardaí working in the airports, for example. But right now, what she was finding hardest to deal with was the complete waste of her bloody time. If a showdown was imminent, it was going to mean blood on the walls, because Dan may have had the time to sip tea and nibble sandwiches, but if anyone thought they were going to take this investigation from her without a fight, they were deluded. As long as she believed she had the best chance of cracking the case, she would battle for it tooth and nail, especially now Foxy had told her that tomorrow was Doubting Thomas's feast day. Jo had no doubt in her mind that if she didn't find their killer before then, she'd have another body on her hands.

Beside her, Dan was trying to control his own agitation by clicking the top of a pen up and down; two seconds exactly between each press.

Jo took the sum of her opposition. She had worked with only one of the NBCI officers before – Jenny Friar – but she knew the other two by reputation. Frank Black was the most recognizable face on the force – fifty-odd, overweight, with a moustache trimmed neatly above a purple top lip. He wore a dapper paisley silk scarf above his gold-buttoned navy blazer and had an ability to wax lyrical about his own crucial involvement in cracking the country's worst crimes when a camera and mic were being thrust in his face, though colleagues who'd worked on the same cases remembered things differently.

Alongside him sat Dave Waters, twenty years younger, ambitious, studious, expensive rimless glasses displaying a vanity to which his looks gave no purchase. With a doctorate in psychology, he was a novelty in a job where the only accomplishment that counted was hours on the streets. In recent years, he had increasingly assumed the role of the force's unofficial psychological profiler. To Jo's mind, he was neither instinctive nor intuitive, and the string of letters after his name had made him fluent only in jargon.

Of the delegation, Jenny Friar was the most formidable. Aged in her late forties, she had a Princess Diana haircut, an expensive wool pashmina and a set of heavy semi-precious gems strung around her neck. At one time, Jo had looked up to her, but that had been before she sold out to management.

Dan asked Jo to take a seat. The old days, when he'd have walked across the room to carry it back to her, were gone. Jo felt the back of her neck and shoulders tighten. 'I'd rather stand,' she said.

He gestured with a hand as he did the introductions. Jo noticed that not one of them had the balls to look her in the eye.

'You may or may not be aware,' Dan began, 'that the family of Father Reginald Walsh switched off his life support today.'

It shouldn't have come as a shock, but it did. Jo felt her stomach constrict. Now she understood why the atmosphere in the room felt so feral. The body count had just risen to four. But she was also bloody livid. As head of the investigation, she should have been informed first. Why had nobody told her?

'The commissioner contacted me today,' Dan continued, 'and he informed me of his intention to add to our resources by assigning these three new members to our team.'

Jo sneaked a quick glance at Dan. It was a relief to know that he hadn't been instrumental in this ambush.

'We're very glad to have you all here today,' Dan said. 'I understand you've each been studying the case notes. Why don't you each give us your assessment?'

Jo folded her arms tightly.

Dan leaned forward. 'Let's get on with it, shall we?' He turned to the profiler. 'Dave, why don't you go first? Who do you think we're dealing with?'

Dave Waters stood up and hooked his thumbs in the waist of his pleated jeans. College stripes hung in a scarf around his neck. 'We're dealing with a narcissist,' he stated.

Jo began to pick the leaves off Dan's geranium.

'He's an egotist who is probably known to the force for crimes in the past.'

'What about Jo's theory of a Roman Catholic motif?' Dan asked.

'I'm afraid I don't think much of it,' Waters replied. 'Sharia law says the same thing about an eye for an eye, so perhaps we should be visiting members of the Muslim community?'

'We don't have time for this now,' Jo interrupted sharply. 'I'm sorry, but I've already established a link between the killings, and who the killer thinks he is . . .'

'Are we to understand that the status of the investigation

has changed and you now have a suspect?' Jenny asked, smoothing the wrinkles in her skirt.

Designer, the kind of clothes only a woman with a salary to spend on herself can afford, Jo thought. 'The killer thinks he's some kind of avenging angel. All these people have wronged him, and once we find out how, we'll have him. Now, if you'll excuse me, I need to get back to work.'

Jenny Friar stood up, walked to the side of Dan's desk and sat on it, crossing her legs at the ankles, blocking Jo's exit.

'Do you or do you not have a suspect?' she asked authoritatively.

'Don't be ridiculous, I've only had twenty-four hours on the case.'

'Well, I've only had twenty minutes, and I have a suspect,' Friar replied. 'He made a confession right here in this station to DI Gavin Sexton. His name is Andy Morris, but I believe his nickname is Skinny.'

29

Jo phoned Sexton as she drove towards the Pearse Street flats where Skinny lived. She kept it curt, telling Sexton to meet her there and refusing to explain why. Sexton had been on his way to see Stuart Ball's mother and didn't sound too happy at having to entertain a change of plan. That made two of them.

Jo's anger was sharpening by the minute. For the second time today, he'd kept her in the dark about a solo run – on her investigation! How could he not have told her he'd interviewed someone who'd confessed to Anto Crawley's murder? She'd get over Jenny Friar rubbing her nose in it, but what she found hardest of all was the look she'd spotted in Dan's eye. He actually felt sorry for her. What the hell had Sexton been thinking?

Jo knocked at the suspect's door, then at his window with the ball of her fist. There was no bell, let alone a knocker on the door. Skinny was either not at home or playing silly buggers. Jo stepped over to the neighbour's door to find out which, but hadn't so much as touched it before an old man in a string vest, glasses with bottle-thick lenses and high-waisted trousers appeared and told her to try St Andrew's Resource Centre, where a Concerned Parents Against Drugs meeting was taking place. In the eighties and nineties, the

CPAD had mobilized the anger of frightened parents who'd lost or were losing children to addiction by organizing evictions of drug dealers. If CPAD were back in action, it was a real sign of how bad the drugs problem was again in this part of town.

Sexton pulled into the complex, just as Jo was driving out. He lowered the window of his year-old, 5-series BMW. 'I did tell you about his statement, I know I did.'

Jo glared at him, then shut her eyes tightly as a pain stabbed through them, causing her to lose her vision momentarily. Then she put her foot down full throttle and tore down Hanover Street towards St Andrews, her exhaust belching black fumes behind her.

Sexton stayed on her tail, a set look on his face every time she glanced in her rear-view mirror. When she crossed to the wrong side of the road to grab a parking spot, he was still there like glue, taking a big chance with the oncoming traffic.

He jumped out before her and leaned in her window, both hands on the car door. 'It's not what it looks like.'

Jo reached over to the passenger seat for Skinny's statement and picked it up by a corner like she was handling a turd. She held it up in front of him. 'Only it looks like you took a statement from someone confessing to Anto Crawley's bloody murder.'

'It was a try-on!' Sexton said. 'The statement isn't even bloody well signed. So he knew about Crawley's teeth. Big deal! But he got the incidentals wrong – he told me they were smashed in. And how could they think him mentioning the knife was corroboration of his knowledge of the crime scene? It was all over the bloody *News* and hardly inside information.'

'So why did you file his statement?' Jo asked, getting out of the car and forcing him back on the pavement.

'What are you saying, Jo? That I filed a confession that's not worth a shit to make you look incompetent? I filed it because it's procedure. That's my job. I wasn't going to waste your time or mine on a wild-goose chase.'

Jo frowned, scanning the building opposite. 'And I'm saying that here is yet another example of you keeping things from me. What else haven't you told me?'

Sexton looked away. He was hiding something, Jo was sure of it, but it would have to wait till they were back in the station.

She crossed the road and headed into the building towards the room at the back where the CPAD meeting was taking place.

Inside, it was cramped and there was standing room only. Sexton stood beside her, nudging her shoulder with his own to indicate the man holding court at the top of the gym. He was dressed in a shiny black bomber jacket.

'That's him,' Sexton said out of the side of his mouth.

Jo noted the green, looped ribbon pinned to Skinny's breast telling her he was a Shinner. The hypocrisy of Sinn Fein's members chilled her to the bone. It may not have been PC, given the sensitive nature of the post-peace process, but it was the fact that they were exploiting parents' misery by using the threat of force to move other drug dealers along so they could take over the market for drug distribution for themselves that upset her most.

She concentrated on Skinny. Part of him was constantly on the move, but not in a synchronized way. His hands would dart in one direction, his head another. He was arguing with an old woman seated up front, a thyroid-related bald patch on the top of her scalp, thick ankles under heavy tights. In between blowing her nose, she was insisting that her son had nothing to do with drugs and she could not evict him from her home.

'I know you from the time you were a nipper, Andy,' the old lady said to Skinny, holding her hand so high off the ground. 'How many times did I take you in after school and give you a hot dinner if your ma wasn't home?'

Skinny stood over her, radiating aggression. 'It's nothing to do with me. The people have spoken.'

Jo glanced at Sexton. She could tell he was having doubts too about his initial reading on Skinny's innocence too.

Meanwhile, the crowd had burst into applause, and then started up the old familiar chant: 'Pusher-pusher-pusher out-out-out.'

The old lady cracked. 'How can I get him off drugs if he's on the streets?' she begged, tears running down her cheeks.

The chanting grew more ferocious.

Every age is here, Jo thought, casting an eye over the crowd. The men in bomber jackets standing at strategic points around the kangaroo court were watching the crowd, not Skinny. One of the heavies had LOVE HATE knuckles folded over his crotch and was looking over at Jo and Sexton. They stood out a mile, she knew this only too well.

The old lady was trying to sidle her way out of the row of chairs past extended legs. No neighbours stood to pat her back or shifted their legs an inch to aid her progress.

Sexton touched Jo's arm. She could see what he was thinking. If these people realized who they were, the mob mentality could turn nasty.

'If he's not gone in twelve hours, every stick of furniture

in your home goes over the balcony,' Skinny called after the woman.

Jo reached out as the woman approached and took her by the wrist, turning her around. The room went silent. Jo led the old lady back to the top of the room, pulled her ID out, held it aloft. Sexton pulled out his mobile, kept it at waist level and started dialling for back-up.

'Proud of yourself?' Jo called as a round of boos struck up. 'Look at her.' The volume of the noise decreased, but not much.

Skinny was throwing furious looks at everyone in a bomber jacket around the room, making hand gestures that all involved removing Jo. Sexton had the phone to his ear.

'What age are you?' she asked the woman.

'You have no business here, copper,' Skinny shouted. 'If your lot could handle the drugs problem, we wouldn't have to deal with it ourselves. Even the prisons are riddled with heroin.'

Applause. Cat calls. 'Out-out-out.'

The bomber jackets started moving towards Sexton, who put his phone away, and gave Jo a nod that said help was on the way.

'I'll only leave if one of you can tell me why you're taking orders from the likes of him' – Jo glanced at Skinny – 'a pervert who has sex with dead women!'

Now she had their attention.

'What the fuck are you talking about, copper?' Skinny asked, his face contorted.

'Did you or did you not confess to the murder of Anto Crawley in Store Street yesterday?' Jo asked him, holding his statement up for all to see.

Skinny shrugged.

'Well, the man we want also likes to have his way with dead women. That you?'

'What's she talking about, Skinny?' a man's voice called from the crowd.

'Don't try and deny it. We record everything that takes place in interview rooms these days, or have you forgotten that?' Jo told the crowd.

Skinny held his hands up. 'I was having a laugh,' he said. 'It was all bullshit, I'd nothing to do with Crawley's murder.'

'I believe you, but others may not,' Jo said. 'And if anything happens to this woman, we'll turn over every flat belonging to anyone in here.'

Without warning, the old lady spat at Jo's shoes.

The crowd applauded.

Jo sighed then walked calmly towards the exit.

'You as bent as the rest of them in Store Street?' Skinny called after her.

30

Jo's car, which now had the word 'pig' scratched on both sides, was refusing to start. After the fifth attempt, Sexton manhandled her into his. Jo protested, until she spotted the crowd emerging from the hall and heading towards her car, shouting angry taunts. Jagged scotoma criss-crossed through her peripheral vision. A migraine was imminent, and it was going to be a big one. *Jesus*, she thought. *Not now. Not when I know the killer's going to take another life tomorrow.*

As he drove, Sexton phoned Dan from the hands-free, explained what was happening and told him to collect the kids and to send a tow truck to pick up her car. Jo could hear the irritation in Dan's clipped answers. She didn't know if he was more annoyed because he was put out or because Sexton was in the driving seat. When it came to Dan, she didn't know anything any more . . .

She pinched the bridge of her nose and held on to the door handle, opening her eyes to identify the smell making her stomach heave. A Magic Tree dangled from the rear-view mirror. Jo pulled it free, pressed the window button and chucked it out. Sexton raised his eyebrows but said nothing.

'You need to get yourself a life,' she told him, staring at a box of tissues perched between the cream-leather seats, pulling one free and spreading it flat on the back of her neck.

'How'd you afford this car anyway?'

He didn't answer.

Jo was sorry she'd put him on the spot. How he spent his money was his business. At least she had the kids, even if it was over with Dan.

'Tell me how well you know Ryan Freeman,' she asked, changing the subject.

'What do you mean?'

'He called the incident room the other day asking for you. Today he shows up at a place where nobody knows you'll be.'

Sexton pulled up at lights and turned to face her. 'He helped me out last year. I was going through a bad patch, and was driving under the influence. I crashed the car.' He brought his hands together, creating angles over the wheel. 'Don't look at me like that. Nobody was hurt, except me.'

'How did you get around a conviction?'

'There was a problem with the warrant.'

Jo groaned.

'I told you, nobody was hurt. The insurance covered everything, but that wasn't enough for the guy who owned the car. I mean, fair enough if he'd been in it, but he wanted my job. He tried to get Ryan Freeman to run an exposé about how I got around the charges. Ryan looked after me, so I guess you could say I owe him.'

'Where was I when this was going on?'

'You were away on maternity leave.' There was another long pause. 'Is it really over between you and Dan?' Sexton asked, after another long pause.

Jo kept her eyes shut. The muzziness in her head was growing.

'I presume it's serious with Jeanie,' Sexton went on. 'I

remember seeing the way they were together, a couple of years back. I think it was the inspectors and sergeants annual conference, down in Westport. I thought it then too.'

Jo wanted to concentrate on anything other than the sick feeling in the pit of her stomach. But even more than that, she just wanted to shut Sexton's words out.

On the N11, Sexton jerked suddenly as the lay-by in which they were driving came to an abrupt halt. He was going to have to merge with the rest of the traffic, but at the top of the queue a driver in an 'I love NY' cap with a row of flashing lights along his front bumper was looking in the opposite direction and refused to let them merge.

With a screech of brakes, Sexton jumped out of his car and held his palm up, forcing the driver to stop and stick his hazards on. After showing him his ID, Sexton checked his tax and insurance and told him to turn off the engine, as he took down his details.

Jo watched in disbelief. For the next ten minutes, other drivers beeped and got out of their cars to see what the hold-up was. They didn't care if Sexton was a plain-clothed garda, they wanted to get home. Finally, Sexton got back in the car and pulled out ahead of the 'I love NY' driver.

'I want the names of each and every cop who ever inter-viewed any of our victims on my desk first thing tomorrow morning,' Jo told him as they neared the Lamb's Cross junction. The sliproad to her house was just beyond it. 'Bar the priest, all the victims were criminals to a greater or lesser degree, so there should be quite a few entries on the system.'

'What's your thinking?' Sexton asked.

'You heard what Skinny said at the drugs meeting: "Are you as bent as the rest of them in Store Street?" What was he getting at? We know our killer is avenging a crime, and he's doing it on our patch. Doesn't that indicate to you that somebody in the station might know what that crime is?'

'You'd take Skinny's word?' Sexton said, sounding disbelieving. 'He's a lying toe-rag.'

A newspaper vendor rapped the window as they waited to turn right at Slate Cabin Lane. Sexton waved him off but Jo signalled she'd take a paper, reaching across to Sexton's window with the change.

The newsprint stank, making her stomach lurch again, but she pulled it in and placed it on her lap. It hurt to read, but as she made out the headline she realized the good news was they'd just found Rita's mother. The paper had an exclusive interview under the banner headline 'My Girl Was No Hooker'. Old Mrs Nulty had probably been holed up in some hotel by the newspaper so no other editor could get her before the story went to print. That meant she was no longer AWOL.

The bad news was that the small print was dancing nauseatingly in front of her eyes. Jo's migraine was about to take hold.

31

Katie was sharing a room in Crumlin Children's Hospital with a toddler suffering from a syndrome that reduced her to a permanent vegetative state. The kid's growth was stunted and a peg in her stomach made her vomit whenever the nurses hooked a feed up to it. She was being sick in her cot right now, making a dragging noise which Ryan knew he'd never forget. Strings from helium birthday balloons dangled over the kid's cot, telling him she'd recently turned two, even though, at a guess, he'd have put her at six months. He wondered who'd brought the balloons – the nurses, or her family? And where was her family now? He rang the bell for a nurse to come, thinking maybe it was possible there were people out there who were in a worse plight than him after all ...

His own sense of indignation came as a bolt from the blue, and he realized instantly why. Him looking down his nose at anyone else's parenting skills was a bit rich. If it hadn't been for him, and the criminal activity he'd been exposing in the underworld, Katie should have been getting ready for school this morning, turning the house upside down for her copy book, demanding the crusts be cut off her sandwiches and begging to be let sleep over with her best friend. 'Please, please, please' she'd have been saying and, of course, he'd have acquiesced. Instead, the choices he'd made in his own life had changed the course of her life for ever.

A nurse came into the room and pulled the birthday girl out of the pool of vomit. She was an Irish nurse, a sign of the changed times. Before the recession, the nurses were all Indian or Filipino. At least they were all kind in Paediatric, Ryan thought, not like their angsty counterparts working with geriatrics.

'Can I help?' he asked the nurse.

She shook her head and rang the bell. Another nurse came and whipped the sheets off the bed and began packing them into sterile plastic sacks. Freeman heard them soothe the toddler by her name – 'Talullah'. He shook his head. What kind of parent would pick a hippy-dippy Hollywood starlet name for a kid with no life expectancy?

He moved to the side of Katie's bed and sat on the chair alongside, watched her sleeping. He felt the lump in his throat rise as he touched her hair. She'd been an IVF baby, conceived after the point when he and Angie had both presumed they'd left parenthood too late. Knowing the lengths they'd gone to to have her and the cotton-wool existence they'd planned to give her added an extra dimension to his guilt.

She'd been admitted yesterday after the convulsion and was waiting for an ECG to establish if there was any permanent damage in her brain that may have caused the equivalent to what one of the docs had described as 'a short circuit in her wiring'.

Ryan glanced at the clock on the wall. It was nearly 7 p.m. Angie was due in any second. On cue she appeared in the doorway, looking thin and over-groomed. She strained her head away as the smell of vomit hit her.

'I'm sorry, but this is not acceptable,' she told the Irish nurse. 'I don't want to seem heartless, but it cannot be healthy having Katie in this environment, not with all the bugs going around in hospitals.'

'I've already passed your concerns on to the matron,' the nurse said, tucking new sheets into the cot. 'As soon as another bed becomes available, we'll try and move you.'

Angie came over to Ryan, taking her coat off as she did so.

'I'd have got back sooner, only for that bloody Mad Cow roundabout,' she said. 'How are you supposed to get through it when it's not a roundabout? And anyway, there isn't even a pub on it any more. I nearly ended up on the Navan road. How is she?'

'No change,' he said.

Talullah started to moan and cough as the nurse changed her clothes. Angie was about to kick off again when a rap on the door distracted her. It was Gavin Sexton.

Both Ryan and Angie stared in surprise.

'I'm sorry, visiting hours are not until –' the Irish nurse began.

'It's okay, we know him,' Angie said.

'It's not okay, there are children trying to sleep,' the nurse insisted.

'Why don't you and I head down to the canteen and grab a coffee,' Ryan said to Sexton.

'Actually, I need to talk to both of you,' Sexton said.

'But one of us has to stay here,' Ryan pointed out.

'It's important.'

Ryan looked to Angie, expecting her to protest, but she put up no resistance. After giving the nurse his mobile number and making her promise she'd ring if Katie woke, he followed Sexton and Angie down the corridor.

By the time they had emerged from the elevator a minute later, Ryan knew two things with certainty. If Sexton couldn't tell them whatever it was en route, it was going to be something very bad. You don't need to get people sitting down if you're delivering good news. He was also convinced that Angie already knew what it was.

'I want to talk about the day Katie was abducted,' Sexton said when they were finally settled over coffee. 'I've got a pal in the computer section who did me a favour and analysed the last digit of the registration and the make of the car caught in the CCTV footage parked at the school gate the day Katie was taken. I know who the car belonged to, and the name of the woman who was seen arguing with Crawley.'

Beside him, Angie started to cry softly.

'Who was it?' Ryan asked, a cold trickle of fear running down his spine.

Angie turned to him slowly. 'It was me.'

32

Jo lay on the bed with the curtains drawn and her eyes shut. Her breath was short and scared. The pain was as bad as she ever remembered it having been and, in the months after the crash, it had been bad. Four bodies in under a week, she thought, feeling shivery. Quick work.

She rolled her head sideways slowly, opening her eyes to try and make out the time on the alarm clock on the bedside locker. The red light of the digital display stung too much for her to focus. Seven something – she was sure the first digit was a seven. She closed her eyes again quickly. Since her visit to the warehouse, she understood that inflicting pain meant every bit as much as creating a spectacle to this killer. She had to find him before he made anyone else suffer. Once the migraine had passed, she could get back to work. She prayed it would soon. Otherwise, tomorrow there'd be a fifth . . .

She could hear Dan and Rory's muffled voices in the kitchen under her room. She wanted to call them, to let Dan know the freezer was fully stocked and that he could have his pick for the boys' dinner. But nothing came out. The tablets were finally starting to take effect: she was starting to drift off . . .

She was in her father's car, in the back seat with Sue. Their dad was laughing at them for flapping their arms like wings, willing the car up a steep hill. They used to do it at the same spot every day on the way to school. He'd laugh every time. She watched him straining around for a glimpse of them, his green eyes twinkling, the same way they did whenever he turned the garden hose on them instead of sprinkling the flowers. Over his shoulder, Jo could see the lorry coming straight for the car. Sue vanished. Jo opened her mouth to warn her father, but the words just froze in her throat. She tried to point, but her arm wouldn't move. Her father turned back around, too late.

Sitting bolt upright in the bed just before the moment of impact in the dream, her skin drenched, her heart racing, Jo gulped deep breaths of air. Her head was pounding, but there was a faint realization breaking through. Tomorrow would be the killer's most symbolic killing so far. He was going to inflict the ultimate act of vengeance. He was moving on from Exodus. He would need to show just how much he hated Jesus Christ. That meant he was going to crucify his next victim.

Thursday

33

When Jo woke, Dan was standing over her with a mug of steaming tea and a plate of toast.

'What time is it?' she asked, getting that same split-second feeling she did every morning when she wondered why his bits and pieces – watch and wallet, the contents of his pocket, his latest book on some infamous military incursion and the alarm clock from hell – weren't on his bedside locker. She rubbed her eyes. She could have done with that wake-the-dead clock now.

'How you feeling?' he asked, placing breakfast on the locker.

Jo glanced down and realized she was wearing one of Dan's old T-shirts. She pushed to the back of her mind the vague memory of holding her arms up last night so he could slip it on. The T-shirt was miles too big for her. He'd gotten it at an old Undertones concert and worn it like a badge of honour for years afterwards, even though it was faded and stretched. It was so old she remembered him wearing it when Rory was sitting against the front of it in a papoose.

'What's the time?' she asked again, feeling her wrist for her watch and wondering where she'd left it. Last night was a complete blur. 'And where are the boys?'

'Relax. I dropped them both off so you could lie in,' Dan

said, drawing the curtains. 'It's almost ten. Don't bother rushing. You might as well be hung for a sheep as a lamb. What's your boss like anyway?'

Ordinarily, Jo would have made a joke of this with something like, 'He's an absolute bollox,' but she couldn't believe the time. Anyway, the way Dan had been acting lately, it would have had a ring of truth. No, she thought. Better to stay on her guard until things were back on an even keel between them. And the one thing she mustn't do was mention that bloody Westport conference Sexton had told her about. Once she brought that up, it was going to trigger World War III. That was the year she had pulled out because of a dose of bloody flu. Dan couldn't have been more understanding. Now, maybe, she understood why. He had been looking forward to meeting Jeanie.

There wasn't time to worry about it now. She was running so bloody late, it was a nightmare. She got out of bed and gave her head a little shake. She felt quivery, like her system had been through the ringer, but at least the terrible headache had gone. For years after the crash, she'd lost whole days because of migraines just like last night's. She'd thought they were a thing of the past and had forgotten how debilitating they could be.

Dan was looking at her bare legs as she headed for the wardrobe. She sighed. He wanted it every way – to treat her like a skivvy in work and to give her the 'come to bed' eyes now they were home alone. Well, she wasn't able for the emotional rollercoaster; it wasn't fair.

'Woah,' Dan said, placing his hands on her shoulders. 'Nice and easy does it. How's the head?'

'It's passed. Look, I've got to go, I've got Anto Crawley's autopsy this morning.'

'I rang Hawthorne. He's moving a drowning up ahead of it.' Jo sighed with relief.

Dan paused, still looking worried. 'When was the last time you saw that neuro consultant?'

Jo shrugged. 'It's most likely all the chocolate I've been eating since I've given up fags.' She slipped her clothes from the hangers. On Monday, Dan had made her fail her training course. On Tuesday Dan'd told her he'd taken legal advice about protecting his financial stake in the house; on Wednesday he'd humiliated her at a disciplinary hearing that was completely unnecessary, then stood by and let Jenny Friar of NBCI sink her teeth into her with a look of pity in his eyes. Pity! She'd show him.

She knelt down and pulled a pair of black heels from under the bed.

Dan seemed to sense it was time to change the subject. 'Is today still bin day?' he asked.

'Shit!' Jo sprang up and moved the net curtain to see if the neighbours' had been collected yet.

'Sorted,' Dan said, moving behind her and pointing to their bin out with the others. He put his hands on her shoulders and turned her round so they were facing each other.

'What am I doing wrong here?' he asked. He'd slipped a tie under his collar and was criss-crossing one uneven length over another.

'Here,' she sighed, stretching up on her tiptoes and fixing the knot.

Dan watched her softly. 'How did you get on with that suspect yesterday?'

'It's a long story. He's a drug pusher, and a Shinner, and he retracted his confession in a room full of witnesses.'

Dan put his hand on her cheek. 'I know you think I've

been too hard on you. It's just I have to do everything by the book. They watch my every move when it comes to you.'

'I understand,' she said, straightening his tie and smoothing the shirt across his shoulders, 'that you're due up for promotion.'

Dan took a step back and folded his arms. 'That's got nothing to do with it, and you know it. For the record, I know, if anybody can find the killer, it's you.'

Jo took a deep breath. 'Then let me, Dan. Stop getting in the way!'

'I'd forgotten how dogged you get when you want something,' he said, turning away.

'What's that supposed to mean?'

'It means if you put half as much effort into your personal life, maybe we'd still have a marriage.'

'I've got to go,' Jo said, bundling up her clothes and pushing past him on her way to the bathroom. 'But if I had time to argue, I'd remind you that you're the one who had an affair and that you're the one living with someone else!'

She slammed the door behind her, then pulled it open again. 'This is why you've been digging your heels in, isn't it? You can't bear to see me managing without you. The job's the only hold you've got left over me, so you've been making sure I don't forget it. Well, it's bloody well worked.'

She slammed the door again.

Jo flicked the shower setting to its most powerful jet setting before stepping under the steaming water. It was so loud she didn't hear the door open. When the water caught the side of her eye she turned suddenly, only to see Dan standing there. She made a grab for the shower curtain, using it like a towel to shield her nakedness. 'What are you . . .?'

'I miss my wife,' he said unapologetically.

Jo wrapped a real towel round herself, rubbing the heavy wet out of her hair. She walked back into the bedroom barefoot.

Dan followed and sat on the edge of the bed watching.

'One question,' Jo asked calmly.

He lowered his head.

'That time you walked out on me during the Phoenix Park child murder investigation . . .?'

He frowned. 'Not that again.'

'Where did you stay, Dan?'

'It's years ago, I can't rem–'

'Fine, forget it,' she said, and turned on the hairdryer.

By the time she was dressed and ready to leave, Jo knew by the way all the bedroom doors were closed that Dan was gone. She was hurrying down the stairs when she spotted the *News* on the hall table. After setting the house alarm, she pulled the front door behind her, sat in the car and read the story by Ryan Freeman under the subhead 'Gardaí Hunt Crazed Cleric Killer'.

Jo's heart sank. Not only had old Mrs Nulty criticized the way Jo had landed on her doorstep while she was still coming to terms with the terrible news, but she'd also put the details of the 'priest's twin' into the public arena. For the life of her, Jo still couldn't see how this story beat the one that Freeman was sitting on involving a serial killer on the rampage. And since there was not so much as one mention of the word '*muti*' or 'foreigner' in the story, she realized without a shadow of a doubt that someone on her team was briefing him. And she no longer had any doubts as to who it was.

34

The killer moved through the chosen one's split-level, open-plan home. His bare feet clacked as they moved, soles sticking to the lacquered wooden floor. He stopped only once in his task, to take a closer look at the tropical fish in their shimmering aquarium. Slowly, he tipped the glass box out on the floor, moving to the side of the downpour. The fish wriggled and leapt on the hardwood. He squelched around until he spotted the one he was after, and then he trod on it, wiping his damp hand dry along the back of a low white couch.

A row of remote controls sat on a nest of wooden coffee tables. He picked one, aimed it indiscriminately, and the framed picture on the centre wall flickered to life as a moving picture of fire flames.

Next, he switched the flat-screen TV on, and then the stereo system. He pitched both volumes at the exact same level to create a hum of confusion.

He headed to the kitchen, all gleaming black-PVC-fronted presses and stainless-steel knives and gadgets. Removing a white tablecloth from the bag, he shook and spread it over the round glass table, pressing out the creases with the flat of his hands, nudging the more stubborn ones out with a finger.

He set two places for three courses – removing the knives, forks, spoons and wine glasses from his carpet bag. A human skull got pride of place as centrepiece, around which he arranged ten candles spaced perfectly evenly apart.

With a stick of chalk, he wrote the word 'Golgotha' on any surface that would take it – the black presses, the dark floor.

He climbed the stairs, shaking silver coins out of a purse made of sackcloth as he headed for the sleeping area.

Finally, removing a rope from his waist, he slung it over one of the exposed beams directly overhead. Once the noose was at a height that meant it could be seen from the front door, he made the sign of the cross backwards – tipping his right shoulder first, then left, torso, head. It takes seven seconds to die, suspended by the neck, and in that time the chosen one would experience what it meant to be divine.

The killer knelt down and began to chant.

35

Jo's car decided to start with no problems next morning, having been delivered on a tow truck to her house the night before. On the way to the station, she used the red-light stops to tidy it, which involved jamming most of the rubbish on the floor under the passenger seat. The driver in front of her had managed to apply her make-up in the same way, and was currently giving her hair a good brush. The man behind was excavating his nose.

As the lights changed, she shifted gear and threw the phone on her lap, loudspeaker on, to make the calls she was conducting during the green-light sections of the journey. She had already phoned the city's newsrooms one by one, informing the duty editors that she intended holding a crime conference outside the station at 2 p.m. sharp.

'Gerry?' she asked as the latest call connected.

'Gerry's sick,' a stranger's voice said.

'Wendy around?'

'She's in a meeting.'

'You new?' Jo asked.

'First day.'

'First day!' Jo said. 'What's your name?'

'Jim. Who's this?'

'Jim, you ever heard of Daithi Bhreathnach?'

'Nope. Who's speaking, please?'

'First day, first lesson in crime and punishment, Jim: the biggest problem with our criminal justice system is that society thinks it's the injured party. You know the way it is with big corporations – the little guy gets lost.'

'I'm sorry, what's this about?'

'It's about a criminal called Daithi Bhreathnach, who shows that the burden of proof has swung too far in favour of the accused.'

'Who?'

'David Walsh, aka Daithi Bhreathnach. That's one of his tricks. He avails himself of all his rights, insists on having everything translated into the Irish language as a delaying tactic. He's so good at thwarting the system he's now running a paralegal school for criminals – teaching them to switch lawyers as often as possible, take judicial reviews – anything and everything that might stall their case, because if it's stalled long enough it gets thrown out.'

Jo heard the receiver change hands, then Gerry came on the line. 'Birmingham, I thought you had better things to do – like bullying old ladies?'

'SLR, Gerry. Tell the minister to read the report by this afternoon. Victims need rights in court too.'

Inside the station's incident room, Sexton's interview with Skinny was replaying on a TV perched on a rack of steel shelves containing a blinking DVD and video player. Sexton was slouched in a chair, telling someone on the other end of the public hotline to call the press office. Mac, Merrigan, and Frank Black and Dave Waters from the NBCI were studying the TV, and a dozen odd detectives were trawling through the paperwork, collating anything that might be of interest.

Sexton gave Jo a 'what's the story?' shrug, ripped the top sheet of paper off his pad and scrunched and fired it in a rainbow shot at the bin. It missed and joined a half dozen others scattered on the floor. He covered the receiver with his hand. 'Thought you'd like the pleasure,' he told Jo, throwing his head in Jenny Friar's direction.

Friar was leaning over Jo's desk, marking up a copy of yesterday's *Evening News* with a pink highlighter. She was wearing a beige-linen trouser suit which made her look chunky but fit. She stood up when she realized Jo had arrived and reached for her pint of Starbucks, a 'good of you to join us' expression on her face.

Foxy sat dead centre in front of the box, wading through a wad of door-to-door questionnaires for anything of significance; Merrigan sat beside him with a pile of as yet untouched paperwork, making a meal of an orange, sucking segments that dripped on to his tie.

On the screen, Skinny was once again insisting to Sexton that he'd killed Anto Crawley. His arms hung down by the sides of the plastic chair behind his back, his legs were wide open and he kept pulling at the tip of his long nose with his index finger and thumb.

Jo strode over and switched the TV off.

'Hey!' Friar protested.

'It's bullshit, it's all bullshit. He admitted as much when Sexton and I confronted him yesterday,' Jo said. 'Come on, lads, we've got work to do.'

'And you believed him?' Friar asked.

Foxy and Sexton jumped up. Merrigan seemed reluctant to follow.

'It's irrelevant what I believe. But one way or another, he's a liar, and now that he's retracted his confession, we'll never get a conviction. You want to do something constructive to contribute to this investigation? Get me Anto Crawley's NSU file.'

Friar glanced at her NBCI colleagues then back at Jo.

Jo understood Friar's reluctance. The gathering of intelligence by the National Surveillance Unit through covert surveillance was routine when it came to persons suspected of serious crime. Crawley's form would contain the kind of highly relevant information that would never see the light of day in court. It would list his daily movements, associates, places he frequented, weaknesses such as gambling or a mistress, any or all of which could potentially throw up a new lead.

'You're joking, right?' Friar asked.

'We're dealing with four murders,' Jo said. 'I don't have to remind you of this, do I?'

'I'm not ready to write this suspect off yet,' Waters, the criminal profiler, said.

'Perhaps you'll view things differently when the killer strikes again today,' Jo said. 'Because Skinny here is going to have a watertight alibi, since Merrigan is going to bring him in and hold him for the day.'

Foxy nudged Jo's foot with his own, telling her not to walk herself into a corner.

Friar made a loud rustling noise with the newspaper. 'You're staking an awful lot of your credibility on a hunch, Sergeant,' she said, not unhappily.

'I'm a DI.'

Friar held up the paper and shook it at Jo. 'Your priest theory is going to limit our potential sources of information. People who may have reason to suspect someone else may now be writing it off because their suspect isn't a priest.'

'Look, I never said our man was a priest,' Jo said. 'On the contrary, he's probably an atheist, and I suspect someone very like us. He probably works in some area of law enforcement, or the military. He's not a bloody Muslim, he may well have come to our attention previously and the locations of his killings are the key to cracking these crimes.'

'Here we go round the mulberry bush again,' Friar remarked.

Foxy stepped up to her defence. 'You forgot to mention that the killer's got a grievance with the church,' he said.

Jo shot him a look of gratitude. 'Yes.'

'And he gets off with dead chicks,' Sexton said.

Merrigan wiped the corners of his mouth. 'And he's a darkie!'

Friar exhaled loudly.

'Thanks for the show of support, lads,' Jo said, leading the trio into the corridor outside.

'Merrigan,' she said, turning to face him, 'I need you to get our colleague's prime suspect in here. Tell Skinny that if he cooperates we won't have him charged with wasting police time over making a false statement. Either way, he spends the day here – okay? Having him under lock and key when the killer strikes again may be the only way I can convince them that they're barking up the wrong tree.'

Merrigan nodded, puffing out his chest as he took off.

Sexton reached into his inside pocket and pulled out some sheets of paper folded in half, which he handed Jo.

'What's this?' she asked.

'The names you wanted of officers who'd had any dealings with our victims,' Sexton said quietly. He turned the top page over for her and pointed to a name at the bottom of the list.

Jo stopped suddenly. 'Is he still down in the incident room?'

'Mac still in there?' Sexton called out to some officers clustered further down the corridor.

'I passed him on his way into the john,' one answered.

'Have him in the interview room by lunchtime,' Jo said. 'And tell him I want to talk to him about Rita Nulty.'

36

Jo drove to the morgue with Foxy, telling Sexton to make his own way there. She was almost afraid to say it out loud, even to Foxy, but discovering that Mac had had previous dealings with Rita Nulty was sounding major alarm bells. He ticked all the right boxes for the killer: knew the law – check; may have been the bent copper Skinny was alluding to – check; and then there was the minor matter that, when attached to the investigation, he had neglected to mention he knew Rita Nulty.

As soon as Foxy clicked his seatbelt on, Jo found it hard to get a word in edgeways. It was only supposition, he explained, but he'd been in Mac's home once.

'His place was to die for, something you and I could only ever dream of, Jo,' he said. 'I'm the first to admit there could be any reasonable explanation – inheritance, gee-gees – what do I know about how he balances his accounts? All I do know is that while the rest of us are trying to make ends meet, he's shacked up there in an IFSC penthouse apartment living like a lord. I'm talking paintings on the walls with red dots in the bottom corner because they've been bid for at auction.'

Jo gripped the steering wheel. She knew it wasn't Foxy's form to gossip, but Mac's IFSC address was too close to the murder scenes for comfort.

'There was this other time,' he continued, 'when I got caught up in the celebrations for one of the lad's promotions . . .' He waved his hand up and down to tell her to slow down.

Jo sighed. In her opinion, Foxy was a worse passenger driver than she was, and that was saying something.

'You know the way it happens, you say no to another pint and someone puts one in front of you anyway. The lads were going to Lillie's Bordello, and I thought, why not? Sal was away on a school trip, so there was no reason for me to go home at all if it came to it.'

Jo smiled. It was like trying to imagine her own father in a trendy nightclub hoping to score.

'I wasn't going there for "action",' Foxy clarified. 'Who'd be interested in an old man like me? I was going to see what it was like. I always got the feeling about that place that, if I'd tried to get in, I'd have been turned away.'

'Go on,' she said.

'So I went with the gang, and Mac gets us all in, slapping the bouncers on the back on the way in. And inside, you should have seen it, the women were pouring themselves over him. Not just any women, Jo. I'm talking about the ones you see in the papers and those VIP magazines, the ones who are all a shade of orange, and they totter into the ladies – arm in arm, if you get my drift.'

'So let's look into his background quietly,' Jo said. 'See where all that money came from, and if we can find anything that might fire a religious obsession, yeah?'

Foxy nodded his agreement.

Sexton had arrived at the morgue ahead of them and was moaning about the distance he'd had to walk across the car park to the road outside for a fag now that smoking was banned from the grounds of all public buildings. Given that the morgue was located at the back of the fire-brigade training grounds, where buildings, cars and containers were regularly set alight, he couldn't even chance a sneaky one.

Jo had no sympathy. She'd have walked ten miles for one, if it was an option. She barely grunted in reply, still angry that he had lied to her about briefing Ryan Freeman.

'What do you make of Mac not telling us he knew Rita Nulty?' he asked. 'You think he's involved?'

'You stay outside here, keep an eye out,' she said to him brusquely. Precautions were sometimes necessary during high-profile autopsies, she reminded him, and Anto Crawley's was certainly that. The grave of the paedophile priest Brendan Smyth, who'd been a prolific child abuser, had had to be filled with concrete. Up until his death, Crawley had been considered public enemy number one.

'You're having a laugh, right?' Sexton said, and then realized what was wrong. 'Are you suggesting I organized that interview with old Mrs Nulty so I could take over from you?' To his credit, he looked shocked.

'Your pal Ryan Freeman's byline was on it,' Jo said. 'Now, unless you want to end up as a glorified security man on this case, I'll deal with Freeman from now on.'

She turned and headed into the Portakabin with Foxy, Sexton dragging his heels behind them. Anto Crawley was lying on the slab, being stitched back together by Hawthorne.

'Couldn't you have waited?' she complained.

'I'm on my own today,' Hawthorne snapped, pointing over to a second unattended cadaver lying on a slab on the far side of the room. 'The other pathologist has had to go to a murder suicide of a family of five in Donegal, and my technician's out sick.'

Jo studied Crawley. It seemed hard to believe the waxy, sunken and musty shell of a man could have wreaked so much havoc on an entire country. His jaw hung slack against his neck, his open mouth was a pit of congealed blood, his wiry dark brown hair was receding, his arms were heavily tattooed and his left shoulder had a list of first names under the letters 'RIP'.

Foxy crooked his neck sideways to try and read them, keeping his hand over his nose and mouth like the dead crime lord 'The General' Martin Cahill used to when he saw a camera. Jo scanned Crawley's flesh for any signs of defensive wounds, while Sexton nudged Foxy's shoulder with his own to tell him to check out the size of Crawley's member.

'Show me the manner in which a nation cares for its dead,' Foxy told him, 'and I will measure with mathematical exactness the tender mercies of its peoples, their respect for the laws of the land, and their loyalty to high ideals and their regard for the laws of the land.' He was quoting William Gladstone. The same words were inscribed over the door of the city's Coroner's Court next to the station.

Hawthorne threw his eyes up to heaven. Considering they were in a glorified mobile home, even Jo thought Foxy's words were over the top.

'See here.' Hawthorne indicated some white specks on Crawley's nostrils. 'The blood patterns tell us that the teeth were removed while he was still alive, and these flecks of froth confirm it. You get splashes if a victim has been struck; smears tend to indicate flailing or thrashing limbs; trails lend themselves to a victim who's been dragged; and, as in this case, spurts indicate the heart was still pumping after the fatal injury.'

'Meaning?' Jo pressed.

'Meaning,' Hawthorne repeated impatiently, 'that the deceased panicked, presumably because someone was wrenching his teeth out, causing his heart to beat faster, making his lungs work harder, resulting in an ingestion of the blood caused by the oral injury. Death was technically due to drowning. The foam you see on his nose is produced by mucus and air. We'll see it again when we cross-section the bronchea and trachea. There was relatively little blood at the scene. I suspect we'll find most of it in the lungs, and they'll be distended when we get them out. They can hold two cubic litres of liquid, you know.'

Jo pointed to the hallmark wound right of Crawley's breastbone, the same one they'd seen on Rita's, which had led to their theory of the Doubting Thomas link. 'Do you know anything about the significance of this wound for the faithful?'

Hawthorne coughed irritably.

'It hastened Christ's death,' Foxy answered. 'I read it last night in one of Sal's books.' He copped her frown. 'After I'd had forty winks of course. Christ died after three to six hours on the cross, which took even Pontius Pilate by surprise.'

'Same analgesic . . .' Hawthorne cut in.

'Any sexual interference?' Jo asked him.

Hawthorne shook his head.

'What about a weapon?' Jo asked him.

'I reckon it must have been a sword, you know, like the ones used by the Roman centurions. The tip could have caused this.' Hawthorne pointed to the breastbone. 'Also, I've been comparing the injuries during the rending of Rita

Nulty's bones and muscle – all very clean, there's no ripping motion at all, suggesting your man probably removed the body parts in one sweep.'

Jo thought back to the notes she'd made in the apartment when she'd revisited the Rita Nulty crime scene, how she'd thought Rita's assailant had been wearing a long coat. If the killer was carrying a sword, he'd have to have been able to conceal it. 'I'll bet you any money our killer was wearing a robe,' she said.

37

Back in the station, Jo lifted the blind to get a better view of the scrum of reporters outside the station. A TV3 van was parked on a double yellow in the lane left of the station, but the girl who'd jumped out in a pair of CAT boots and a puffa jacket was more concerned with setting up a camera tripod than the garda beside tucking a ticket under her windscreen wiper. An RTÉ van pulled up alongside. Jo watched as a guy jumped from the sliding door while the van was still moving and headed for the garda with the ticket book.

Rubbing the sticky dust from the blind off her finger with her thumb, Jo turned around to face Mac. He was sitting with his legs spread apart and his size-twelve Dr Martens' soles flat on the ground. Sexton sat in the chair beside the door at Jo's request, because she hoped a friendly face might help put Mac off guard. The good-cop-bad-cop routine had become clichéd for a reason: it worked.

She took a seat opposite Mac and opened a folder containing a slim stack of sheets.

'Smoke?' Mac reached under his fleece into the pocket of his uniform shirt.

Jo leaned across, took the box from him and dropped them in the waste-paper basket at the side of the table. She was not having him set the pace. 'This is a no-smoking room,' she said, lifting the foil ashtray that had started life as a Mr Kipling apple tart off the table and disposing of it too.

Mac caught Sexton's eye. 'Nazi,' he joked. 'Reformed smokers are always the worst.' He gave a short, derisive laugh.

'Why didn't you tell us you'd arrested Rita Nulty and let her off with a caution?' Jo asked.

Mac looked surprised. 'It was irrelevant,' he said, pulling his fleece up over his head. His shirt lifted and showed his midriff – taut stomach muscles that required a lot of work to achieve, Jo realized.

He shook his shirt back down. The dark string of a religious scapular jutted up from under his collar. The sight of it made goose pimples break out on Jo's skin.

'You knew the murder victim of a case you were assigned to personally, but you don't think that's relevant?' she asked.

No reply.

'So what was she like?'

'Can't remember.'

'Let me help you. New Year's Eve last. 2 a.m. You were returning from your shift when you spotted her soliciting outside the IFSC . . . Come on, you must remember! It's a bum shift for a party animal like you. It's just across the road. You live there, don't you?'

Mac shook his head. 'Is this a formal interview? Only I haven't been cautioned. If it is, I'd like to have my solicitor now, please.'

Jo referred to her papers. 'You were driving back to the station with Detective Inspector Healy, now in CAB. He filed the details of the incident on PULSE before signing off.'

'That right?'

'I've just spoken to Healy on the phone, and he remembers it clear as a bell. He says after telling him you knew Rita, you left the squad car and went over to her for a little chat.'

'I want my brief. Is this being taped?'

'Think of it as an off-the-record chat. Did you know her?'

'No.'

Jo sighed. 'Look, Mac, if you want to do this the hard way – fine by me. I'll get Healy's deposition and it'll be your word against his. Think about how it will look. He says you knew Rita. You say you didn't. So why did you let her off with a warning on New Year's when your only hope of promotion is with a half-decent conviction rate? What's your basic at the moment, €25,000? Not much, is it? Though from what I hear, that hasn't stopped you living the high life. How do you manage it then?'

Mac shifted uncomfortably in his chair.

'So let's try that last one again, shall we?' Jo said. 'Did you know Rita Nulty?'

'Yeah, to see. You couldn't not know Rita. She got around. I wouldn't be doing my job if I hadn't come across her, would I?'

'But you kept it quiet after she was murdered . . . Did you know she was being pimped by the Skids for drugs?'

Mac was silent.

'What if I said she kept the names of all of her clients written down, would that ring a bell?'

'You're having a laugh. Rita couldn't even remember to brush her teeth in the morning . . .'

'Just knew her to see, eh?' Jo asked, holding his eye. She took a little black contacts book that had been sitting on her lap from under the table and flicked through the pages.

'Makes for interesting reading . . . When did you say you last saw her?'

'I want my solicitor.'

Jo reached for the sheets in the file on the desk. 'I'd like to talk about the boy who died in the cell on your watch now,' she said.

'What? That's years ago. What's he got to do with Rita Nulty?'

'You tell me. Do you even remember his name?'

'What the hell is this?' Mac stood up and lunged at her. 'What did I ever do to you, eh?'

Sexton moved to intercept him, but Jo held her arm out to tell him to sit down. 'You too,' she told Mac.

He slouched back into his seat. Sexton sat down slowly.

'It was a long time ago,' Mac said. 'It may come as some news for you to learn, Sarge, but I was cleared of any wrongdoing.' He turned to Sexton. 'Now, my solicitor's name is Jasper Flood.'

'It says here that the family of the kid who died on your watch was taking a civil action against you,' Jo went on. 'That must have come as a shock. Especially when you thought it was all over and done with. A kid died in a cell, the way they do . . .'

'It was all hot air. They'd never have gone through with it.'

'You sure?' Jo asked. 'Only I rang the kid's father earlier. He says you called to his house after the writs were served and warned him you'd make his life "hell on earth". He said you told him you'd "friends in low places", and I quote. What does that mean? Who've you been hanging around with, Mac?'

Mac looked at the floor.

'I also asked Foxy to put together a list of any other cases in which you were involved over the last twelve months. Guess what? He's only found your name on a warrant relating to some Skid whose charges were dropped because of a mix-up over the dates. I bet if we go further back we'll find more Skids, won't we?' Jo leaned forward, forcing Mac to look at her. 'You were on their payroll, weren't you?'

'Don't you know that, if you ask the same question more than once, the courts consider it an interference with a suspect's right to silence?' Mac said finally.

'Of course,' Jo said. 'You know all about your right to silence because you know the law . . . You're on the take, Mac, aren't you? You don't need to worry about your status, or your conviction rate, because you've found a much more lucrative nixer.'

Mac's face was white. 'Prove it.'

'As a matter of interest . . .' Jo said, holding up a seven-by-twelve school photo from the file. The image showed a portrait of a kid more boy than teen. 'What was he like?'

'The truth? He was a little prick. Not PC to say so, but then life isn't, is it?'

'So you thought you'd put some manners on him?'

'I never touched him.'

'So you said. Just like you said you didn't know Rita.' Jo stacked the papers back together and closed the file.

'For Christ's sake, what's your problem with me, eh?' Mac shouted suddenly. 'Not getting any at home? Want to get some of my special attention?'

Jo swallowed. He was making her nervous. 'Stuart Ball – did you know him?'

Mac gave her a look of contempt. 'Frigid bitch.'

'What about Anto Crawley?' Jo asked, glad Sexton was there.

'Now I'm your serial killer, is that it?' Mac asked, looking at Sexton like it was a wind-up.

Sexton looked away.

'You tell me,' Jo said.

'You're pathetic,' Mac said to her. 'You swan in here, looking down your nose at everyone, having married the boss to get ahead. You dump him when things don't go your way then do the bleeding-heart routine to give the impression you're married to the job. I feel sorry for you. Well, if you think you're going to stitch me up, you got another think coming. I go down, I'm bringing everyone else with me.'

'And that means?' Jo asked.

Mac ran his fingers over his lips like he was zipping them shut.

'If that's a reference to Sexton's car crash, he's told me all about it.'

Mac didn't so much as blink.

'You work out a lot, because you're watching your back, right?' She walked over to him, pulled the string of the scapular from around his neck and studied the image of the Sacred Heart stitched into the felt. 'Didn't have you down as the holy type,' she said, curling her lip.

'Keeps me safe,' Mac sneered.

Suddenly, Jenny Friar rapped and entered, without waiting for the all-clear. 'We need to talk,' she told Jo, gesturing towards the street. 'What the hell is going on out there?'

Jo stood up. 'I'm all finished here,' she said, tossing Sexton back his contacts book. 'Get him his solicitor, and get me a buccal swab.' She turned to Mac. 'I want your DNA.'

38

Jo's watch read 2.30 p.m. when she left Mac and Sexton in the interview room. She rubbed her hands over her face anxiously. It wasn't stacking up. If Mac was being bribed to help Skids evade charges, why would he start knocking them off? Maybe he'd wanted out because the Skids were blackmailing him but, if so, would he really kill four people? And why go to so much trouble with each killing, when a bullet in the back of their heads would have dispatched them far more effectively?

'We've got a situation,' Jenny Friar said. 'The place is crawling with press, a journalist from the *Sun* has just turned up hiding in a cubicle in the john . . .'

'Any missing-person reports yet?' Jo asked, changing the subject as she branched right towards the stairs.

Friar had headed straight on towards the incident room, and now looked round. 'Not that feast day palaver again . . . Where are you going?'

'My photo call,' Jo replied.

'Are you saying you're the reason they're here?' she shouted as the weighted door slammed shut between them. 'You are way out of order.'

'I am still technically in charge of this investigation,' Jo answered, continuing down a flight of stairs.

'You need clearance from the press office!'

'Technically, given my rank, I don't,' Jo answered.

'So what are you going to tell them, Jo?' Friar asked. 'The killer thinks he's Doubting Thomas; he hates the Christian code of law so much he mutilates the victims to remind people of the way things used to be done; he drugs them the way Christ was drugged; oh yeah, and he's never been in trouble with the law before, which he knows inside out. Where's that supposed to get us? You planning to ask Joe Public if anybody knows anyone matching your description?'

Jo stopped and looked up. 'Maybe.' She turned and, squaring her shoulders, strode out past the front desk in reception, past the oil painting of the city's rooftops, through the door into daylight and down the curved granite steps.

Somebody let out a shout as she emerged, and immediately a round of flashes made colour spots burst before her eyes. Squinting, she continued to descend to where a dozen-odd jostling reporters swarmed into an arc around her, plunging hand-held tape recorders in front of her face. Two sound muffs appeared over her head, the men holding them trying to angle them at the end of long poles. A couple of photographers stood on stepladders with long lenses, even though they were only six feet away.

Jo waved her hands for some hush. 'Apologies for the delay, and the next one of you who pulls a stunt like Piddling Pete from the *Sun* gets themselves a court date . . .'

Immediately, there was a burst of indecipherable questions. Jo held up her hand again. 'I'm not taking questions right now, I'm here to give you a statement.'

'Detective Inspector . . .'

A blonde with shiny make-up wearing a shiny black PVC stripper's mac was talking. 'Three murders in three days, no arrests: have the forces of law and order lost control of the city?'

Jo tucked loose strands of hair behind her ears.

Another voice, this time from a young bald man with red flaky skin on his nose. 'Detective Inspector, these three killings have now hit every strata of society. Are we in the grip of a crime epidemic?'

Jo looked at her watch. 'You've got precisely two minutes to listen. If you want to waste it, keep going. First of all, my deepest sympathies to the families and friends of the victims now coming to terms with their losses. And for the record, we're dealing with four, not three, killings, which we believe are linked.'

The questions started up again, twice as frantic.

'But the main reason I've called you here today is to appeal to the public to be extra vigilant,' Jo continued. 'I wouldn't be doing my job if I didn't warn people to take all precautions necessary. We will find the killer. But until then, we need people to be on their guard – and especially today.'

She looked straight into one camera lens. 'And to the killer, I want to say: find the strength to show what true power is and stop. Don't hurt anyone else. You can talk to me at any time, and I promise you I will try to rectify the wrong done to you. You can contact me through the station.'

She gave the incident-room number and took another deep breath. 'On a happier note, I can tell you that some good is about to come from this. As you all know, the balance of our criminal justice system is heavily weighted against victims. Fortunately, our justice minister is about to realign one aspect of the system in the victims' favour. I understand he is going to recommend Separate Legal Representation, so that rape victims no longer have to consider themselves ancillary to the judicial process. That's it, thank you for your time.'

She turned and headed back up the steps.

'Inspector . . . what's the fourth victim's name? Are you saying there is going to be another killing today? What are your lines of inquiry? Do you have any suspects?'

The questioners didn't wait for one to finish before another piped up.

Jo ignored them, and kept going, catching sight of the blinds askew in the incident room overhead.

'They're after your head,' Foxy said, holding her coat, keys out, and the files she'd asked him to organize on the case as she got inside.

'Back entrance,' she told him.

'What if he doesn't kill today?'

She shook her head. 'Why am I the only one who is taking today seriously?'

'But why did you tell them it's the same killer?' Foxy asked. 'We won't have a minute's peace now.'

'One, because my conscience has enough baggage already, thank you very much. And two, I want to see how Ryan Freeman covers it now he has to. Did you notice? He didn't even bother to show up. Get your job book out. I want every spit and cough on his background. I want to know why he wasn't out there. There has to be a reason. You should check the phone exchanges between him and Sexton – has the frequency gone up in recent days? I want to know what he had for breakfast, if he wipes his arse with double-sided toilet paper – everything. Did you find anything on Mac?'

217

'Nothing leapt out, Jo. Apart from those dropped cases that we know about already, he's a model officer.'

She took the keys out of his hand. 'Don't let him out of your sight today. I've asked the lab to see if they can cross-match the drugs in the apartment where Rita died with that Skids sting organized from the station a few months back. It's just a hunch, but if we get that drug link, we can keep him for a week. I want him here till the last second. Him and Skinny – aka Andy Morris. You got that?'

Foxy nodded. 'Where are we going now?'

'Who said anything about "we"? I need some time alone to think. Oh, and can you get one of the uniforms to ring around the cemeteries in the city. See if they can find out about any grave desecrations or disruptions in the last five years. If nothing comes to light, widen it to the rest of the country.'

Foxy noted it down.

She tipped his chest. 'And today's study topic is necro-philiacs, specifically in the Bible. It's not something you can consult Sal about, so you're on your own.'

''Course,' Foxy said, tucking his pen behind his ear and holding out Jo's jacket for her to put her arms in. 'If you're wrong about today, it's all over. They'll shaft you – you know that, don't you?'

'If I'm wrong about today, I'll go myself,' Jo told him over her shoulder. 'But I'm not wrong. Today is a big day for our killer. Today will be the most spectacular so far.'

'Professor Hawthorne rang and left a message for you to call him. Said it's important,' Foxy called after her.

Jo nodded as she strode away. Her watch read 2.47 p.m.

39

Mac paced up and down the cramped space in the holding cell trying to get his head straight. The job; the few quid he'd put aside; the dream of running a little Irish bar on the Costa Del Sol – it was all about to go down the Swanee, and it was all because of that bitch Jo Birmingham. But she still wasn't satisfied, and she wouldn't be either, not till she had him completely stitched up. He still hadn't seen his lawyer, and any minute now they were going to come and take his DNA – she'd said as much. They could use 'reasonable force' to take a cheek swab, and Mac knew only too well what constituted 'reasonable'. It wouldn't have mattered if he just opened his mouth and said 'ahh'; he could just picture some of the lads queuing up to have a go once word went around of what he'd been up to. He had to get out of here. Mac knew what pain did to people.

He tucked his fists under his arms. He didn't want any part of him touching the scabies-ridden walls, though he could have done with punching one of them. He should have been on a one-way flight the second Anto Crawley asked him if Ryan Freeman's kid had been reported missing, he now realized.

He walked over to the cistern in the corner, unzipped and had a slash. When he was finished, he pulled his sleeve over his hand so he could turn the sink faucet in the corner without making contact, then splashed the water on the back of his neck and face, shook it off and exhaled tightly.

If he told them the name of the person who'd paid him to list who was involved in what had happened to the Freeman kid, he was a dead man. Every one of them – Stuart Ball, Anto Crawley, Rita Nulty, Father Reg – had been dispatched since.

He threw a glance at the coarse grey blanket covering the bed. If he had to stay here tonight, just thinking about the prison sentence Birmingham had in mind for him would drive him out of his mind. He sniffed under his arm. He needed to get home, to shower, to change and to get the numbers of his contacts. He could phone someone, organize for Birmingham to be taken down a peg or two. Everyone had a point at which they were willing to back off; the Skids had taught him that. It wasn't enough for Birmingham that his career was dead in the water anyway. Any chance of promotion had gone by the wayside the night the kid in the cell died. Yes, he'd been helping some lowlifes jack poison into each other's arms ever since. It was called enterprise in his book. But Birmingham still wanted her pound of flesh. She hadn't been here that night, seen the way the kid in that file had answered him back. So Mac had given him one dig too many, so what? Some might say he'd done society a favour. It cost €100,000 to keep a prisoner inside for a year. He'd saved the taxpayer a potential fortune.

The key clanked in the door behind him and he turned jumpily. It was probably just some cheeky fucker going to offer him lunch. Mac knew exactly what bodily fluids were mixed up with any tray that slid under that door.

But when he saw the face looking back at him, he grinned. 'Thanks be to fuck,' he said. 'Get me out of here.'

40

By 5 p.m., Jo was checking a roast chicken in the oven after taking a break from studying the files on the case. She was all fingers and thumbs with the food, her concentration a million miles away. She knew there'd be hell to pay for walking out at the time she had, but she couldn't handle any more interruptions from Friar and her NBCI team, or the constant challenges to her authority. Time was too precious now. Foxy, Sexton and Merrigan were going to drop by for a late-night conference once her boys were fed and bedded down for the night. Until then, Jo needed some peace and quiet to pore over the details in the mountain of paperwork stacked on her desk containing background information on the victims and anything relevant that had turned up during interviews in the house-to-house enquiries. There had to be something in there that would crack the case, Jo told herself as she fiddled with the dials on the cooker.

'The drug addict Stuart Ball was murdered on New Wapping Street,' she said to herself. Scooping a handful of cutlery out of the clattering drawer, she pulled a knife free of the others and placed it on the bench to represent New Wapping Street. 'Rita Nulty was killed on Castleforbes Road, which runs parallel to New Wapping Street,' she said, picturing the building site where she'd found Rita and placing a knife side by side with the other.

'First sign of madness, talking to yourself,' Rory remarked from the kitchen table behind her.

Jo looked over her shoulder and back before he saw her smile. He had his school books spread all over the kitchen table, and the corner of his mouth was marked with an inky blob from where he'd been chewing his ballpoint pen. Harry was sitting on the floor beside him, grinding a rusk to pulp.

Jo grabbed a roll of kitchen towel and bent over to wipe the rusk off the floor before Harry scooped any more of it into his mouth. 'Make yourself useful and either set that for dinner, or relocate to the desk in your bedroom so I can,' she told Rory.

His chair screeched back as he stood up, sniffing over her shoulder as he headed out, making Jo jerk the potato peeler straight into her thumb. She sucked it painfully.

'The drug baron Anto Crawley was whacked on Spencer Dock, which runs parallel to both New Wapping Street and Castleforbes Road.' Jo pictured the abandoned warehouse, pulling another knife out of the drawer. Three knives sat in a row. All three streets were joined at one end by North Wall Quay and on the other by Sheriff Street, where Father Walsh, the priest, was found. She sandwiched each end with a fork. 'It has to mean something,' she said quietly.

Spotting Rory's books still spread all over the kitchen table, Jo called down the hall for him to come back and take them so she could set it. She was primed to give him an earful, but when she pressed the cordless house phone against her shoulder to answer it, while using her hands to scoop up his books herself, a reporter on the end of the line asking about recent developments got lashed instead.

Realizing Harry was attempting to climb up the leg of the chair, Jo put the phone down and rushed to his rescue, startling him so much he took off and managed to totter his first few steps in the process before stopping and wobbling precariously. She froze, feeling her tears well up. Then she knelt down in front of her baby turned little man and put her arms out. 'Come on, sweetheart,' she whispered. 'That's it, you can do it, come to Mummy.'

Harry managed another couple of steps before collapsing into her arms. Jo held him very close and planted a series of kisses on his soft head. *Thank Christ!* she thought, closing her eyes and rocking him from side to side. *Thank Christ I didn't miss that!*

The smoke alarm ripped through the moment with piercing urgency. With Harry still in her arms, Jo ran to the oven and turned everything off, then grabbed a dishcloth and ran out to wave it frantically under the alarm. Finally, Rory appeared with a kitchen chair, climbed up and killed the ear-splitting noise.

'Where've you been?' Jo asked, swinging Harry up in the air. 'Somebody's baby brother has just started walking, haven't you, my darling angel?'

'Thought I'd help you get the garden in order, Mother,' Rory said, tussling Harry's hair, then pulling the lawnmower fuel from behind his back and holding it up. 'The less time Dad has to spend on it, the better for everyone's sake.'

'Rory,' Jo began, sitting Harry down. 'Dad's move home, it doesn't mean . . .'

The doorbell clanged to life and she put her hand on Rory's arm to stop him answering it. As she pulled the door open, she remembered where she'd seen the black mac before.

'Hi, we've met, I'm Linda from the *Mail*,' the woman said in an over-familiar tone. 'Can I have a word?'

'Absolutely not,' Jo replied, starting to close the door.

'Where do you find the time with a serial killer on the rampage?' she asked patronizingly, looking over Jo's shoulder at Harry on the floor behind her.

Jo began to close the door but stopped when she noticed the way the reporter had stepped sideways, then looked over her shoulder to a car at the end of the drive. Jo spotted a long lens balancing on the driver's wing mirror.

'Mind your baby brother, son,' she instructed Rory over her shoulder, before pulling the door behind her, pushing past the hack and storming over to the car.

'What the hell do you think you're playing at?' she asked, wrestling with the photographer for the lens. 'We've got privacy laws in this country.'

'Damage that and you pay for it,' he warned.

She spotted his name engraved on a tarnished gold bracelet – Darryl. 'Now you listen to me, Darryl, and listen good . . .'

'Why don't you concentrate on your job and let us do ours?' Linda had followed her over to the car. 'You're the one who's put the country on high alert, telling them a madman was going to strike again today. And now you're home. Couldn't you get your overtime approved? Your childminder call in sick? People are dying, you know!'

'Get out of here, Darryl, before I have you charged, and take her with you,' Jo warned.

'With what?' Darryl asked aggressively.

'Trespassing and loitering with intent, for starters,' Jo warned.

'Come on, Linda, she's not worth it,' Darryl said.

'Wait a second, where did you get my home address?' Jo asked, leaning in the window.

Linda caught her eye, and Jo thought she was going to say something. Then Darryl revved the engine and she got inside the car.

Shaking her head, Jo went back into the house. 'Leave the garden for now,' she told Rory. 'And get your coat. We're eating out.'

In the Eddie Rockets restaurant, Jo's mood lifted as Harry started sucking happily on a cheesy chip. 'Your dad and I broke up for a reason. It wasn't working between us,' she said to Rory.

Rory sucked Coke through three straws. Still just a big kid, Jo thought.

'We did the facts-of-life talk years ago, Mother,' he said, 'and believe me, it was only mildly more embarrassing.'

'I'm just saying, things have moved on now. Dad's got Jeanie.'

'But you haven't met anyone,' Rory said.

'Yet,' Jo corrected him.

'Does that mean you're looking?'

'Of course I'm looking,' Jo lied.

Rory's eyes moved to the window. He jabbed his middle finger at it.

'Rory!' Jo remonstrated, turning anxiously and spotting Linda and Darryl parked outside, angling their camera straight at them. Smug didn't cover the look on their faces. She gave them the finger herself.

The camera captured that moment too.

'Now I'm the kind of mother who stuffs her kids with

additives and resorts to vile hand gestures, as well as being a bad cop,' said Jo, sighing.

'Maybe they could run it as an ad in the singles section,' Rory suggested.

Jo laughed. But there was an uneasy feeling in the pit of her stomach. She wondered if she wasn't willing the killer to strike again, just to bail her out.

41

By 10.45 p.m., Foxy and Merrigan were taking seats on Jo's couch. Jo hadn't had to ask them when she opened the door, their faces said it all – still no body.

'The good news is Hawthorne's been in touch,' Foxy said, clearly trying to lift morale. 'His prelim on Father Reg showed that the priest had pierced nipples.'

'Not your average celibate then,' Jo reacted, mood improving slightly.

'Certainly opens up a whole range of possibilities as to what he'd been doing and the reasons why he might have come into contact with the Skids,' Foxy said. 'Also, the forensic lab phoned in to say you were right. They had a positive match on the drugs we found on the coffee table at Rita Nulty's crime scene and that recent Skids sting the station brought in, which means you can keep Mac longer if you want.'

Jo bribed Rory to go to bed by unhooking the DVD player and scart lead from the telly and handing them to him. Rory gripped them with the kind of enthusiasm that suggested she'd have a job on her hands ever getting the player back out of his bedroom and disappeared upstairs. It was past his bedtime, but she'd let him stay up because he'd studied hard all evening, after a mild argument in which he'd demanded to know what possible contribution to his adult life half of the stuff on his curriculum could make.

'Half an hour to help you unwind, that's it,' Jo warned him, crossing her fingers behind her back as she watched him head up the stairs. She didn't want to curse the thought passing through her head, but the move home seemed to have done the trick: Rory was really knuckling down . . .

Back in her living room, Merrigan and Foxy were arguing over which channel to watch. She walked over and switched off the TV.

Merrigan threw his hands up then whacked them off his legs with a sigh.

'Thanks for coming,' Jo said. 'I know we all have private lives, and I just want to say, I appreciate it.'

Merrigan pretended to play a tiny violin.

'I'm being sincere!' she warned. 'Any luck on the door-to-doors?'

'Yeah,' he said reluctantly. 'One of the uniforms found out that the dead padre had got his knuckles rapped for putting Rita up in his home. Father Reg claimed he was doing God's work, but some of his parishioners believe she was doing him. Someone wrote to the bishop.'

'Gives us a start on who was leading him by those nipple rings,' Jo said, looking at Foxy anxiously. 'Any luck with necrophiles in the Bible?'

Merrigan covered his nipples playfully and made a coy face. Jo was starting to get narked. It was all a big joke with him. Someone was going to die in the next hour and a quarter, if they hadn't already.

'Yes, actually. According to the Bible, there was one very famous necrophile . . .' Foxy said.

'Who?' Jo asked.

'Get me a sarnie and he'll tell you,' Merrigan said. 'Doreen scraped my dinner into the bin when I said I'd to head out again.'

Jo sighed as he and Foxy followed her into the kitchen. Merrigan started pulling open drawers. Jo took over, reaching into the bread bin, grabbing a bread knife from the drawer and cutting a slice of white bread.

'Go on,' she prompted.

'Only King Herod,' Foxy said. 'You know, the one who had all the male babies killed when he heard about the birth of Christ, the one who had John the Baptist beheaded for Salome after her Dance of the Seven Veils.' He opened the fridge and retrieved a tomato. 'Herod's supposed to have kept his dead wife Mariamne – whom he murdered, by the way – seven years in his sleeping quarters for sex . . . after he'd killed her.'

Jo took a sharp breath in. 'So our killer is honouring his enemies like we thought.'

'Thought you'd be pleased,' Foxy said.

'It also explains why Rita's body was the only one sexually interfered with,' she said slowly. 'I must've missed something with the other three victims. Foxy, can you think of any more of Christ's enemies?'

'What are you thinking?' he asked.

'Our killer paid tribute to King Herod with Rita. I want to know which of Christ's enemies Stuart Ball, Anto Crawley and Father Walsh represented in his mind.'

'Judas – he was the main one,' Merrigan said, picking up his bread. 'Can I have a slice of ham with this?'

'The Pharisees – according to one of Sal's books, they were the moral equivalent of priests and the ones who judged Christ,' Foxy said.

'Father Walsh would fit that bill,' Jo said. 'The killer will have left us a sign if so. Can you check out any biblical references to them, Foxy? We'll need to study the crime-scene photographs and see what symbol our man left there.'

'Any chance of a cuppa?' Merrigan asked.

'You asked me to look into necrophilia, and I've got that list of desecrations you wanted,' Foxy continued. 'A couple of graves were robbed, but the bodies were left intact . . . Also, I spoke to a psychologist and a leading expert in the area, who says the research suggests that 90 per cent of necrophiles are male, so no surprises there but, interestingly, half of those who actually killed so as to take ownership of the victim's body are gay. Oh yeah, and it's mostly morticians who offend.'

Merrigan sat down at the kitchen table and took a mouthful of bread. 'Great, our man's a faggot as well as everything else,' he said.

'It's all to do with fear of rejection,' Foxy went on. 'Most necrophiliacs are either trying to control someone who previously resisted them, or to reunite with someone who's died, or to overcome isolation.'

Jo filled the kettle and switched it on.

'Previous serial killers with this particular attraction to the dead – Ted Bundy and Jeffrey Dahmer,' Foxy said. 'But most famous of all . . . Jack the Ripper.'

'You know any of Christ's other enemies?' Jo asked him.

'Pontius Pilate,' Foxy said, sitting down beside Merrigan. 'Though he did appeal to people to come to their senses after they chose Christ over Barabas.'

Jo clicked her fingers. 'I'll bet that's who Crawley represented. We need to look for the symbol in the warehouse near Crawley's body – didn't Pilate wash his hands? It has to be there somewhere. I'll check the scene-of-crime photos tomorrow. Can you get me the names of the others? And a detailed description of the scene where Stuart Ball was found.'

Foxy looked up at Jo, his face worried. 'We also need to talk about Mac. Am I the only one who thinks he's in this thing up to his neck?'

'Steady,' Merrigan said. 'He's one of us.'

'He's a bad one, and you know it,' Foxy said sharply.

'I'll worry about Mac,' Jo said. 'We can keep him in custody till next week now, don't forget!'

'Mac could have got his hands on the cocaine we found at Rita Nulty's crime scene,' Foxy said cautiously. 'He could have taken some from our batch and brought it there.'

'I agree,' Jo said as the doorbell rang. She sighed. 'If that's a bloody reporter, I won't be responsible for my actions.'

'It's probably just Sexton,' Foxy said as she got up.

The door opened before Jo got to it. Dan appeared in the entrance with two suitcases hanging from either hand and his key in one.

'You said Friday,' Jo said.

Dan looked at his watch. 'Sorry, I'm an hour early. Tomorrow's not good for me.' He looked up and saw the heads peering from the kitchen. 'Am I interrupting?' he asked.

'We're just finished,' Jo said.

'Any developments?' Dan asked.

Foxy and Merrigan avoided his eye and Jo shook her head. Dan turned and headed up the stairs.

'How about my cup of tea?' Merrigan asked, as he stood up. Foxy gave him a shove in the back to keep going.

'Thanks, lads,' Jo said. 'See you tomorrow.'

'I'm bloody gasping,' Merrigan told Jo as he passed her in the hall.

Behind his back, Foxy patted Jo's arm. It was his way of telling her not to lose heart.

After they'd gone, she stood with her back to the door trying to think. She was more certain than ever the killer was going to crucify his next victim. What she needed to do next was work out who.

42

11.10 p.m., and Rory and Harry were asleep, the TV was on mute and a Sinéad O'Connor album was playing low on the stereo. Jo was on the couch, legs tucked under her chin. She was studying a Dublin city centre street map. Her mobile and car keys sat on the coffee table in front of her, her shoes were on the shagpile rug directly underneath. She was taking regular deep breaths, trying to inhale the smell of nicotine from the jumper she had retrieved for that specific purpose from the laundry basket.

Dan arrived, bringing a fresh soapy smell; his hair was still wet. He'd gone straight to the spare room to unpack after Foxy and Merrigan left and then must have taken a shower.

Jo did a double take. He had changed his clothes and was wearing a Tommy Hilfiger T-shirt open to the third button, Wranglers, a cowboy belt and black winklepickers. Mid-life-crisis clothes, she thought, also noticing a chain glinting around his neck. She'd never seen him wear jewellery before.

'You going somewhere?' she asked.

'Yeah, heading out for a couple of late pints.'

'A club?' she asked, appalled. Him heading out on the tiles wasn't exactly a ringing endorsement of her theory that the killer was going to strike again in under an hour.

He shrugged and sat down beside her on the couch, glancing at the map. 'What are you thinking?' he asked.

'Doesn't it strike you as strange that all the bodies were found in 'C' District?' she said, picking up a pen and marking the spot on the street where Rita had been found. 'In the building where we had our hostage-training exercise, remember?' Jo crossed another street. 'This is where Stuart Ball was found, but look.' She pointed. 'If it had been on any of these adjoining streets, it would have been the Bridewell's jurisdiction. We've got every one of them.'

Dan gave a short hum.

'We need to get Anto Crawley's surveillance records from the NSU,' she told him. 'I'm hitting a brick wall with NBCI on the subject . . .'

Dan stood up dismissively.

'Think about it, Dan. Somebody like Crawley sleeps with a bulletproof jacket under his PJs. He's always prepared. He's not going to let any Joe Soap near him to kill him. Rita, too – she had the Skids pimping her. How did the killer get past them, carrying the tools he needed to hurt her like that? Rita and Anto Crawley have to have trusted whoever killed them, or at the very least known them. That's why we need that list of Crawley's associates.'

'I'm not arguing with your theory, Jo. But you know how tight that information is kept.'

'And you know whose head is going to roll if we don't find the killer soon,' Jo said. 'Mine will be splashed all over the *Mail* tomorrow morning as it is.'

'I can't get you out of the hole you've dug yourself into,' Dan said, sighing.

'You won't have to,' Jo answered. 'I'm going to find him.'

Dan's mobile bleeped with an incoming text. He glanced

at his watch. 'Stupid of me to forget. It's all going to change completely any second, isn't it? You're going to be proved right and everyone else wrong when a mutilated body shows up – oh yeah, crucified . . .'

Jo stared at his watch. It was new too, and looked like a fake Tag. She really wanted to know what he'd done with her dad's old leather-strapped one . . .

'You really think I'd say anything if I wasn't sure?' she asked.

'I'm just asking if you're out of your depth, Jo.'

'I wasn't until the second you asked me,' she said.

He sighed, walked to the curtain and pulled it slightly aside to see out.

'Here's my lift.'

'Ask him to wait a few minutes, I need to talk to you.'

Dan shook his head. 'It's not a cab.'

He pulled on a jacket – a windbreaker, shiny on the outside, fleece lining. He looked all wrong in it.

'So how is this living-separately thing going to work when you get back tonight?' Jo asked. 'Is Jeanie planning to stay too? Is that what this is about? Think the green-eyed monster will do the trick?' She stood up and began plumping the scatter cushions. 'Because two can play at that game . . .'

He lunged and grabbed her by the wrist, dragging her over to the window. She was stunned. In all the big, ugly rows they'd had over the years, he'd never resorted to force. If the boys hadn't been asleep, Jo would have screamed at him to let go. Instead she whacked him repeatedly with her free arm. Dan pulled the curtain aside to show her that the car waiting was being driven by one of his rugby mates. Then he let go.

Jo stared at him staring back at her. She knew they were

both thinking the same thing – how had it come to this? They'd both been to domestics, seen how septic a relationship becomes when it turns nasty, how much damage it does to the kids.

After a long pause, he said, 'You want to know where I went during the Phoenix Park investigation? The Quality Hotel, Pearse Street. Room 112. And yes, to save you the trouble of a follow-up call, it was a double room.'

43

11.32 p.m. Jo moved the street map she was studying off her lap and went to the window, which someone had just rapped. She pulled back a curtain, to see Gavin Sexton standing there with a bottle of red wine in one hand and two wine glasses in the other. He'd changed out of his work clothes and into his civvies – a denim jacket and chinos. His hair was gelled into a spiky style. He lobbed his head in the direction of the front door.

Jo went to the hall and pulled it open. 'Where've you been?'

'Down the station,' he said sheepishly. 'Letting Mac go.'

Jo presumed he was joking. 'You don't have the authority,' she ribbed.

'I know, so I used your name, said you'd ordered it.' He held her stare.

'You what?'

When he didn't blink, Jo headed down the hall for the phone.

'Can you just listen to me for a second?' he asked, following and pressing a finger on the hang-up button.

Jo glared at him.

He took his hand off the phone, twisted the cap off the bottle and started to fill a glass. 'I can't do this without a drink.' He held it out to Jo. She ignored him and started to dial again. He placed the empty glass beside the phone. 'I let him out so I could follow him. I thought if he's our man, and Jo's right about today, he's going to lead us straight to the next victim,' Sexton continued, pouring another and taking a big mouthful. He swallowed hard. 'And there's something else I haven't told you about the case.'

Jo hung up. She looked towards the bedrooms and then pointed into the sitting room. He walked in and sat on the couch.

'Go on then,' she said, remaining standing.

Sexton didn't look at her. 'It's got to do with Ryan Freeman's little girl. Her name is Katie. She was taken by the Skids, a couple of months back. It's the crime that links all our killings.'

Jo sat down slowly, keeping her eyes on him as he kept talking.

'I don't know what they did to her. I've been trying to help the Freemans to find out. Whatever it was has messed her up really bad . . . She's only a kid, Jo. I mean, can you imagine something like that happening to either of yours? How scared you'd be? . . . I know you'd go to any lengths to help her recover. Well, as you already know, Ryan and I go way back, and he asked me to help.'

'Tell me everything,' she said.

'Anto Crawley ordered Katie's abduction, no question,' Sexton explained, speaking between big gulps of wine. 'And he made sure Ryan knew it too.' He told her about the CCTV footage. 'And it looks like Rita Nulty was chief babysitter while they were holding on to Katie. Stuart Ball probably helped cart her off, and I suspect Father Reg found out what happened, I'm not sure how yet.'

Jo sighed. 'And all this time I've been running around like a blue-arsed fly, and people have been dropping dead left, right and centre . . .'

'You think this has been easy for me?' Sexton said, leaning forward, his face even more lined and tired than usual. 'I promised Ryan I'd stay quiet for Katie's sake. If we went tramping in there making arrests, we'd no chance of anyone in the Skids telling us what they did to her. We're still trying to bring her back, Jo. She hasn't talked properly since this thing happened.'

Jo sucked air through her teeth. 'She's still sick?'

He nodded. 'She's in Crumlin at the moment.'

'So why are you telling me now?'

'I was always going to tell you, Jo. But yesterday, I found out that Ryan's wife, Angie, was being blackmailed by Anto Crawley before he died. I've spoken to her. She said her only part in it was to give Crawley advance warning on what Ryan was going to print about the Skids. Crawley would use her tip-offs to get his act together before the stories appeared in print. If Ryan was about to publish the fact that Crawley has a container of hash sitting in Dublin port, Angie tips Crawley off, and it's too late – the container's empty. The story dies. I believed her, and so did Ryan. Anyone would have done the same to save their family.'

'*Believed* her?' Jo pushed. 'Why the past tense?'

He took a swig from the bottle.

Jo took the bottle out of his hand and put it down on the table. 'Now tell me what happened when you released Mac. And then how long you spent doing yourself up since you tailed him?'

'I just thought that, if I followed him, we'd get to the bottom of it, finally. But he went straight home.'

Jo grabbed her keys and phone.

Sexton jumped up too. 'You can't just go barging in on Katie. She's in a bad way. She can't cope with any more trauma.'

'We've got it all wrong,' Jo said. Her hand shook as she dialled Dan's number. 'Mac isn't the killer. He's next.'

Friday

44

12.29 a.m. The first thing Jo saw when Sexton kicked Mac's door in was two bare size-twelve feet hanging limp at that grotesque angle that instantly suggests suicide – big toes touching. They dangled from the far side of a mezzanine, which was obscuring the top half of the body.

Sexton clamped his hands on Jo's shoulders like he was going to use them to vault over. Jo spread her arms to block him from rushing to Mac's aid, pointing to the heavy pool of blood congealing under the body.

'Out,' she told him over her shoulder, speaking over the racket the TV and stereo were making. 'In the same direction you came in, close as possible to your original footsteps, and we'll need your shoes.'

The way Sexton exhaled behind her suggested that he realized he was in some part to blame for Mac's death.

'Make the calls,' she reminded him tersely.

She braced herself, then moved stiffly across the open-plan apartment, registering the strange words scrawled on the walls. Foxy was right, she thought, staring at the white, distressed-leather couch running the line of the apartment walls and the paintings on the wall – Guggi, Graham Knuttel. No civil servant's salary had paid for this place. The hairs on the back of her neck lifted as she got closer to the body. Mac's apartment was also in 'C' district.

She was standing by Mac's feet, just beyond the pool of sticky blood. She could have turned and looked up, but she wanted to delay it for as long as possible, as she had a mental image of what she would see. She pulled a face as a bad smell – like soggy stems of flowers left in stagnant water – hit her. Her gaze moved to an overturned aquarium and the dead fish scattered about.

'It's not like you to lose your temper,' she told the killer, voice shaking.

She took her pad and pen out of her bag and noted the precise spelling of the strange words on the walls then turned and looked round slowly. Mac had been nailed to the balcony that ran round the apartment. His arms were fully extended, bound at the wrists to the chunky wooden rail that formed the balcony's barrier, and his hands had also been secured to the wood with metal spikes. Blood had run from the wounds down to his elbows before dripping on to the cream carpet, and his head was drooping sideways, so that his chin touched his chest. A crown of thorns sat on his forehead. Bar his Y-fronts, he was naked. And, yes, there was the signature wound, left of the breastbone, Jo observed, trying to concentrate on anything other than the chill she felt in the pit of her stomach. Not revulsion. It was fear.

She headed for the clear glass stairs connected to a side wall and climbed to the gallery floor, taking in the silver coins scattered about. 'Judas,' she whispered.

The noise was making her so jumpy she couldn't help looking over her shoulder. 'Come on, Jo, the killer's gone, keep it together,' she told herself. 'This is what you're trained for. You need to see things the way he did.'

She looked at Mac's unmade bed. It was low, a Japanese crate job, dressed with black satin sheets, the kind single men like and women don't.

Then slowly, concentrating on her breathing, she looked across at the back of Mac's head and torso, which were close enough to touch. She noted the marks and welts on his back, suggesting he'd been whipped.

As long as she was rationalizing, processing, she could do this, Jo told herself. She moved closer so she was looking down on the top of Mac's head. The crown was made of hawthorn branches and the spikes had torn open wounds in his scalp. She swallowed her rising sense of panic and looked at the rope wound several times around his wrists. It was blue and thin – the sort used for a washing line. They might strike lucky if they could analyse it down to a year of manufacture, she thought. If only there was more time . . .

She looked over the balcony at the rear of the apartment, at the stainless-steel kitchen, and she spotted two glasses in the sink. Did Mac know the killer too? Had he had a drink with him before he'd died? There was no sign of breaking and entering.

'Five dead,' she said to the killer. 'It doesn't get any better than this for you, does it? You must feel like a god yourself now.'

Now she was back in control. Fear was being replaced by anger. Leaning over, she put a hand on Mac's chest and felt his body temp, recording it as 'still warm to touch'. She inspected the rusting nails in his palms; from the size of them they could have been used in the sleepers of a railway track. They could be sourced too, she thought. She crooked her arm, trying to work out how Mac's killer could have held Mac's body in place while hammering the nails in, then spotted the red bruising round the neck where the rope – probably the same as used on the wrists – had looped.

'Why did this one get the special treatment?' she asked, talking to the killer again. 'If it was Crawley's idea to abduct Katie Freeman, all the others – even Mac – were minor characters. Why not give Crawley the worst death, on what you consider your special day . . . Unless . . .'

She looked over at the aquarium as she put it together. 'Mac made you most angry . . .' she said, understanding suddenly. 'Judas was the traitor – Christ's greatest enemy. That's why you chose Mac . . . You're not wiping the victims out because of what they did to Katie, are you? You're murdering everyone who can tell what happened to her. Judas was the whistleblower, after all.'

She ran down the stairs and over to the kitchen sink where the glasses sat – in an ideal world, they'd be stained with fingerprints. Depending on who'd been drinking, they might have a hope of more DNA if there were saliva.

She went to the tall cylinder bin in the corner, pulled her hand into her sleeve and lifted the lid carefully. The only item inside was an empty bottle of wine. She made a note to have it taken, and all the rubbish in the apartment block sifted. She headed over to the table and studied, without touching, what she'd first thought was food but now looked like a molten-candle wax stain.

She reached for her phone and scrolled through the contacts then hit the dial button.

'Gerry?' she said as the call connected. 'It's Jo Birmingham . . . Yeah, I know what time it is . . . Never mind where I got your home number. No, it's not about getting support for victims in court. I need a big, big favour.'

45

Angie Freeman was sitting in front of the TV in her sitting room watching a panel discussion on a late-night news show. She'd kept the lights off and the volume down out of pure habit, as if Katie were sleeping upstairs and not in hospital.

Jo Birmingham's press conference was being replayed for the commentators on the telly. After each sentence, the programme's host would freeze the frame on a big screen behind a group that included a member of the opposition party, a psychiatrist and a tabloid-newspaper editor and invite the participants to analyse exactly what Jo had meant. Angie rubbed warmth into the tops of her arms as goose pimples began to spread. She was only wearing a light negligée. She turned to identify the draught as the sound of the key in the front door told her where it was coming from. Ryan had entered and was looking at her as if he'd seen a ghost.

'Where've you been? You know what time it is?' she snapped.

With a sigh he closed the door behind him, giving their dog Cassie time to slink in around his legs. 'She didn't get a walk today with everything.' He paused as he saw what was on the TV. 'Why are you watching that?'

'Because it's only a matter of time before they start putting two and two together – and what's going to happen then? If you're sent to prison, how am I supposed to cope? How'll I pay for Katie's medical bills? If I've to go back to work, who'll take care of her?'

Ryan made a noise that went with a sneer.

'What's that supposed to mean? Are you calling me a bad mother?'

'Me? And there I was thinking it was your friendship with scum like Crawley that got us into this mess.'

'I didn't sleep with him.' Angie stood and moved towards Ryan. One of the straps of her negligée fell down her shoulder but she didn't hitch it back up. She slid her arms around his waist and pressed into him, resting her head on his chest.

'I just think we should start to get our story straight and start looking out for each other, like old times.' She tilted her face up to his.

He put his hands on her shoulders and pushed her away, holding her at arm's length. 'You think I killed Crawley, don't you? But I had nothing to do with any of it. Much as I wish I had, it wasn't me who killed him.'

'Well, somebody did, and they're trying to make it look like it was you.'

He reached for the zapper and switched off the TV.

'Put it on, I want to see it.' She sprung at Ryan suddenly and slapped him hard on the face. Cassie whimpered but Ryan didn't so much as lift a hand or step back to defend himself.

'What kind of fucking excuse for a man are you?' Angie screamed at him. 'Don't you understand anything? Tell me you killed Anto Crawley. Tell me you did it!'

46

Jo sat on the covers of Rory's single bed in a terrycloth dressing gown and a pair of novelty Tasmanian Devil slippers which stared back at her like a ridiculous antidote to the horrors she had witnessed tonight. It was four in the morning, but she couldn't sleep. A man had been crucified. A man she knew, whom earlier in the day she had accused of being in the wrong, a man who had died an agonizing death because she still hadn't solved the case.

She closed her eyes and listened to the sound of snoring in the next room. Friday, early morning, and Rory and Harry were fast asleep in her bed. Rory must have checked on his baby brother then fallen asleep on the covers of her bed. Jo had pulled an eiderdown over him and headed for his bed instead. Rory was a good kid, she reminded herself, and right then the sight of Harry's chubby little hand jutting through the bars of the cot and sitting bang smack on Rory's face was just what she needed. It had melted some of the perversions of what she'd just seen done to Mac, whose full name she now knew to be Dave MacMahon. The stiff whiskey she was nursing in her hand was helping too, but it couldn't change the overriding sense that everything was going to change tomorrow. There'd be the public reaction to her eating out while a killer went on the rampage, and there'd be the change in the station. You killed a cop, whether he was good or bad, and it became personal for other cops.

The sound of the front door opening made her back straighten. He'd arrived at Mac's apartment just as Jo was leaving and grilled her in front of the mules about why she hadn't done things by the book instead of barging in. Jo could have argued, but she was all done arguing with Dan.

She could hear him banging the presses in the kitchen, then a noise which she presumed meant that the gammy press door had just fallen off. He's probably looking for the whiskey bottle, she thought, glancing to it on the bedside locker.

On the landing, he stopped outside the door. She guessed he'd spotted the light under the door and presumed Rory was still awake. He rapped once and put his head around, looking surprised to see her there. He was about to back out when she patted the side of the bed.

Dan looked exhausted as he closed the door behind him and sat down, the dark circles under his eyes more prominent. He leaned forwards on his knees. His windbreaker had bloodstains on the sleeves. He must have helped get Mac down. She could also smell smoke off him. Dan hadn't smoked in years. Jo handed him her glass, which he drained. She topped it up.

'Aren't you going to say it?' he asked, staring into the glass.

'What?'

'I told you so.'

Jo opened her mouth, intending to remind him that she hadn't wanted this to happen, but said nothing.

'Hawthorne went ballistic,' he went on. 'He'd been at his

annual hunt dinner and arrived in his dinner jacket, bow tie
– the lot. Said we shouldn't have interrupted him for something he could have seen to in the morning. You wouldn't
have left a dog strung up like that for the night, Jo. Mac was
one of our own.'

Jo's heart went out to him. The way you treated the dead
mattered to good people like Dan. She put her hand on his
shoulders and rubbed his back.

'I've been such a bloody fool,' he went on. 'You know he
came to me, years ago, and told me what happened that
night with the kid in the cell: how he'd given him one slap
too many, how he'd fallen and cracked his head against the
metal frame of the bunk, and he never meant it to happen. I
believed him.'

Jo pulled her hand away. 'And you said nothing?'

'Don't start. Not tonight. There's only one thing to talk
about. How are we going to stop this killer? It was one thing
when the victims were all linked to gangland – the public
doesn't care about scrotes knocking off scrotes – but now
we've got a priest, and a cop. Middle Ireland is going to start
baying for blood, and it's going to start right now.' He
turned and looked at her, his face taut with worry. 'You have
to find him, Jo. You're the only one who understands why
he's doing this and what he might do next.'

47

Flanked only by Foxy and Sexton, because nobody had bothered to inform Merrigan, Jo crossed the yard of Mountjoy Prison towards Justice Minister Blaise Stanley, who was posing for photographers at a pre-arranged press call. It was 10 a.m., and the country had woken up to the news that a garda had been murdered. On *Morning Ireland*, Aine Lawlor had sounded even closer to tears than usual. The *Mail* story about Jo not being up to the job looked off the wall, because the radio stations had moved on to the story of the cop 'with her finger on the pulse . . . who'd predicted the crime'.

Jo had learned from Gerry on the phone during the previous night's conversation that Stanley was scheduled to launch a new policy document on Temporary Release for prisoners this morning. The prison location had originally been chosen to send out a zero-tolerance message on criminality. But given last night's development, Stanley had gone into fire-fighting mode and was about to add a state-of-the-nation address. The original plan to pose outside the modern red-brick and ice-block-fronted prison on the North Circular road had been abandoned in favour of the view from behind the prison walls. Inside the grey steel gates, it was strictly infirmary-style granite. Jo knew that the

Victorian attitude to justice conveyed by the location had been picked purely because it suited the public mood.

Either way, the prison looked like what it was, Jo thought, turning around – a moral sewer. Usually drugs, mobile phones and even bottles of vodka came sailing in over the wall. In Wheatfield Prison, the contraband-missile throwers were so prolific an 'X' had been spraypainted on the side of the wall that bordered Cherry Orchard Hospital to show the best pitch point. There was nothing that couldn't be got in prison. During one prison raid, the authorities had even discovered a couple of budgies.

Gerry had agreed that Jo could have the minister's ear before he was whisked off to Baldonnell aerodrome, in return for which she had agreed not to call him for a month. Now, as she approached Stanley, Jo suddenly realized the real reason he'd been so uncharacteristically amenable.

'I've been set up,' she told Foxy, watching the way Gerry moved behind the minister to pat his shoulder, whisper in his ear and gesture to Jo with his chin.

Stanley had been holding up a state-published book with the hallmark harp on the front at various angles – thrust out front, over a shoulder, above his head – for a bunch of photographers clustered in a pack in front of him, lunging towards him on one leg or angling cameras sideways as they clicked. His scowl never changed from shot to shot.

After listening to what Gerry had to say, Stanley looked up, registered Jo and waved her over.

The photographers, in various styles of flak jacket, started calling Stanley's name to get him to pose again. One snapper was lying prostrate in front of the minister, aiming his long lens at Stanley's chin. The name of the newspaper on the press pass around his neck told Jo why – it was the paper that gave above-fold half-pages to arty shots.

Jo studied Stanley sceptically, thinking that the only part of him that didn't look groomed was the hair on his fingers. His face shone with the glow of a weekly exfoliating face mask and the space between his eyebrows was an unnatural width. You'd have to get a lot of people sucking up to you before you'd treat yourself to that much pampering, she thought.

Foxy leaned in to tell her what he'd found in the photographs of the Stuart Ball murder scene.

'Tools,' he explained. 'A chisel and anvil. Turns out they're the stock tools of a silversmith's trade.'

Jo shook her head in confusion.

'The silversmith Demetrius was another of Christ's enemies,' Foxy explained. 'He wasn't happy with the impact of the messiah's message on his trade of idols dedicated to the goddess Diana. I think it's Demetrius who the killer wanted Stuart Ball to represent.'

'And you were right about Anto Crawley representing Pontius Pilate. There was a bowl of water set in the ground. Oh, and the word "Golgotha" scrawled in Mac's apartment means Calvary.'

Jo slapped him on the shoulder, and he nudged her back to indicate a reporter, identifiable by the spiral-bound notebook he held in one hand and the folded newspapers he had tucked in both waxy jacket pockets, who had begun moving towards her. The rest began to follow like sheep.

Stanley waved Jo over to join him again, but she crossed her arms and firmly stood her ground.

Stanley looked put out but quickly reined in his true feelings for the sake of the cameras. He approached Jo, reached for her hand and shook vigorously, then turned to the cameras as if to say, 'You getting this?' Then he clapped her upper arm and leaned in for a quick hug, which was delivered with a paternal pat on the back. 'They're all gangland killings, that's the line,' he whispered.

Jo was spitting mad. It was infuriating to have him turn on the charm as if they were old friends, and to have him give her instructions as if he'd a day-to-day, hands-on involvement in the case. The truth was that, without cameras around, she couldn't have got a call put through to him.

'Detective Inspector Birmingham,' a reporter called. Jo couldn't see which one. 'Another killing, just as you predicted yesterday. How did you know? Is the killer in touch with you?'

Jo put her hands in her pockets and looked at her shoes.

'Inspector,' another one – that bald guy from yesterday – called, 'the public are calling you the prophet policewoman . . . When is he going to strike next?'

Before anyone else cut in, Jo said: 'I'd like to take this opportunity to extend my deepest sympathies to the family of Garda Dave MacMahon. I want to assure them we are doing everything possible to find the person or people responsible for this grotesque act, which is a crime against every right-minded member of our society.'

Jo tried to move off, but Stanley had one arm around her back and the other on her elbow, which he gave a little pull.

'I'd also like to extend my condolences,' he said, in a well-practised tone that was as effective as 'Quiet!'. 'As you know, the last time we lost a member of the force to gangland was when Detective Garda Jerry McCabe was murdered by the IRA when they raided a bank escort. But these are changed times. Since then my party has seen the IRA decommissioned; we have lengthened the powers of detention for gardaí holding drugs suspects; we have created the Criminal Assets Bureau to disassemble the tier of drugs money; and we have put gangsters on the run.'

Jo wondered why they were letting him run with the political party broadcast when the garda helicopter, which was equipped with heat-seeking equipment, was circling overhead – not to hunt down fugitives, but to provide extra security detail in a place supposed to be the biggest deterrent to crime in the first instance.

But the reporters were too busy scribbling frantically and thrusting tape recorders inches from his face.

'I have every confidence in Detective Inspector Birmingham and her team,' Stanley was saying. He gave her the kind of proud look that parents give to children at school plays. 'As she proved yesterday, she knows exactly what we're dealing with here, and it's only a matter of time before she catches this maniac.' He looked straight into the camera. 'And I can promise you, when we do catch the Skids responsible, they will feel the full rigour of the law.'

'Inspector, are all the killings linked to the Skids?'

'Inspector, can you tell us anything about the circumstances of Garda Dave MacMahon's killing?'

'Minister, what are you doing to offset public panic?'

'I'm allocating forty more officers to the incident room, to work under Detective Inspector Birmingham. I can assure you that, whatever the Senior Investigating Officer on the case wants, she will get. I've no further comment,' Stanley stated, opening his arms to give the impression of doing the precise opposite.

The questions started up again, but Stanley had turned to Jo. 'We'll talk further in my car,' he told her. 'Find the killer and I'll give you whatever you want.'

48

The state Merc was parked in the bus lane outside the prison, hazards on. After arguing with the garda on Stanley's driving detail that there was no way her team was going to drive behind them so Stanley could keep moving towards the private Lear jet, Jo climbed into the back seat.

Stanley was already there, going through the morning's papers. Gerry was in the front passenger seat, his thumb jerking madly across the keyboard of his BlackBerry. He nodded at the driver, who stepped out of the car.

'Do that to me again, and I won't be responsible,' Jo said as soon as she'd the door closed behind her. 'You know as well as I do we are not in the middle of a gangland turf war!'

Stanley's legs were crossed, and a soft leather shoe pointed towards Jo. She could just about see the sole – and reckoned from the light scuffing that, before today, it had only ever traversed expensive wool carpets.

She leaned towards him. 'The killer we're looking for is working alone, and not motivated by the money to be made from the drug trade. He's got a biblical take on revenge, and he knows exactly what he's doing. These are not – I repeat, *not* – gangland killings.'

Stanley sighed. 'That's not how we're going to play this. The party's come under enough criticism for bailing the Roman

Catholic Church out financially on the compensation for sex abuse victims deal. I will not have the public whipped into a frenzy by talk of a religious maniac until you find him.'

Jo stared at him in disbelief. 'Let me guess. The youngest in a house full of sisters, right? Wait, don't tell me . . . Mithered by your mother, alcoholic father – how am I doing so far?'

Stanley didn't answer.

'Married a woman who only speaks when she's talking about you and insists that she, and not your housekeeper, should be the one to iron your socks?'

Stanley looked unsettled.

'I'm right, aren't I?' Jo said. 'I'd go so far as to suggest the last time you had sex with your wife was more than ten years ago. But there's a blonde behind the scenes somewhere . . .'

'Your husband's up for promotion, isn't he?' Stanley said, turning on Jo.

'Ex-husband.'

'Still, matters of the heart are never clear-cut, are they?' he said. 'You got kids? Think they'll forgive you if Daddy is transferred to the back of beyond because of you?'

'Is that a bloody threat?' Jo said, looking straight at him. 'That is a bloody threat! Gerry, I want that logged for Labour Court hearing . . .'

Gerry shifted uncomfortably.

'Do you really think anyone will give a flying fuck?' Stanley continued. 'People are losing their jobs left, right and centre, taking pay cuts, having their homes repossessed. Do you think anyone will listen to poor little Ms Job For Life complaining her ex-husband has to move station?'

Jo reached for the door handle.

'Wait,' he said, clasping her wrist.

She stared at his hand.

'You badly want rape victims protected in court, right? Well, I'll recommend it – on one condition.'

In the front of the car, Gerry stiffened. He knew what was coming.

'You find the killer, and stick to my line until he's brought to justice.'

Jo thought about it for a few seconds. 'I need the NSU file on Anto Crawley. That's why I'm here. The team from NBCI won't hand it over. They say it's life and death for the touts. I say people are dying anyway.'

'You'll have it by this afternoon. But I need you to bring someone in. I don't care if he was arranging flowers in the church at the time of the killings – bring him in and let the papers know you're questioning him. That way you get both of us off the hook.'

Jo opened her mouth to protest.

'I'm not asking you to lock him up for good. You can release him again later, and no harm will be done. Justice must be seen to be done, Detective Inspector, as must the pursuit of justice.'

He reached out his hand to shake hers. Reluctantly, Jo took it.

'One other thing,' she said, before getting out. 'Your favourite artist of all time would be Constable, am I right?'

He frowned. 'Turner,' he answered.

On the pavement next to the Merc, Sexton and Foxy were waiting.

'This afternoon, when I give the word, and not before, we are going to make our first arrest,' Jo said.

When she told them the name, they burst out laughing.

49

Before leaving the prison grounds, Jo told Foxy and Sexton the jobs she wanted actioned. Foxy was to have any working girls who'd had warnings about soliciting in the last year brought into the station; Sexton was to bring Stuart Ball's mother in so Jo could question her herself. After hailing the team a cab, she commandeered Sexton's Beemer to drive to Crumlin Hospital.

'Don't worry, I'll take care of it,' she told him.

He groaned as she revved up.

'Relax,' Jo said, bunny-hopping away – a trick she'd perfected when Dan was teaching her to drive.

According to the girl on the administration desk in the hospital, Katie Freeman was on the second floor. Jo spotted Ryan Freeman as soon as she pressed the release button to the ward. He was standing midway down a narrow corridor painted with Disney cartoon characters, talking to a doctor in a white coat. The conversation with the doc ended before Jo reached him, but he stayed in the same position, apparently lost in thought.

'What the hell . . .?' he began when he saw her.

Jo stopped and gave him a weary look.

'Harassing sick children now, are you?' Ryan demanded. 'Not mine, you're not. Nurse?'

A nurse poked her head around the nurses' station then began making her way towards them.

'The easy way, or the hard way?' Jo asked, leaning in close to him. 'The former means I go into Katie's cubicle and get a sense of what I am dealing with. You never know – maybe, just maybe, it will help.

'The alternative is actually quite easy for me but hard on you. I do things by the book, go and get my warrant for your arrest, and the case makes headline news. How long do you think you can keep what happened to Katie quiet then? Because despite how it looks, I don't think you had anything to do with the killings.' She paused. 'I'm not sure anybody reading about it will agree with me, though.'

'What's going on here?' the nurse asked.

Jo waited.

'Nothing,' Ryan said, looking at the floor. 'I'm sorry to have bothered you.'

'I saw you on TV this morning in connection with those killings, didn't I?' the nurse asked Jo. 'You're a garda. You can't come in here without authorization.'

'She's family,' Ryan said.

The nurse looked unconvinced but was distracted by some children in pyjamas whom she shooed back into the play-room at the far end of the corridor.

'I'm warning you,' Ryan said, leading Jo into Katie's room. 'If you upset her in any way . . .'

A sick toddler was lying in a cot on the right-hand side of the room. Jo took a deep breath. She'd always found visits to hospital wards a reality check – how fragile things were; how easily it could all be taken away; how day-to-day problems became trifling when compared with what some people were going through. But a kids' ward, that was different. How would you cope if that kind of thing came to the door? And why shouldn't it come to your door, as against anybody else's? Like most people, she tried not to think about it – until days like this, when it was rammed home.

'Darling,' Ryan said, heading to the bed at the window where Katie was sitting listlessly. 'This is a lady I work with.'

Katie didn't look up.

Jo's face softened as she looked over his shoulder. Katie's fair hair was in two plaits and wisps had escaped around her hairline. She had on a pink cardigan, with the big-stitch look of having been knitted by a granny, over a pair of Hannah Montana pyjamas.

Even a cursory glance at Katie told Jo that the girl was going through a lot. There was something seriously wrong with the way her eyes moved, as if the lights had gone out behind them.

She suddenly felt overwhelmed with sadness. If somebody did that to your kid, you'd want to hurt them – of course you would. Ryan Freeman could be their killer: he knew the law, and he knew the victims, who must have known him through his reputation; and he had more motive than anyone else, given his daughter's condition. But Mac had ticked all the right boxes too, Jo realized. And could Ryan really have murdered five people in cold blood? She didn't think so. There was something about the way he was fumbling for a tissue to wipe a string of drool that was running from the corner of Katie's mouth that told her that such murders required way too much planning for a man as shattered as he seemed to be.

'You may well just be the prettiest little girl I have ever seen,' Jo said, sitting on the edge of the bed and putting her hand over Katie's. 'You know, when I was younger, I was in hospital too. I lost my dad. Nobody blamed me, but I blamed me. I wished so hard I could go blind that I used to keep my eyes closed for days on end. It didn't make any difference, though; in the end, I realized how sad it would make my dad up in heaven if he thought I couldn't see, so I opened them.'

Katie glanced over to her dad.

'Who hurt you, my darling?' Jo asked. 'Did somebody tell you they would hurt the people you love if you said anything? But your dad and mum are safe. Nobody can touch them. All they want is for you to get better, do you understand?'

Tears began to spill from Katie's eyes.

Ryan put a hand on Jo's shoulder, warning her she'd gone far enough.

Jo reached into her bag and pulled out a jacket of photographs. She pulled one out and held it to Katie. It showed Anto Crawley's mugshot. 'Him?' she asked. 'Was he there?'

Ryan took a step and reached for the photos but dropped his hand when Katie responded with a stiff nod.

Jo held up a picture of Rita Nulty – her mugshot.

Katie fanned her fingers in front of her face and looked through them at Jo. She started to shake.

Jo took this as a yes too. Ryan sat down on a chair as if his legs had gone weak. The next photo of Stuart Ball – taken from a line-up – made Katie's fingers close tight together.

'What about him?' Jo asked, taking Katie's hands down gently and showing her a picture of Father Reg.

No reaction.

'This is the last one.' Jo held up Mac's picture.

Again nothing.

It didn't matter. Jo hadn't expected to find either Mac or Father Reg on site.

'You see, we know who they are, which means they can no longer hurt you,' she told Katie. 'Nothing will happen because of anything you say – do you understand, sweetheart? The only thing that matters now is that you get better.'

But Katie was still shaking. Jo leaned towards her. 'Somebody else was there, weren't they?'

Katie opened her mouth to say something – and then gagged, doubling up on the bed and choking in distress.

'What's going on here?' Angie demanded, appearing in the doorway.

50

'How dare you! What the hell do you think you're doing? You have absolutely no right to be here!' Angie Freeman shouted.

They were outside Katie's room in the ward corridor, and Jo was glad of the chance to stare so she could take Angie in properly and work out what it was about her that didn't feel right. She was very pretty, in a Melinda Messenger kind of way – big teeth, big hair, and big boobs on a small, stick-like frame.

Jo put her as mid-forties, with signs of resistance – she had that puckered-hem collagen look going on around her top lip, and too much concealer under her eyes was making her blusher look like stripes of war paint.

'This isn't ending here,' she continued. 'I want the name of your superior officer.'

Jo noticed a slight tremble in Angie's hand as she took a pink mobile out of her WAG-style glam handbag and tried to turn it on. She was wearing skinny white denims, a studded, big-buckled belt and high, shiny, white faux-crocodile-skin ankle boots that must have cost at least three figures, and possibly four.

'I'm also going to complain to the registrar! And if Katie has suffered any setback because of this, I'm going to sue the Minister for Justice . . .'

Jo frowned. 'Do you always blame other people when things go wrong?'

Angie blinked. 'Are you out of your fucking mind? Have you any idea what I am going through in all this?' She walked over to a stack of plastic chairs shoved against the wall, lifted the top one down and sank into it, spent.

Jo had figured out what it was about Angie that just didn't fit. She got the same irrational feeling any time she saw a drop-dead gorgeous man holding hands with a girl in glasses, an Alice band and socks under her sandals. It wasn't fair, but it was life. Angie was way too glamorous for Ryan Freeman. He came across as all square edges – like a union official. He was clever, sure, but his accent was from the wrong part of town, and his clothes never quite fit. Jo would have brought them together as a couple if he'd had loads of money, or a great job, but he didn't have either of these. He was a hack writing about the kind of people Jo suspected Angie looked down her nose at.

Jo sat down too. 'Here's what I'm thinking,' she said. 'Katie's abduction happened a month ago, but your high-lights are no more than a couple of days old.'

Angie looked at her disbelievingly.

'Don't get me wrong,' Jo said. 'I'm not going to judge you for having your hair done. But I've seen what happens to people when someone they love is hurt or killed. Personal appearance is one of the first things to go after a trauma. What this tells me is that either you know more than you've let on about what happened to Katie. Or you don't care.' Now Jo was looking at her too. 'Personally, I'm leaning towards the former.'

'I know your sort,' Angie hissed. 'Career first, kids last. Just because I don't work, you think I should be wearing a tracksuit with gravy splashes on my tits. Some of us take a bit of pride in our appearance. That doesn't make me a bad mother.'

'Let's go through this together, shall we?' Jo said, thinking back to what Sexton had told her late the night before. 'You're filmed on a CCTV camera outside your daughter's school rowing with the country's most well-known drug baron. You drive off, and Katie is taken from school by the person you argued with. Later, Katie is released untouched. The way I see it, the only way that could have happened is if you contacted your friend Anto Crawley to say sorry. Is that why he let her go?'

'You stupid bitch! You call what happened to her untouched? She can't speak, for Christ's sake! Do you know what selective mutism is? It's a rare psychological disorder caused by extreme anxiety contributing to chronic depression. She's nine years old!' Angie put her face in her hands. 'I was trying to protect her by telling Anto Crawley what Ryan was writing about to keep him away from Katie. He'd sent his scumbags to my home and threatened to hurt her if I didn't. What was I supposed to do? What would you have done?

'I thought, if I can just get Ryan to stop writing about Dublin criminal gangs, the nightmare would end. I kept telling him, it's too dangerous, get out, nobody cares! What difference does any of it make? The laws don't change. The politicians don't resign. The gangsters get rich, get out of prison, go back to their villas in Marbella. I said to him, everyone is on the take. You can't change that. We have a child. Think of her! The newspaper won't protect you. They argue over your expenses bill for this, your expenses bill for that. They don't care about the cost to you, to us, to Katie.'

'But your insurance policy didn't work like that, did it?' Jo asked.

Angie gave a sort of sob. 'Crawley wanted more. He wanted the names of Ryan's sources. Crawley was waiting for me at Katie's school. I told him I'd tried to get the names, begged him to give me more time, but he wouldn't listen. I drove away thinking he'd follow. I thought that would get him away from Katie. Instead he took her. Do you have any idea what that was like for me?'

Jo leaned back. 'So why didn't you say something? All that time she was gone, you didn't think to yourself, I'd better tell the police that Anto Crawley's involved in this, to help them find Katie. You must have thought it possible he would harm her – kill her even?'

'I was up the walls! But I still thought that this was between me and Crawley, and that if I told the police, he would harm Katie.'

'And you needed to keep in with Crawley, didn't you? Because, without him, who'd look after your cocaine habit?'

Angie's jaw fell open in shock, and she touched her nose self-consciously.

Jo leaned towards her. 'You were there, weren't you? Is that why Katie won't talk? She's protecting you. Isn't she?'

51

Lunchtime. Jenny Friar had just slammed the phone on Jo's desk down as Jo arrived back in the office. Friar's NBCI colleagues, Dave Black and Frank Waters, were standing on either side of her, looking uncomfortable.

'That it?' Jo asked, reaching for the file on her desk.

Friar clamped her two hands over the paperwork. 'First, I want an assurance that you won't go off half-cocked,' she said.

'Request denied,' Jo said, walking around to her chair. 'As Senior Investigating Officer on this case, I reserve the right to explode if the mood takes me.'

'Have you any idea what you're dealing with here?' Friar asked, her hands still on the papers.

'Yes, yes,' Jo said. 'Life and death, the importance of protecting sources, yada yada. Now, I've got a killer to catch and, while you may consider obstructing me your priority, my murder investigation takes precedent. I want the name of the cop who was handling Anto Crawley, and you're the only person left in my way.'

'It's not going to make a blind bit of difference to the investigation,' Friar argued.

'I'll be the judge of that, thank you very much.'

'I don't see why you need to find out who Anto Crawley was feeding information to,' Friar said.

'Anto Crawley was bringing drugs into the country, drugs that we intercepted but which wound up back in one of our victim's crime scenes, strongly suggesting he was briefing someone in here,' Jo answered, sitting at her desk. 'The garda handling him has a case to answer.'

'But if the name gets out, all our sources will stop talking. The handler's life could be in danger,' Friar said.

Jo put her hand on the paperwork. 'I promise not to tell.'

Putting her feet up on the corner of her desk, she raised the document to read it, and scanned through. It was called a Suspect History Antecedent form and was only to be completed in respect of persons believed to be involved in serious crime. This meant it contained the kind of information that would never have seen the light of day in a court of law, which, in Jo's opinion, meant it might actually be useful.

CRIME ORDINARY: Yes
SUBVERSIVE: No
1. **FULL NAME:** Anto Crawley
   DATE & PLACE OF BIRTH: 13/6/70 or 13/6/71, Dublin
   ALIAS & NICKNAMES: 'Anto'; 'Mr Bad'
   DCR NO.: 1232/08
2. **DESCRIPTION:**
   HEIGHT: 5'10" **BUILD:** Broad/fit **WEIGHT:** 11 stone
   EYES: Blue **HAIR:** Sandy **COMPLEXION:** Fair
   ACCENT: Dublin **GENERAL APPEARANCE:** Casual
   GARDA PHOTO: Attached
   FAMILY PHOTO: Attached
   DISTINGUISHING FEATURES (include scars,

tattoos, physical disabilities): Tattoo 'RIP' on right
forearm, along with names of deceased Skid
lieutenants – Frank, Johnno, Smurf (see appendix
for biogs)
**TYPE OF DRESS SUBJECT NORMALLY
WEARS:** Leather jacket, hoodie, jeans, T-shirt,
trainers, trucker cap.

3. **PREVIOUS ADDRESSES:** Crumlin, Rialto (see appendix)
   HOME ADDRESS: Oliver Bond
   COMMENTS RE. SURVEILLANCE ON ABOVE:
   SDU carried out surveillance on his flat.
4. **HABITS & HOBBIES:** Pitbulls, pigeons
5. **HOTELS, CLUBS, PUBS, CAFES & SHOPS FRE-
   QUENTED BY SUBJECT:** Liberties, Smithfield
6. **WEAKNESSES** (drink, drugs, gambling, women, homo-
   sexual): Likes to watch his girlfriend with othe men,
   or have her describe it in detail – cf phone recordings.
7. **HEALTH:** Treated for irritable bowel syndrome. Part
   of colon removed.
8. **SUBJECT'S DOCTOR:** Varies
   DENTIST: Varies
   CHEMIST: Varies
   OPTICIAN: Varies

Jo reached for a pencil and chewed the top, speed-reading
the rest of the headings for the one she needed to find, planning to study the answers in depth later.

9. **ASSOCIATES** (names, DCR nos, extent of criminal
   involvement and relationship with subject):
10. **MODUS OPERANDI** (include days and times of
    particular activity):

11. GARDAÍ TO WHOM SUBJECT IS KNOWN
    PERSONALLY/GARDAÍ WHO PREVIOUSLY
    CHARGED SUBJECT/GARDAÍ WHO INTER-
    ROGATED SUBJECT:

Jo was annoyed to see black lines blocking the answers to
this information. She read on:

12. SUBJECT'S SOLICITOR & COUNSEL:
13. DETAILS OF ALLEGATIONS AGAINST GARDAÍ
    MADE BY SUBJECT:
14. PREVIOUS CONVICTIONS (Last three and others if
    pertinent):
15. ACQUITTALS AND GROUNDS FOR SAME, IF
    RELEVANT:
16. TELEPHONE NUMBERS (inc. telephones to which
    subject has access):
17. VEHICLES TO WHICH SUBJECT HAS ACCESS
    (Reg. no., colour, make, type; owned or used;
    mobile/radio or C/B):
18. CAR-HIRE FIRMS (used by subject):
19. BOATS TO WHICH SUBJECT HAS ACCESS OR
    OWNS:
20. AIRCRAFT TO WHICH SUBJECT HAS ACCESS OR
    OWNS:
21. INFORMATION AVAILABLE AS TO OTHER
    MODES OF TRAVEL:
22. OTHER PLACES HERE OR ABROAD
    FREQUENTED BY SUBJECT:
23. PRIVATE GARAGES TO WHICH SUBJECT HAS
    ACCESS:
24. GARAGES AT WHICH SUBJECT NORMALLY

PURCHASES PETROL OR HAS VEHICLE MAIN-
TAINED:
25. GARAGES TO WHICH ASSOCIATES HAVE ACCESS:
26. DRIVING LICENCE NO.; SEAMAN'S BOOK NO.;
SOCIAL SECURITY NO.; PASSPORT NO.;
EXCHANGE, TIME & DATE OF ATTENDANCE;
PHOTOGRAPH REFERENCE NO.; BANK
ACCOUNT/CREDIT CARD; BANKER'S CARD/
BUILDING SOCIETY PASSBOOK NO.; FOREIGN
BANK ACCOUNT:
27. SPECIMEN HANDWRITING (where available):
28. FIREARMS CERTIFICATES HELD BY SUBJECT:
29. RELATIVES (include full name, maiden name, address,
DOB, occupation, place of employment and attitude
towards criminal activities of subject):
30. GIRLFRIEND/BOYFRIEND:
31. EMPLOYERS (current and past):
32. QUALIFICATIONS OF SUBJECT (skills, education,
etc.):

The last question was the one she was most interested in,
and it made her put her feet back on the floor.

33. HANDLER:

Jo looked up to Friar, who was standing over her. The space
where the answer should be also had a black bar running
over the type. 'What the hell is this?' Jo put a finger over the
bar, then looked up accusingly. 'The ink is still bloody wet!'
  Friar said nothing.
  Jo tapped the sheet. 'Whose name have you blocked out?'
  'I can't tell you,' Friar said.

Jo reached for the phone. 'You can explain why to Blaise Stanley. I don't remember him appointing you chief censor.'

'She won't need to . . .' a voice said in the doorway.

Jo didn't need to look up to identify the speaker.

'It's me,' Dan said. 'Anto Crawley was my agent.'

52

Jo slumped back.

'You happy now?' Dan asked, striding over. 'You know how many people will have seen that file, just to indulge you? Once word gets out that Crawley was working for us, everybody will become suspect. All that bloody surveillance, all that overtime – wasted. I've got two undercover officers on the ground monitoring a Skids consignment due in the next week – heroin and coke with a street value of €50 million. Those men will have to be recalled in case they get their heads blown off!'

He looked at Friar and gave a stiff nod in the direction of the door. Looking none too pleased, she took the hint and headed out, Black and Waters following hard on her heels.

Dan sighed, reached for a chair and positioned it directly in front of her desk.

Jo leaned forwards. 'You gave the country's biggest drug dealer carte blanche to operate with impunity – in return for what?' she asked.

'Don't give me that shite! You know as well as I do that the only people with information worth trading are criminals,' Dan blasted back.

'Oh, I understand perfectly,' Jo said. 'Your informant Anto Crawley tips you off about what drug deals are going down, and when. You extend the long arm of the law as nec-essary. It's a win-win. He gets rid of the competition, sometimes sacrifices some of his own who've got a bit too ambitious, builds up his slice of market share, and you get promoted for all the drug seizures that are put down to you. What I don't quite get is what's in it for the parents of the kids dying out there from heroin rubberstamped by our bloody Customs!'

Dan straightened his tie. 'When you can come up with an alternative, let me know.'

'Why didn't you tell me?' she asked, turning to look at him properly.

'Maybe I knew you'd react like this,' he said.

'But what about Mac? The Skids were paying him to get them off charges. How did that work? If Mac was being paid, were you? I have noticed you have a nice new wardrobe, and what was that I heard about your plans to buy a new place?'

Dan slammed his hand hard on the table. 'Now you're taking the piss . . .'

Jo stared at him.

He dragged his hands through his hair and sighed. 'Crawley didn't have carte blanche, that must be why they recruited Mac. I had no idea he was on the take. If I had . . .'

'What about Ryan Freeman's little girl, Katie? Did you know Crawley had abducted her?'

Dan rubbed his jaw. 'Not until recently, no.'

'Only there was another kid hurt by someone connected to this station, and you managed to keep that to yourself too.'

'What are you raving about now?'

'That kid who died on Mac's watch. Last night, you said

that Mac had come to you to 'fess up.' She paused. Dan said nothing. 'Do you even know his name, Dan? It was Jimmy Wren. For future reference.'

Dan turned his palms up on his thighs. 'Look, Crawley told me that Ryan Freeman's wife had a bit of a problem and was visiting one of his dealers. So I thought, why look a gift horse in the mouth? So I asked him to try and get her to get her hands on Freeman's contacts book. I wanted to find out who was leaking stories to him from the station. If I'd had any idea Crawley would go to those lengths, I'd never have –'

'Did you ever find out what happened?'

Dan shook his head.

'Katie Freeman is in hospital because her mother couldn't come up with that book. Everyone associated with her is dead. Maybe you should think long and hard about exactly the calibre of criminal you're dealing with in future.' Jo stood up. 'Full of secrets, aren't you? There have been five bloody victims, Dan. How many more would it have taken for you to tell me, just as a matter of interest?'

'I had nothing to add to your investigation!' Dan roared. 'I've got kids too, remember? If anything happened to either of them, I'd –'

'Either, or just one of them?' Jo asked, pulling her coat on. 'You didn't want me to have Harry, remember?'

Dan closed his eyes. 'No, I didn't want any kid of mine so embarrassed by the sad old fart collecting him or the other kids calling me his granddad. I was wrong. I love Harry.'

Jo took a breath and reached for her keys and phone. 'Right,' she said.

'Where are you going?' Dan asked, as she pulled out the door.

'To interview Stuart Ball's mother.' She clicked her fingers like she'd just remembered something. 'Oh yeah, and after that I'm going to talk to the man we brought in for questioning today, purely to keep the papers off your boss, the minister's, back, who, by astounding coincidence, happens to be another of your moles. Do you think I don't know that Merrigan's been briefing you on my every move behind my back? You can release the details, if you like. I was thinking something along the lines of: "A 52-year-old male is currently helping gardaí with their enquiries. When gardaí called to his home, he agreed to present voluntarily at the station rather than risk arrest." Keep his name to yourself, though. We don't want any more bad press, do we?'

53

Sad as it was to see Stuart Ball's mother still in the throes of overwhelming grief, Jo was a lot more comfortable in her company than she had been with Rita Nulty's mother, who seemed more concerned about herself than with catching her daughter's killer. In the two minutes since introducing herself to Valerie Ball in the interview room, Jo had been handed Stuart's laminated mass card, asked to listen to Stuart's voice on a saved message on Valerie's mobile and shown a hologram of his face hanging from a gold disc on a chain around her neck. Tears flowed freely down her face.

Jo passed over a tissue, suspecting that the scaly skin on the interviewee's hands was caused by over-exposure to water and cleaning agents over the years.

Valerie Ball was younger than Rita Nulty's mother too. She was dressed in jeans and a sweater, sported trainers on her feet, and her thick, russet hair was cut in a no-nonsense style.

'There's a tradition in Connemara, where I'm from,' she began, blowing her nose. 'Mourn for a month, and then get on with your life. But the second I saw my baby on the slab, I knew that I'd never be able to feel good about anything again.' She started to cry again.

Jo patted her on her back. 'You mustn't think like that.

You're still in shock, my love. I'll organize some tea, with lots of sugar.'

Valerie sighed heavily. 'I'm sorry. Please, don't worry about tea. Just ask me what you need to. I want you to catch the bastard that did this, and not waste any more time. A serial killer, I read. That means more mothers are going to have to go through this.'

Jo sat down and reached across the table for Valerie's hands. 'Let's start with some pictures, to see if you recognize them for me.' She held up a picture of Anto Crawley.

Valerie sighed again, heavily, then sniffed. 'That's the bastard my boy owed money to. Sent his cronies to my house looking for money, and called a couple of times himself. Anto Crawley thinks he is somebody, or did, before ... I paid him whenever I could, got loans off the credit union. Then, a couple of weeks before Stu died, the amount shot up to €50,000. How was I supposed to get that kind of money? I'd have had to sell my home. I'd have done it, 'course I would, but then out of the blue Stu told me it was sorted. Said he owed nothing, but wouldn't tell me what had happened. I asked him did he kill someone for them ... How do you write off €50,000?'

She looked at Jo guiltily. 'I'd tried everything to get him off drugs. Nothing worked. Got him on a methadone programme – that was just an excuse to pump more poison into his system ... Did the tough-love thing – put him out, till he told me he'd been selling himself on the street. What would you do? 'Course I took him back in. He was my boy.' She shook her head and sniffed. 'Even tried locking him in his room once, with the help of my neighbours. But he threatened to kill himself. I couldn't take the chance. Stu was all I'd got. I got pregnant when I was fifteen, my family turfed me out, it was just me and him for so long. Even in the worst of it, he was a good boy, always looked after me. Always made sure I had enough, did more for me in his short life than my parents ever did. Twenty-four years old, that's all he was when he died – twenty-four!'

She broke down again.

Jo walked around the desk, knelt down and handed her Rita Nulty's picture.

The blood drained from Valerie's face, 'She's the reason my boy's dead in the grave. She was Stuart's girlfriend years ago, the one who got him on the drugs in the first place. She'd have sold her own mother, that one. He'd been calling her again, I found out.

'My bill was through the roof,' Valerie continued. 'It was through the roof this month. I got it itemized; this mobile kept coming up. I rang the number and recognized her voice the second she answered . . . That's why he's dead, isn't it? That bitch as good as killed him, just like I always told him she would! Said it to her face too when she tried to gatecrash his funeral.'

Jo pulled Father Reg's picture from the bottom of the bundle.

Valerie's face hardened. 'Dirty bastard. I caught him in my house once.' She covered her face and started to cry again. 'Stu'd have done anything for money for drugs.'

Jo showed her Katie's picture. 'Who's that?' Valerie asked, confused. 'Is she dead too? She's only a kid, poor mite!'

'No, she's still alive,' Jo said.

Jo produced the last of her images – one of Mac. He was in the foreground of a group shot which had been pinned to the staff noticeboard a few months back after a big trial had resulted in a conviction and the officers attached to the investigation celebrated in the pub. Jo pointed out Mac from the others. He was carrying a tray of pints. Valerie shook her head. 'Never saw him before.'

Valerie's finger moved to a face behind Mac and tapped. 'But this one called to my flat the day Stu died. I was on my way to work. I didn't like his attitude. He said he wanted to talk to Stu about something that happened to a little girl he knew personally. He said that he was a copper. Thought that kind of thing wasn't allowed – conflict of interest, isn't it? I told him to call back later when I was finished work. Thought I'd seen him off. Stu was still in bed! I couldn't stay around, I'd have been late. But when I got home, my house had been turned over and Stu was gone.'

54

It was 4 p.m., and Jo was in her car, speeding towards Sexton's home.

She was absolutely furious with herself. She didn't deserve a badge, let alone the chance to head up an investigation. She covered her mouth as she thought of all the warning signs she'd ignored, which, when put together, were so bloody obvious. She should have realized the instant she'd seen him showing Freeman around Anto Crawley's crime scene what he was up to. So Sexton had been to visit Stuart Ball on the day he died, had he? And was driving around in a car worth several years' wages. Maybe Katie was in danger even now? Jo hit the accelerator and overtook a car on two continuous white lines. Sexton had been one step ahead of them all the time. Now she knew why.

'Sexton's wife . . .' Foxy said, as Jo pulled back on to the right side of the road.

Jo glanced over. He was holding the bottom of the passenger seat with his right hand and had hooked his left into the overhead handle. Jo had been so lost in thought, she'd forgotten he was there.

'Suicide,' Jo answered.

'Do you remember the incident at the funeral?' Foxy asked quietly.

Jo nodded. The same memory had struck her the second Valerie Ball had identified him. Sexton had punched the parish priest before Maura was even in the ground for announcing during the ceremony that he'd like to see a return to the old days, when suicide victims were not allowed to be buried in consecrated ground, because at least it had some chance of discouraging others. Jo had known the killer would have a big gripe with the church for some personal reason – and here it was.

'What was his wife's name again?' Foxy asked.

'Maura,' Jo said, slamming in the clutch, hitting the indicator and guiding the car into the kerb as she reached for the handbrake.

'What?' Foxy said.

Jo flicked the visor down and pulled the street map free. She flicked the fold open on the north inner city and traced her finger along some of the streets. 'Dear God,' she said, flinging the map into Foxy's lap and glancing into the wing mirror before taking off again. 'The streets where the victims were found form the letter M for Maura, at least they will when the last body is found in East Wall. I don't think we'll find Sexton at home – he needs to leave one last body to form the last leg of the letter.'

'Let me see,' said Foxy, studying the map. 'In the O2?'

Jo nodded. 'That's what I was thinking.'

Foxy reached for the radio. 'Maura was buried in Deansgrange. I'll dispatch a couple of the lads to the grave, see if there's any signs of disturbance.'

Jo stretched across and blocked him with her arm. 'Sexton could pick up the call,' she reminded him. 'Phones only.'

They were still negotiating traffic when Dan rang Foxy, who relayed each sentence, covering the mouthpiece in between.

'The O2 is all clear, Jo,' he said, pausing to listen. He drew a breath, and held the phone on his lap. 'Still no sign of Sexton, and his phone's off.'

Jo frowned.

Foxy put the phone back to his ear. He grunted, and hung up. 'Dan wants us back there now, Jo.'

'Fuck that,' Jo said. 'I'm going to Sexton's home.'

'You can't go in there without a warrant. Anything you get without one will be inadmissible.'

'Life always takes first priority, remember?'

'Not when we don't have any missing-persons reports to justify a search.'

'Spare me,' Jo said, pulling up. 'Station's a ten-minute walk from here.'

'I'm not leaving you.' Foxy folded his arms obstinately.

Jo thought for a few seconds. 'Why don't you call Dan and tell him we're on our way back? We don't have to mention we're going via Sexton's. Okay?'

Foxy grunted, and did as he was told.

Jo pulled out again into the traffic.

'I say the name Gavin Sexton to you, what's the first thing you think of?' she asked.

'The job,' Foxy said. 'Someone who lives and breathes the job.'

'That's what I was afraid you were going to say,' Jo said.

'What do you mean?'

'I mean, in all the time I've known him, I've never known him not to call in even when he's on holiday – that's when he takes his holidays.'

'He went to Old Trafford a couple of years ago.'

'So he supports Man United – so do half of all Irish males. I don't know anything about his private life, though. Do you?'

'It's not easy, to get over something like that,' Foxy said. 'Finding yourself suddenly alone, I mean. It's hard.'

'I know, Foxy, I know,' Jo said, pulling up outside a bookie's on Dorset Street. Sexton lived in the flat above it.

'You know, he never once asked me in,' she said as they approached Sexton's door, at the side of the shopfront. 'All those times I dropped him home, or he kipped in my house, he never so much as offered me a cuppa.'

After picking up a key from the manager of the Indian restaurant next door, whom she knew was leasing the place, Jo opened the door to a narrow set of stairs.

'Stairs?' Foxy said, reading her mind.

Access to and transport from off-street parking without being noticed would have been difficult, next to impossible even, especially if Sexton was trying to haul anything life-sized in or out.

Jo's eyes travelled the skirting for any stains. Nothing. She climbed the stairs and rapped the door then, realizing it had been left unlocked, pushed it open.

The place was the kind of bedsit that gets called a studio flat in a classified. It was sparsely furnished: an armchair facing a TV, a computer on the dinner table. It all looked desperate for a woman's touch. There wasn't even a carpet on the floor.

'Christ, it's a hovel,' Foxy said. 'I wouldn't leave my dog here for the night.'

'Wouldn't the dust rising from the concrete play havoc with your lungs?' Foxy asked.

'Or sinuses,' Jo replied, glancing at the two doors on the back wall and crossing the room.

'Do you remember how Maura died?' she asked Foxy

over her shoulder as she pushed the first door open. It led to a toilet. 'With a vacuum-cleaner cord, wasn't it?'

The second door led into the bedroom. Jo headed to a bedside locker and started going through the drawers.

'You think that's why he's got no carpet?' Foxy asked.

Jo pulled out a credit-card receipt and held it out to Foxy. It was dated 9 p.m. the previous night and was from an off licence, showing the purchase of a bottle of red wine.

'Sexton brought one round to my house last night, but there was one in Mac's bin too.'

Foxy nodded. 'I know the place. It's right beside the IFSC. Where Mac lived.'

'And died,' Jo said. The receipt put Sexton at the right time and place for Mac's murder. It was all the proof she needed to get a warrant for his arrest.

55

Sexton slid the glass door open and stepped inside the porch, knocking gently on the front door. He never rang the bell when he called to the Freemans', in case Katie was sleeping.

Stepping back into the tarmac driveway, he lifted the flap of his jacket, eyeing the box he had tucked under his arm critically before readjusting it to make sure it was well hidden. He expected Katie would already have Barbie in her showjumping costume, but he hadn't had time to look for something original – he was up the walls with work on the investigation. Still, it was better than arriving with his hands empty. And it was his way of letting Ryan and Angie know that Katie would always come first with him, no matter what either, or both of them, turned out to be mixed up in.

He opened a couple of the buttons on his shirt and pushed his sleeves up. He'd only come because Ryan had texted him it was urgent. Sexton had tried phoning him back to tell him there was no way he could walk off the job, not with Mac's body having been found in the early hours of this morning, but Ryan hadn't answered. After failing to get any answer from Angie's mobile, or their landline either, he'd stood up from his desk in the incident room and announced that he was heading to the newsagent's across the road to grab a sandwich. Then he'd switched his phone off and hopped into his car to speed over.

He looked over both shoulders, checking the street both ways, nervously. It was still only mid-afternoon, and he knew from having switched his phone on briefly to check his messages that nobody was looking for him, yet he was jumpy as fuck. He hadn't had a wink's sleep last night after seeing Mac strung up like that. It reminded him of how he'd found Maura, and that opened up a whole other can of worms, which had required a lot of high-percentage alcohol to close again. Still, if Jo Birmingham found out he was here, there'd be no excuses. And she could stop here at any stage, given their conversation last night. Now she knew about what had happened to Katie Freeman, it was only a matter of time before she called.

In front of him, the door creaked half open. A man in his late twenties peered back at him through the gap. He had a shaved head and a familiar face, but Sexton couldn't place him or see the rest of him from the neck down. 'All right?' he asked him. 'Ryan home?'

The man shook his head and went to close the door.

Sexton put his hand flat on it and held the door open. 'I'm not selling anything, mate. I'm here because Ryan told me to come around.' When the man still didn't budge, he felt his heart speed up. 'What about Angie?' he asked. 'Is she here?'

'No.'

Sexton leaned back and placed a hand on the bonnet of Angie's car, which was parked in the drive directly behind him, not taking his eyes off the man. It was still warm.

'You sure?' he asked, springing forwards with his arm extended so that the ball of his hand knocked the door straight into the man. The man stumbled back. Sexton put one hand around his throat and pushed him up against the hall wall inside. The Barbie box fell to the ground.

The man held his two arms up in surrender. He was barefoot and wearing an overwashed Metallica T-shirt and jeans.

'Who are you?' Sexton demanded. Pulling his wallet out of his jacket pocket, he let one half fall open to reveal his ID.

'Relax, mate, I'm Angie's brother,' the man replied. 'I'm just housesitting for them till they get back. They're on a visit to the hospital.'

Sexton heard a whimper from upstairs. He tightened his grip. 'Who's that then?' he asked.

'Their dog,' the man answered calmly.

Sexton released his hold. Taking another couple of steps into the house and down the hall, he picked up the landline and dialled Ryan's number, not taking his eyes off the guy. A phone in the sitting room rang.

The man met Sexton's stare. 'He'll have forgotten it, that's all,' he said.

Sexton pushed the door to the sitting room open to get the phone and saw Cassie lying motionless on her side. He pushed past the man, who'd moved to the doorway, grabbed the banisters and took the stairs two at a time.

There was no mistaking the sound when he got to the top. It was someone crying. Turning right, he pushed open the bedroom door. Ryan and Angie were bound and gagged and lying on their backs on the floor, eyes frantic.

56

Am I in a coffin? Sexton asked himself. He was in pitch darkness and relying on his other senses to work out what was going on. He remembered seeing Ryan and Angie, then there was a blow to his head that made stars burst before his eyes and another bang as he chipped the banister rail; he recalled feeling his legs buckle beneath him – and now this. *Have I been buried alive?*

It was so cold. Freezing. His teeth were trying to chatter, but his mouth was gagged with a wad of something foul-tasting, his tongue wedged against a rough texture, like gauze. The taste and the smell were overpowering. It was chemical, and he could feel it stripping his mucous membranes. *Formaldehyde?* His stomach gagged, and the effect almost choked him. *Don't*, he thought. *Don't resist. Save energy.*

There was a hardness against his back, and his wrists and ankles were bound with zip ties; his fingers could feel the tail of the plastic. He'd already tried to sit up, but had banged his head. Whatever the ceiling was over him, it was so low he couldn't even turn sideways either. He banged again with his head and listened to the zinging noise the bone made against steel. *Hollow, I think it's hollow. That means I'm not underground.*

How long had he been like this? he wondered. *Not long in this cold. You could not survive for long in this cold.* He could hear his rasping breath, his lungs heaving for air. There wasn't much of it, he realized. The thought made him panic. He could feel his throat restricting. And he hated confined spaces at the best of times. What had happened?

It's a fridge, he thought, watching his breath cloud in front of him. Not a coffin, because it was not made of wood and the walls were cold, hard and silky. Steel. As he kicked the enclosure surrounding him, he realized he was naked. The bastard had stripped him. What was the smell? *Bleach?* He could hear the wheeze in his chest, and concentrated on his breathing. He thought about a case some years back in which two bachelor brothers were burgled in the west of Ireland, tied up and left to die. A neighbour found them a couple of days later, but they'd died of cadavaric spasm. *If I'm going to die, I'm going to die fighting, not because this evil bastard has scared me to death*, he thought. 'You'll have to kill me, you bastard,' he tried to call. But his tongue didn't move. *Think, think. Like in an investigation, build up the picture.* He lifted his hand and hit a solid wall.

He could hear something. He held his breath so he could hear over the pounding of his heart in his eardrums. Footsteps.

A scraping noise, a rattle, like a filing cabinet, a slide of wheels against a runner, and he was out in blinding light. He blinked rapidly. When his corneas had shrunk to the size of pinholes, he realized he knew where he was. He was in the morgue, on a slab, on one of the storage shelves. He heard the steel rattle of a trolley as it was wheeled up to him. He tried to rotate his head to see who it was, and found he was staring at a face under a hood.

'Matthias,' a voice said gravely. 'Do you not know me?'

Sexton shook his head.

The man was dressed like a monk. He lowered his hood.

Sexton stopped moving. He knew him now – it was the man who'd introduced himself as Angie's brother, and who was also, he now realized with blinding clarity, Hawthorne's assistant, the man who'd helped perform Rita's autopsy in the morgue, but his beard was gone.

He groaned as everything fell into place and watched as the killer reached for a scalpel off a kidney-shaped tray. He felt its cool, slick point at the base of his neck. He shook his head desperately, almost choking on the gag, and felt a trickle of wet roll down the side of his neck. *Had his throat been cut? No just pricked. If it had been cut, there'd be a gush. There was no gush.*

Sexton stopped moving as he realized something else. If Angie's brother worked in the morgue, it meant he hadn't broken in. No alarm bells would go off. Nobody would come looking.

It was Friday evening, and they had the whole night ahead of them.

57

It was 6 p.m., and the station was a hive of activity. Every uniform who had ever asked a question at a checkpoint, sat in on an interview or so much as passed on a phone message was there. Condensation was rolling down the walls and fogging up the windows. There were more officers out on the corridor, shouting in to find out if there were any updates. Mac had been murdered, and now word was spreading that Gavin Sexton was missing. All the phone lines were being used, and as soon as one phone was put down, it started to ring again, mobiles going off in between. This was the atmosphere Jo pushed her way into when she and Foxy got back from Sexton's flat.

Dan was standing at the top of the incident room alongside Jenny Friar, arms folded, listening and nodding as she pointed things out to him on the wipe board. Dave White was immersed in a file. Frank Black was on the phone, covering his ear and then shouting the word 'minister' often enough to let everyone know who was on the other end. Merrigan was recounting the story of how his colleagues had got one over on him and hadn't let him in on the joke all the way to the station after they'd picked him up, but as soon as people realized he was talking about himself, they turned away. All conversations dimmed as word went round

Jo was there. Dan headed over to a desk and sat on it, facing her.

She rolled up her sleeves. 'Right! Anyone not attached to this investigation leaves now.' Nobody moved. 'Full time!' she clarified.

The crowd began to vibrate.

'What's happened to Sexton?' a voice called.

More questions followed hard on its heels, officers demanding more information, not giving Jo a chance to answer. She raised her voice. 'You'll all find out what's going on soon enough. Right now I need some organization in here. Out, the lot of you!'

The crowd began to disperse begrudgingly.

'You too,' Jo said to a straggler, motioning a thumb to the door.

Ten uniforms who'd been attached to the incident room full time, most of them given the task of trawling painstakingly through the CCTV footage, remained behind. A couple of them went back to work in front of monitors and put their headphones back on. The rest were on the phones, or inputting information from the paperwork into the system.

'Is Sexton dead or alive?' Jenny Friar asked baldly.

Jo ignored her. 'We have five victims, all of them known to each other, one of them known to us all,' she said to Dan.

'Boss, if Sexton's missing, shouldn't that be two of them we all know, and six victims?' one of the uniforms asked.

'We don't know that yet,' Jo said. 'What we do know is that our killer has got a Bible fixation and that he's wiping out everyone connected with a crime against a little girl who is unable to talk. We know Gavin Sexton has been conducting his own parallel investigation, and we have reason to suspect that he's either going to be the next victim – or he could be the killer. That's all we've got.'

'Sexton's a good cop,' Dan said. 'You're barking up the wrong tree there, Jo.'

'You also brought Mac in for questioning,' Friar said. 'Or are we all on your suspect list?'

'Look, I don't want to believe Sexton is the killer either,' Jo said. 'Of course I don't. But not one of you suspected Mac was on the take – and look what happened to him.'

Nobody said anything.

'Now, let's stop this maniac today – whoever he is. The way I see it, we have to split up and approach it from either end. At one, we've got our victims, and at the other, the killer. Victim-wise, we don't know if anyone else was involved in what happened to Katie Freeman, but if they were, we have to presume they are now in serious trouble. Everyone else has been wiped out.'

'Doesn't that make you a possible victim?' someone called from the back. 'If the killer knows you're trying to stop him, he's going to consider you fair game.'

Jo kept going. 'Foxy has a team over at the Freemans' house now to bring her parents in for questioning. We'll work on this end of the investigation when they get here.' She looked around. 'Any questions?'

Again, there was silence.

'The other end we could use to crack this case is the killer himself. He's got a modus operandi, and his victims are all linked, meaning we've got a pattern. Most importantly of all, it's looking like his next and last killing will be in the O2. Dan, can you look after setting up the surveillance inside and outside the venue?'

Dan looked startled. 'You been there lately? It's a huge place,' he said.

'We're in the closing stages,' Jo said. 'We don't find our killer there, we never will. But we will find a victim, that I promise you. Let's just pray it's not Sexton.'

'I was at a concert there recently,' one of the uniforms piped up from the back. He was fresh-faced, and looked no more than twenty-one. 'They got cameras everywhere, which means there'll be a control room.'

'Good thinking,' Jo said. 'You head down there now and find out more about the surveillance. Oh, and organize a blueprint – you know, drawings of the O2 layout. And bring it straight back here. Pronto, yeah?'

The uniform stood up so quickly his chair fell over.

The phone on the computer desk rang and Merrigan answered. 'They don't have enough people in reception to deal with the ladies of the night,' he said accusingly. 'Shall I tell the lads to send them home?'

'No,' Jo said. 'We've got to cover this from both ends. Those women are going to help us research the victims. I want six of you to pair off and split the working girls up. One uniform, with one member of the team from the NBCI.' Jo looked at Jenny Friar. 'You're in the first team: I need you to separate the girls who knew Rita personally from those who didn't, and find out anything you can about what happened to Katie Freeman, and what Rita's role was. Also, we need to identify anyone else involved in Katie's abduction.'

Jo turned to Frank Black. 'You're in team two. I want you to show all the women Gavin Sexton's picture to see if any of them recognize him, and in what capacity.'

'Third team: I want you to establish if any of the women came across any nutters in recent weeks. Remember: our man knows his religion. Keep this to the forefront of your minds. You got that? The good news is that we've finally got a hit on Rita's mobile number, which the computer experts are triangulating as we speak.' Jo paused and looked around the room. 'Who did Foxy ask to check out Maura Sexton's grave?'

A rosy-faced garda put up her hand.

'How'd you get on?' Jo asked.

'Nothing,' she said. 'The grave was untouched. Quite well kept actually.'

Jo sighed. 'That's a relief, as it lessens the likelihood of Sexton's involvement. I'd have banked on our man having some kind of obsession with the dead, especially after Professor Hawthorne's student's results. Unless the killer didn't need to dig them up in the first place . . .' Jo's voice trailed away. 'Now, listen –'

Jo's phone went off. Foxy's name flashed up. 'Excuse me.'

'Shit!' she said, after listening for a few seconds. She walked over to Dan and leaned in close to his ear. 'We've got signs of something not right at the Freeman house. Nobody's home, and the furniture's been knocked over. Can you get the crime-scene people over there?'

Dan nodded.

'I'll be back in an hour.'

'Where are you going?'

'To the morgue.'

'Why?' Dan asked.

'I'm going to tackle this from the other end. I'm going to research the killer's point of view. Professor Hawthorne's technician is doing a research programme on necrophilia. If he's doing a PhD on the subject, he's going to be a bit of an expert. Don't you have to contrast and compare at that level? Either he came across another instance of someone interfering with a body, in which case I want to know who, or he's using a controlled sample of semen on the bodies, in which case I want to know whose. I want to ask him more about how he sets things up.'

'Bring a uniform with you,' Dan said.

'No,' Jo said. 'I want every available spare body at the O2.'

58

'I last saw Rita outside the Ashling Hotel down near Heuston Station,' a girl called Kinky Kelly was telling Jenny Friar, 'about a week before she was killed.' Kinky smoothed the flyaway hairs on her long, Coca-Cola red wig. The female officer paired off with Friar, who was sitting at the interview table taking copious notes, because the video link-up was on the blink, made the most of the break and shook her cramped hand. Foxy was sitting in the seat beside the door, having inveigled himself in the minute he heard the girl knew Rita. 'I was waiting for her to finish up business with a punter,' Kelly said.

Friar frowned, 'Wouldn't it have been more enterprising to keep working yourself?'

'Wha'?'

'What were you waiting for?'

'Rita owed me, and I wasn't taking any chances she didn't pay up once she got her money, not again. Speaking of which, will I be paid for this?'

Friar stood up impatiently, giving the distinct vibe that this interview was going to be a complete waste of time. Foxy's presence seemed only to add to her irritation. Friar was clearly sick and tired of answering to Jo Birmingham, and she didn't mind letting Foxy know it.

'Pay you?' she asked. 'Take it as a bonus that you'll be allowed to go home after this, as against being charged with soliciting and concealing a crime, for starters.'

Foxy looked startled.

Kinky stretched a string of pink gum from her mouth and, when it snapped, rolled it between her fingers and stuck it under the table. She couldn't have been any more than in her early twenties, with dark eyes and sallow skin. A sloping scar down her right cheek had put paid to her prettiness.

'In the questionnaire you filled in, you said you got the impression Rita wasn't too keen on going with this particular client that you were waiting for her to finish up with. Why was that?' Friar continued, referring to a sheet of paper.

Kelly gave her a look of contempt.

Foxy walked over to the table. 'Listen love, so you know, we do have a fund to cover any of your expenses.' He caught Friar's eye, and shook his head. 'We really appreciate anything you can tell us that will help. We need to catch this man before he hurts another woman.'

Friar looked absolutely livid, but before she could say anything, Kinky had started talking again: 'He'd knocked Rita about the last time, wanted to do some weird stuff, then wouldn't pay.'

'What was the weird stuff, do you know?' Friar asked.

Kinky looked through Friar like she was invisible, and didn't say anything. With an audible sigh, Friar got up, headed for the door and slammed it behind her.

'Go on, love,' Foxy said gently.

'You know, that strangling shit they're all into now.'

'Auto-eroticism?' Foxy asked.

'Whatever it's called. Only he wanted to strangle her, not

the other way around. Rita said she'd actually passed out, he got that carried away. Made her wear a strap-on too, the freak. And then he left her there, out in the open. The choking didn't kill her, but the hypothermia nearly did. He'd used her tights on her neck.'

Foxy knew he wouldn't find a report on the incident. Working girls didn't report crime, not as long as the law regarded them as being on the wrong side of it. 'Where did that happen? Did Rita tell you?'

'Castleforbes Street. They were building apartments down there at one stage, but it's just a wasteground now.'

Foxy breathed in sharply. It was exactly where Rita had ended up.

'Why did she go with him again?'

Kelly rubbed her thumb off her first two fingers. 'He paid what he owed, up front this time. I already told you – she owed it to me. She had to do it. But she wasn't taking any chances, so she told him it would have to be in his car this time.'

'You saw the car. Do you remember the model?'

''Course. Silver Skoda. Everyone knocks them cars but that's what I'd buy if I'd a few quid. They've got an Audi engine!'

'You know your cars,' Foxy said, smiling kindly.

'Started an apprenticeship as a mechanic a couple of years ago,' Kinky explained. 'I dropped out because I was sick of being skint, but to tell you the truth, if it was me, I'd have preferred to go back to that wasteground where he dumped her the first time.'

'Why'd you say that?'

'He'd got this doll thing in the front seat.' Kinky frowned as she remembered. 'Closest thing to a real person you ever saw. Proper size, beautiful hair, fully dressed. Expensive designer stuff it was too. It scared the fuck out of me. First I thought it was a woman, then I thought it was a dead woman, then when I asked him what it was, he introduced me to it, like he thought it was alive or something.'

'Christ,' Foxy said, scratching the back of his neck.

'I saw a programme about them once, on the telly,' Kinky went on. 'They make them in the States. Weigh nearly as much as a person. Even use real human hair on their privates. If they catch on, they'll put me out of business!'

It was an attempt at a joke, and Foxy tried to smile.

'Did I tell you what he called the doll? He said it was the Virgin Mary. He was having a go at me and Rita. Cheeky sod.'

Foxy breathed in sharply. He needed to get this information to Jo. 'You talked to him, then?'

'He pulled up beside me. I thought he was touting, but he only wanted Rita. Said he heard she could get him a little girl. Dirty bastard. Rita said that's what he said last time too.'

'Did you know him?'

'Never seen him before in my life. But I'll never forget him now either.'

'Did Rita tell you what happened?'

Kinky shook her head. 'She was out of it, to be honest.'

Foxy sighed and leaned back in his chair. 'Thanks, love,' he said, 'you've been a great help. I want you to talk to an artist before you go, so we can draw up a sketch of the man. You'll be looked after, don't worry. You should go back to it – the cars, I mean, and your apprenticeship. It would be a lot kinder than what you're doing now.'

'Maybe I will,' Kinky said, 'once I kick horse. Can't do nothing when you're on it.'

Foxy started for the door. He needed to tell Jo how close they were to the killer. He stopped suddenly.

'Took down his reg if you want it,' Kinky was telling the uniform. 'Rita asked me to. Just in case he hurt her again. If that's any use. I wrote it down and kept it in my bag.'

She pinched the clasp open. 'Was it him then? Do you think he killed her? Did he give her a bad time, before she died, I mean?' Looking worried, she handed the scrap of paper over.

'Too soon to say,' Foxy said, taking it. 'Get yourself clean, then go back to the cars. You got to keep yourself safe – okay?'

He gave a quick victory clench of his hand to the uniform and hurried out the door.

59

Evening was closing in as Jo swung into the morgue's parking lot, pulling in behind the only other car, a silver Skoda. She was glad to see it, having heard that Hawthorne had gone to help out with the murder suicide case in Donegal. Her calls to him and to the office from the car on the way had gone unanswered. At least someone was working after hours and could give her contact details for Hawthorne's technician. She wondered how the interviews were going back in the station as she stepped up the metal steps of the first Portakabin and rang the bell. It was the one used by Hawthorne and his assistant as an office. There was no answer. She was heading for the second cabin, situated just behind it, when her mobile started to buzz. Jo answered as something inside caught her eye – a flicker of light from a window of the third Portakabin used as the morgue.

'Congratulations,' Dan said in her ear.

'Go on?' she said, full of anticipation.

'We've got a match on the DNA found in Rita's body.'

'Yes!' Jo said, feeling a leap of joy. Her mobile started to beep that another call was waiting, but she wasn't about to cut this one short for anyone. 'Who is he?'

'George Whelan, unemployed, father of three, two previous convictions back in the eighties, minor. Sixty-two years old. Will I go on or are you going to come back here to join the team who go and pull him in? This is your moment.'

'Sixty-two? That can't be right,' Jo said.

'It's his sperm!' Dan said huffily.

'He's too old. Come on, Dan, you know better than to waste my time.'

Hanging up, she checked to see whose call she'd missed. Foxy rang before she even got the chance to call him back. 'Don't tell me you buy the pensioner line too?' Jo said.

'What pensioner?' Foxy sounded confused. 'Jo, we've got our man's reg!'

The door to the third cabin had opened. Was it the technician? Jo squinted into the light. He looked different. She couldn't be sure.

'Can you hear me, Jo? The car our killer's been using is owned by Ryan Freeman.'

But Jo's line was dead. Her phone had split apart as soon as she hit the tarmac.

60

Jo woke to the sight of plastic cables pressed against her face – hundreds of lengths, different colours. She tried to blink them away more quickly, but her eyelids felt like they'd weights attached. It was so cold. Her head thumped and her jaw ached. She was biting down on something like gauze that was wedged so tight the strings had cut into her tongue and she could taste blood. There were sounds of dripping water and a slight echo.

Her last memory, of standing outside the morgue and the door opening, hit her. She felt a punch of panic and tried to breathe evenly, hyperaware that she was going to need to have all her wits about her. There was another smell now, one that reminded her of church – frankincense? Jo felt her heart rate quicken again as she realized exactly what had happened. The killer had her, and she knew what he was capable of. She also knew that she was beyond help. Back at the station, the team would be concentrating on the DNA link, bringing the 62-year-old suspect in. It could be hours before they realized she'd gone and came looking for her at the morgue. And was that where she was now?

Think, Jo, think. Work it out. I am lying face down, arms and legs zip-tied together behind my back.

She could hear someone else breathing quietly nearby and

turned her head to one side then the other. She was lying on cables, on a concrete floor. Above her the walls of her tomb were concave; it was like being inside a drum. With a supreme effort, she rolled on to her side and looked straight ahead – she was in a concrete tunnel, maybe six foot tall, not much more wide, so dimly lit by intermittent strips of encased light running along the top that visibility was practically nil. She tried to touch her head and felt the robe cut into her wrists. Her jaw began to jerk, no space for her teeth to chatter . . . Where the bloody hell . . . It was so cold.

Ahead of her, the tunnel ran as far as the eye could see, and smelled of a mix of copper and mildew.

Jo rolled back on her front and tilted her head up towards the source of the sound of breathing. In front were the soles of a pair of bare feet, bound, too, to wrists. Sexton was staring at her, willing her to look him in the eye, a gag in his mouth also. His eyes warned her to stay quiet. Jo nodded. She squinted a 'Who?', but Sexton had closed his eyes, presumably to indicate it was unsafe to do any more. She could hear something in the background – humming, easily identifiable as a man's voice, and it was getting louder.

Jo closed her eyes. Sexton was naked, but she was fully clothed and, in the breast pocket of her leather jacket, was an old lighter she'd forgotten about when she'd given up smoking. If it still worked, and if she could get hold of it, it was a weapon, and cause for hope.

Jo concentrated very hard on the tune the killer was humming. What was it? A hymn, or something religious, the mad bastard. And now she also knew what the taste in her mouth was: petrol. There was another sound in the background, more distant, not really a sound, more a vibration travelling down the bolthole. Think, Jo told herself. If it's from cables, it means we're probably underground. That means the noise is coming from above, and that it must be very loud to travel this far. She heard the killer's feet crunching closer and could just make out the sight of the robe, dark brown like a Franciscan's. He was passing her now, his feet inches from her face. He knelt in front of her and put two fingers to her neck. If she'd kept her eyes open a fraction, she would see who he was, but Jo let them close completely, just like Sexton wanted. The killer was checking her pulse and making sure she was still alive, so he could hurt her like he had hurt the others. If she moved the right way, maybe she could dislodge the gag and sink her teeth into his foot, which was right beside her face. But the look she'd seen in Sexton's eye stopped her.

The Book of Exodus quote began to replay in her mind because she knew now exactly what the killer was planning for them. An eye for an eye – Stuart Ball; a tooth for a tooth – Anto Crawley; a hand for a hand – Rita Nulty; a foot for a foot – Father Reginald Walsh; a wound for a wound – David MacMahon. That left fire for her and Sexton.

Then Jo understood. The noise overhead, the tunnel shape, the smell, wires underneath . . . *We're not in the O2,* she realized. *We're under it.*

61

Foxy stood in the busy incident room staring at the phone in his hand. 'Where's Jo?' he asked.

Dan was standing over the blueprints – giant white sheets spread over several desks – smoothing the puckers in the folds with the flat of his hand and asking questions of the jittery venue manager of the O2, who looked to be still in his teens and was explaining what they were looking at. Ten members of the Emergency Response Unit stood around him, looking at the maps too, chipping in queries and discussing the access points. The ERU was the only garda elite squad trained and equipped for siege situations, and they were armed to the hilt. Dressed in black combats and swat jackets, they also stood around the table, wearing the trucker caps with the squad's logo that distinguished them and offset any chances of friendly fire.

Jenny Friar was handing a colour photograph to Jeanie for photocopying. The suspect thrown up by the DNA match was about to be circulated throughout the station.

'I said, "Where is Jo?"' Foxy asked, louder.

The incident room suddenly went quiet. Heads turned.

'The morgue,' Dan said, his finger still pointing to a spot on the map.

'But her line's just gone dead,' Foxy went on, holding his

up. 'She's not on her own, Dan, is she? Please tell me right now that you did not let her go to interview anyone on her own.'

'We are talking about Jo,' Dan said, this time not bothering to look up.

Foxy banged the phone down. 'One of the working girls has just nominated a suspect,' he said angrily. 'She got his reg. I've run a check. The car belongs to the crime reporter Ryan Freeman. His brother-in-law, Walter Kaiser – Angie's brother – is a named driver on the insurance. Walter works part time in the morgue.'

Dan straightened up. 'We've got a DNA match, Foxy. I want you to concentrate on helping Friar find him and not get sidetracked by some prostitute's story, okay?'

'But why did she go to the morgue in the first place?'

'She wanted to find out more about how some PhD student went about his research,' Dan snapped. 'Come over here and have a look at our suspect's picture. Have you seen him before?'

Foxy headed over to Friar. He peered over her shoulder. 'Pull the other one, he's older than I am!' He headed for the door.

'Hang on!' Dan said.

'Oh for God's sake,' Foxy said. 'Jo said the next time the killer strikes will be in the O2. I'll bet he's got her there right now. If we're too late, I'll –'

'I've got the place under surveillance,' Dan cut in. 'There's nobody there, not a dickie bird.'

'Yeah? So how come she's been right about everything so far?' Foxy asked.

Dan turned to the two officers on phones behind him. 'The morgue now, lads. Get down there and, if you find Jo, get her back here. I don't care if you have to use your hand-cuffs. I don't want her leaving my sight again.'

'It's too late for that,' Foxy snapped, coming over to the maps and looking them up and down. 'Any other concealed entrances in the O2 we don't know about?' he asked the venue manager. 'Sometimes those pop stars don't want to go in the main gate, do they? They're afraid of being papped without their make-up on, or with some groupie they don't want their missus to know about.'

'There's a helicopter pad on the roof to get them in and out,' the kid said.

'You think our man is going to arrive in a helicopter?' Dan said dismissively.

'If you had given her the support she needed, we wouldn't be in this situation,' Foxy pointed out.

Dan strode over to Foxy and took him by the collar. 'Give me a break! You were the one who accused her of thieving in the first place.'

'I withdrew it. You're the one who's been persecuting her.'

Jeanie stepped in and removed Dan's hand from Foxy. 'This won't solve anything,' she said. 'Why don't we take a breather, get a bite to eat maybe?'

Foxy and Dan both looked at her like she'd two heads.

'We do need to keep our strength up if we're going to think clearly,' Friar said. 'Think about it, Foxy – how the hell is the killer going to set something up in a venue like that? It's full of people most of the time. What's on in the O2 tonight?' she asked the kid.

'A musical,' Merrigan piped up from the other side of the room. 'My Doreen's got tickets.' He was peeling an orange, and the smell permeated the incident room. 'It's *Jesus Christ Superstar*.' He looked at the astonished faces. 'She booked them months ago. I quite fancied the idea of seeing some women in togas, that's all . . .'

'Fuck!' Dan cursed, his hands on his head.

'What time does it kick off at?' Foxy asked Merrigan urgently.

'Eight.'

The venue manager looked at his watch. 'Right now.'

62

Sexton had pulled the gag from Jo's mouth by clamping it in his toes, the way she'd intended. Now Jo was trying to angle her head close enough to the breast pocket of her leather jacket to grip the lighter with her teeth. If she could just nudge it up another inch with a jolt of her arm . . . Shit! Jo bit her tongue as the lighter came out of her pocket and lodged itself between the tightly packed lengths of cable.

She looked over at Sexton, whose eyes were trained on the far end of the tunnel, then, staring at the lighter desperately, she tried to wriggle closer. The killer had just drenched them with one of those sprinklers she'd only ever seen priests use at funerals.

Biting between the cables, she could feel the lighter's edge between her teeth and tried to dislodge it another bit with her tongue. The taste of dirt, oil and mildew was disgusting, but it was better than the gag.

The lighter moved, she bit hard – *got it*, just about one corner. She sucked hard, walked it in with her lips and began to wriggle towards Sexton.

The big problem was going to be trying to burn off the bind with all this petrol everywhere without turning the whole place into an inferno.

*

Dan had every inch of the O2 covered. The ERU snipers were in position on the rooftop and on facing rooftops, hidden from view. There were more armed gardaí dressed as members of staff in the venue. A team of gardaí posing as plumbers was 'tending' to a leak on the roadside directly outside, causing all traffic to be diverted away from the car park, much to the annoyance of irate commuters thinking they'd gotten over the worst of it once they came off the Westlink.

Dan had taken the decision not to interrupt the musical, and Foxy agreed. If they halted the production and the killer realized they were on to him, they might lose him for good – and Jo, plus, by the looks of it, Sexton. The search of the morgue had led to the discovery of Ryan and Angie Freeman. Ryan had been bound and anaesthetized and left on a slab in the refrigerator unit. Angie had also been tied up, but was unharmed.

Shaken and in floods of tears, Angie had identified their captor as her own brother, Walter, and had also volunteered the information that he was Katie's godfather – all of which made sense to Foxy. Walter had been avenging his sister, and protecting Katie by killing everyone who'd had anything to do with her abduction, and this of course included Sexton, whose only crime was that he'd tried to help. Angie also told them that the Skoda was Walter's car but it had always been in Ryan's name to avoid the hefty insurance bill that came with being a young male. And she was insisting that it was Walter who'd given her a present of a new mobile phone and that she hadn't known it had previously belonged to Rita.

There was no question about the identity of the killer any more. The problem now was finding him. Every inch of space in the O2 had been searched, to no avail.

Foxy and Dan were sitting in the front of Dan's car, watching the entrance. Three ambulances were on standby, the back doors open, the crew sitting on the vehicle floor, watching. Dan was staring fiercely straight ahead. He had one arm over the steering wheel. In his other hand, he held a Bic ballpoint which he fiddled with constantly.

Finally, Foxy spoke. 'Don't worry. We'll find her.'

'If you fly in, you get seen,' Dan said, jabbing his pen up at the heli-pad on the roof. 'How's Walter doing it? Angie said he's a medical student, got a degree in law, and that he started out as an electrician. None of it makes him a cat burglar. Put it together, Foxy. How's he getting in there unseen?'

'He was a spark?' Foxy said slowly. 'Did you know that one of the things Merrigan was supposed to find out was who was paying for the power in the old harbour warehouse where Crawley's body was found? If he'd done what he was supposed to, I bet you any money we'd have had him before now.'

Dan looked down at his hands guiltily.

Foxy sat up straight. 'That could be it – this city's built on a network of tunnels. The Victorians loved them, as did the Vikings, way back. There's one running under the Phoenix Park linking Heuston to Connolly, another one rumoured to link the Mansion House and the Dáil to facilitate the escape of the state's most important citizens in the event of a popular uprising. You won't find it on the maps, it's supposed to be a big secret. There's even one at the casino in Marino, right beside where the morgue is, and it runs all the way into Parnell Street.' Foxy paused, thinking. 'Thing is, there's one under the Liffey too, which would go straight into the O2. The ESB are the only ones with access to it, though – for their power cables.'

'Call them,' Dan said.

63

Jo could hear him coming, his sandals slicking against the cables. Her teeth were chattering, and she clamped her jaw tighter so he wouldn't hear. She and Sexton had managed to free themselves from the restraints. Once she'd gotten the lighter in her teeth, she'd wriggled up to Sexton's hand, and he'd gripped her binding and managed to burn it off.

Closer and closer the footsteps came, till they were just beyond her face, and then Sexton made his move. Lunging forward, he grabbed one of the ankles and struggled with the killer, till he let a roar at Jo that he had him. It was pitch black – so dark she couldn't see anything, so she clawed at the air to find him, felt his limbs thrashing, distinguished him by his cloak and threw herself across what turned out to be the back of his legs.

'You want everyone to live, you'll have to let me go,' he said.

Jo held the lighter up, and in its glow saw Sexton pointing to the explosives strapped around the killer's waist. Sexton pointed up, and she realized the faint sound overhead was the muted roar of applause. The O2 could seat almost ten thousand; all of them were at risk if he managed to detonate.

'You insane bastard,' Sexton snarled.

Jo reached out to touch him. The killer had won. They couldn't risk it. Sexton stepped back.

The killer reached into his cloak and pulled out a button, smiling beatifically.

The lighter flickered out.

The sudden explosion of sound was deafening.

64

As the tunnel flooded with blinding light, Jo closed her eyes. Her pupils couldn't constrict against the dazzling brightness, her eyes felt as though they were burning.

But it wasn't light from an explosion. There was a flood-light pouring down the tunnel, and she was still standing. The sound had been a gunshot.

Beside her, the killer lay, explosives still strapped to his chest, the top half of his head missing. As she squinted into the light, she saw the marksman's cap further down the tunnel. He was kneeling in the distance, weapon still cocked.

And then she heard Dan calling, 'Jo?'

Saturday

65

Walter Kaiser had lived in the basement flat of a four-storey house on Elgin Road, in Dublin's embassy belt. Jo travelled to his home with Dan from the hospital, where she'd been kept in overnight. She followed Dan into the flat slowly, not out of fear, but so she could take it all in. He knew better than to treat her with kid gloves. Sometimes she thought he knew the way her mind worked better than she did.

The poky flat was neat, and clean, but creepy all the same, Jo thought as she entered. The ceiling thumped from the muffled sounds of dance music being played at full volume in a flat overhead. There were houses like it all over Dublin: chandeliers in the lobbies, but running to dereliction. Yet what was a few steps inside made her catch her breath. The room was filled with life-sized mannequins in various states of undress and sexual positions. Four of them were posed in the living room; she guessed there'd be more in the bedroom.

'They call them Real Dolls,' Dan said, rubbing his temples with a spread finger and thumb.

Jo pulled a face. 'And I thought he'd a thing for dead women.'

'You were pretty close,' Dan said, examining one, which was dressed in a school uniform and sitting on a poof in front of the TV, all glassy stare and sandy pigtails. Her legs were open. There was a redhead lying on the couch dressed like a cheerleader in a cropped top and short skirt, legs open too. A brunette had been dressed head to toe in office chic, glasses on her nose as she bent over at the window, a chain hanging from her waist and bolted to the ceiling keeping her upright. The fourth one, which had blonde hair, was dressed like a hooker in long, shiny boots and a latex skirt – again, legs open.

'There's one more,' Dan said, reading her mind.

He led Jo into the bedroom, where she saw a fifth, dark-skinned doll lying in the bed.

'$10,000 a piece,' Dan said. 'Angie said he came into some money a few years back, so that's probably how he paid for them. He even had them serviced when their bits fell off. They were shipped to and from the States in crates.'

'No wonder he'd such a big problem with the Church. They're staunch on this kind of thing – isn't there something about going blind?'

'Angie said his problems started as a kid, after their mother died,' Dan answered. 'As a kid he'd wanted to play weird games like run and jump on the dead cat; drown the puppies – feel the last wiggle; spent all his free time at the dead zoo. She said he was diagnosed at one stage with something antisocial, but their father didn't believe in medication or in keeping his psychiatric appointments. She was the only one who cared about what happened to him. Walter was inappropriately grateful. When Katie disappeared, Angie asked him to help get her back.'

Jo picked up a Bible from a coffee table. Her hand trembled slightly. Dan took her wrist. Jo didn't pull her hand back. 'At least this place explains the hatred towards the Church. But how'd he know we'd be in Castleforbes Road to find Rita that day?'

'Ryan said he remembers Sexton mentioning it to him on the phone, and Walter being in the house at the time,' Dan said. 'Maybe he overheard.'

'How did Walter link Stuart Ball and the others to what happened?'

'Probably Crawley,' Dan answered. 'He'd have talked to anyone if it served his own interests, and if Walter was torturing him, it was in his own interests.'

'I thought the letter the streets made was an M,' Jo said.

'Turn it upside down and you get a W,' Dan consoled.

Jo sighed as she thought how near they'd come to him – and how narrowly they'd escaped.

'Any idea about how that 62-year-old's semen turned up in Rita?' Jo asked.

'He was her last paying punter,' Dan answered. 'It was Walter himself who claimed that Rita had been interfered with after death, remember? We've visited the old punter, and he nearly had a heart attack when he heard he may be a suspect. He's legit.'

'I knew he couldn't have been involved.' She pulled her hand free. 'Let's get out of here. I need a drink.'

In the Waterloo pub nearby, Dan carried a Guinness and a G&T over to their table.

'Last time I was in here it was a spit-on-the-floor job,' Jo said, admiring Dan's midnight-blue eyes.

'Yeah, it's a bit too flash for my liking. Want to go somewhere else? I think there may still be sawdust on the floor in Mulligan's.'

'Pity to waste it,' she said, eyeing the drinks.

'Come on, let's go nuts,' Dan said, getting up. 'It's Saturday. We're off duty, remember?'

*

At the window of Mulligan's pub, they finally sat down side by side. 'We used to come here when we first started going out,' Jo said, taking a sip.

'I remember,' he said, putting his arm around her shoulders. He let his forehead touch hers. 'Take next week off, yeah? After what you've been through, you need it.'

Jo nodded.

'And when you come back, I want to hear no more talk of a transfer, right? You're needed where you are.'

Jo looked away. When you came as close as she had to losing everything, it was a wake-up call. She knew now what was important in her life – and how quickly it could all be taken away.

'What are we going to do about Sexton?' she asked, trying to change the subject.

Dan sighed, his eyes still on her face. 'He's a big boy, he can take care of himself.'

'That's just it. Clearly, he can't.'

After a silence which Jo did not have the head space to deal with, she asked, 'What are we going to do about Rory's truancy?'

'Have dinner with me tonight, and we can discuss it.'

She felt a flicker of excitement. 'Are you suggesting a meal alone, Mr Mason?'

'You got a babysitter?' he teased.

'My place,' she instructed.

'Half nine,' he said. 'And don't cook – no offence. I'll organize a Chinese.'

Jo tipped back the drink with a grin on her face. 'Make it an Indian, and you've got a date.'

66

When the doorbell rang, Jo hopped down the hall dressed up to the nines in a sexy little black dress, hair still sopping wet, one shoe in her hand and make-up not yet applied. It was only eight thirty, and she was still hot-footing around trying to get on top of the cleaning, grabbing clothes from the radiators. She wanted the place right was why. Dan had his own key, and she suspected he was only ringing to keep up the pretence. Not that she wasn't going to give him an earful. He was too bloody early! A woman needed time to get ready for a date, even with a man she'd known most of her adult life – no, especially when it came to that man. She still needed to set the table, do it properly: candles, wine, the works. And she'd yet to settle Harry down for the night. He was still standing in his playpen, walking around it with a big, rosy-cheeked smile on his face. Rory had only just left to go to the cinema with Becky, and she was still picking up after him.

Still, Jo thought as she reached for the door, all things considered, she was in good form. She'd got her car back, with a new coat of paint, and a new engine. She'd driven by the Quality Inn on the way home and realized she didn't care any more about flashing her badge to access the hotel's records. What was done was done. It was water under the bridge now. She didn't want to know if Dan had stayed there single or alone. What she'd realized from her near-miss yesterday was that she and Dan belonged together. Her cuts and bruises were on the mend, Angie Freeman was going into rehab, Katie was finally coming out of her shell and Walter Kaiser was cold as the grave where he belonged. All in all, it was turning out to be her kind of day.

But it wasn't Dan standing on her doorstep. It was Jeanie, red-eyed.

Jo pulled the door open with a sigh of resignation.

'I know what you're doing, you bitch,' Jeanie said angrily.

'With respect, this is my home, and if you can't be civil, I want you to go,' Jo said.

Jeanie wedged her foot inside the door. 'Has he told you I'm pregnant?'

Jo gasped as she absorbed the blow. In the background, Harry let out a peal of laughter.

'I've come to say that I'm sorry for what I did to you. Now I know what it feels like, eh?'

Jo watched Jeanie walk away in the pouring rain then looked back at Harry, who was still smiling at her cherubically from his playpen.

Pulling off the single shoe on her foot, she dropped it on the ground and, letting the other one fall from her hand, she closed the door and slid the bolt across. Padding down the hall, she took the backs off her jangling costume earrings and was placing them on the hall table when the phone started ringing. Ignoring the tears running down her cheeks, she answered it.

'I know it's Saturday evening and you're probably on your way to meet a hot date,' Gerry in Justice said, 'so I'll cut to the chase, shall I? Your proposal for SLR for rape victims has been approved. It's in the pipeline.' He paused. 'Are you crying, Birmingham?'

'Of course not.' Jo wiped her eyes on the back of her sleeve. 'I've just got everything I wanted, haven't I?'

Leabharlanna
Fhine Gall

A NOTE ON SEPARATE
LEGAL REPRESENTATION

Victims don't take priority in court. If they're lucky enough to have survived their ordeal, their role in court is as a witness to a crime against the state. If they've passed on, their memory tends to be assassinated by the trial process, because that's what is required when proving the defence of provocation. Their loved ones sit in the back of the court and weep. They have endured the tragedy of violent loss, and now they must hear harrowing evidence such as the post-mortem findings. The weight of the deceased's brain, heart and liver is information that is par for the course, as are descriptions of how, for example, the skull was incised across the scalp from behind one ear to the other, with the front half peeled forwards and the back half peeled back so the tissue underneath could be examined for bruising, when head injuries are a factor.

Regularly, it all becomes too much, but a family member who shouts out in distress or protests in any way can be held in contempt and be transferred to a holding cell until they purge the contempt by apologizing to the court. All they generally want to say is 'who' they have lost and how the person being depicted in court by the barrister of the accused is a stranger to them. Some will make a Victim

Impact Statement. Since the trial process has concluded anyway by this point, for most families, it's cold comfort.

Rape Crisis campaigners argue that one way of empowering victims in court is to provide them with Separate Legal Representation, so as to help put an end to a system which puts the victim on trial. However, the powers that be have reacted to the campaign for SLR as if it would cause the pillars of the temple to fall.

Like Jo Birmingham, I too feel that the scales of justice are too heavily weighted in favour of the accused and need to be rebalanced back towards the victims of crime. This novel is our opening salvo.

Niamh O'Connor
April 2010

ABOUT THE AUTHOR

Niamh O'Connor is one of Ireland's best-known crime authors. She is the true crime editor of the *Sunday World*, Ireland's biggest-selling Sunday newspaper, for whom she has written six true-crime books which were given away with the newspaper. Her job, in which she interviews both high-profile criminals and their victims, means she knows the world she is writing about.